They stood opposite each other, dimly visible, ten paces apart.

"When that dog howls again," said Rhiannon.

"All right," said the sheriff.

But he added: "If you need a hoss afterward, you'll find 'em in the shed behind the house. The black one is the best."

Rhiannon said nothing.

And then the dog howled in the distance, shrill and long. The sheriff drew his Colt with practiced speed and fired from the hip—

SINGING GUNS was originally published by Dodd, Mead & Company, Inc.

BOOKS BY MAX BRAND

The Bandit of the Black Hills
Blood on the Trail
The Border Kid
Destry Rides Again
The False Rider
Flaming Irons
Larramee's Ranch
On the Trail of Four
Rippon Rides Double
Rustlers of Beacon Creek
Singing Guns
Steve Train's Ordeal
The Stingaree
The Tenderfoot
Thunder Moon
Tragedy Trail
The Untamed
Valley of the Vanishing Men

Published by Pocket Books

Singing Guns

MAX BRAND

PUBLISHED BY POCKET BOOKS NEW YORK

SINGING GUNS

Dodd, Mead edition published June, 1938

POCKET BOOK edition published March, 1942

25th printing.........July, 1971

This POCKET BOOK edition includes every word
contained in the original, higher-priced edition. It is printed
from brand-new plates made from completely reset, clear, easy-to-read
type. POCKET BOOK editions are published by POCKET BOOKS, a division
of Simon & Schuster, Inc., 630 Fifth Avenue, New York, N.Y. 10020.
Trademarks registered in the United States and other countries.

L

Singing Guns

Chapter One

SHERIFF CARADAC'S mule gave out and stood beaten at the bottom of the slope. He dismounted, made a small pack to sling over his shoulders, cached the rest of his luggage in a slicker in a tree fork, and then abandoned the mule to look after its own interests.

He swung up the slope once more, swinging his rifle in his hand to make it lengthen his stride. Over his head was a vast forest of Engelmann spruce; under his foot was the compacted litter of that forest, sodden with water, but seeming like a set of springs as he strode along. Fallen trees had decayed to make that bedding. Whole branches were lost in it, and through the interstices the unceasing rain of needles had sifted everywhere. The sheriff did not stop to admire the lofty gloom of the forest or the strange carpet over which he walked. He was too busy to feel admiration. With every step he made, his glance swung through an arc, to right, to left, like a pendulum.

Steady effort tells the tale, not sudden spurts. But such a steady effort as the sheriff was making, uphill, no man could maintain very long. Every half hour he would pause. When he halted, he put his back against a tree and faced down trail. For even that halting space should not be wasted. He had to be armed with infinite precautions. However, that was what they paid him for in that county, and that was why, at the end of every term of office, they made up a purse for him. There was twenty-five hundred dollars in one purse. With salary, donation, and what one could pick up in the way of state rewards, Caradac managed very well. He liked to make money and he liked to save it; it was his nature to enjoy thrift—his nature was Welsh.

But if there had been not a penny in the game, still he would have loved the work for its own sake. Let others go to far Africa to kill lions or elephants, or to steaming India to bag tigers. They had frightful expense, frightful waste of time; and what was their reward? A chance shot at a flying shape among the woods! But Owen Caradac hunted men; and in his county they took a good deal of hunting, at that; and when they were brought to bay they fought like devils. The jagged white scar that ripped the side of his face was a proof of that. There was another scar that brought a silver seam from under the sleeve of his coat onto the brown back of his right hand, and there were still other marks of battle distributed about his person.

Someday they would get him, he knew. But he always was unreasonably sure that it would be tomorrow, not today, and in the meantime there was the constant joy of the chase! He loved it with all his heart! And as a famous hunter, no matter how many his trophies, will go with beating heart on a new trail, marking the great spread of foot of some king of tigers, so Caradac's heart thumped heavily against his ribs when he thought of his quarry. A big man, like Caradac. A strong man, like Caradac. Fierce, like Caradac again, and also Welsh! Witness the name! Annan Rhiannon!

Caradac's grandfather had printed a maxim on his memory: "Three things that are not often heard: The song of the birds of Rhiannon; wisdom from the mouth of a Saxon; an invitation to a feast from a miser!"

Rhiannon, in the legend, was a woman. To hear the singing of her birds, men were frozen in silence for eighty years!

He paraphrased that thought in grim humor. To hear the singing of the birds of this Annan Rhiannon, men would remain silent until the last day of time. His singing birds were the guns in his hands! Such thoughts trailed through the mind of the sheriff as he conducted his march, but they were dim words which formed, and never enough to darken the keenness of his attention to all around him. He was in the land of Rhiannon now, and it was like walking in the den of a lion.

It began to rain; the torrents of water seemed crushing and breaking the trees; and when a great billow of wind struck them, he could hear the branches straining, crackling. He came out from the woods into a region over which a forest fire had swept. It was lost now in water-dust that filled the air, half stifling Caradac; he could only see dimly the black stumps, holding up misshapen arms. But he was glad of the rain. No matter that the whole face of the mountain was covered with a rushing sheet of water and that the labor of walking was trebled. The important thing was that this mighty curtain of rain shielded him from the possible observation of Rhiannon. So he marched on, vaguely giving thanks.

He came to the river where it lurched over a cliff fifty feet high. So deeply was the current laden that it hardly could be called water. Rather, it was liquid mud that carried rocks as large as a man's head. At the base of the falls was a cloud of yellow foam, like steam, ever springing aloft, ever beaten down again by the sheets of rain; and the ground shuddered with the trampling of the cataract.

Caradac, watching the strife, drew a great breath. So it would be when Caradac and Rhiannon met, man to man!

Then he strode on once more. He made a big detour to the right, because it would be folly to stick too close to the course of the river. Ten days before the inspiration had come to him that perhaps "hole-in-the-wall" Rhiannon used one of the caves near the source of the stream as his hiding place. In the middle of the night he had started on this march. He had ridden a horse into the ground. The mule had given out. Now he must not throw away chances, however small!

So Caradac made his detour and came in again through the thunder of the rain to a place where the river was a little white-robed torrent, springing past the roots of great trees. Just below him the forest gave way to a wild jumble of rocks. Among the rocks and the caves he must try to find Rhiannon, unless the dream had been no omen at all!

Then the rain wall began to clear away and break up. Thunder roared. The rocks stirred under the battering of the heavy echoes, and long-armed lightning struck down from the sky. A fifty-foot fir, not far off, was struck. Fire blasted it. Then it lay on the ground in shreds.

Caradac observed this with satisfaction, and deep content; for such things were symbols and proper settings for the day when Caradac might do battle with Rhiannon!

The rain ceased. Still the vast clouds were piled incred-

3

ibly from earth to zenith like another mountain range; and the water dripped steadily behind him, from the trees.

He went out a little further, to the head of a sharp slope of small rubble—pebbles and rocks the size of one's fist. From this elevation he was able to regard the boulders beneath more closely. Particularly when the clouds broke up and sailed down the curving sky and let the sun come through.

He flashed and glittered on a world of silver. Smooth rock surfaces were a mirror to give back his face, but that splendor rapidly faded. The western wind is as dry as sand, and it will "eat snow," as the Indians say. It breathed upon these dripping mountains and tarnished their glory!

Caradac was not bothered by greater or less beauty, however. He was troubled only to find his quarry, so he remained beside the wet trunk of a fir and continued to scan the region at the foot of the slope. He was about to descend and had actually made a pace down the steep slope of the hill face, rifle at the ready, when he saw a sombreroed head move out from the shelter of a big boulder. Caradac brought the rifle to his shoulder. The man was only thirty yards away, and now he stepped out so that he was completely visible from head to foot. It was Rhiannon!

And Caradac smiled grimly. After all, dreams will not lie to one. There is something sacred about dreams! God bless that which had sent him here.

He did not fire at once. He would wait until the other turned toward him; he would even speak a word. One does not shoot birds until one has flushed them! So he reveled in his victory for an instant, letting the rifle muzzle wander over the body of Rhiannon. Through the head he must send the bullet. There was no surety in firing at the body, particularly a body like that of Rhiannon's, cased in ribs of iron.

The sheriff felt the most unusual pleasure he ever had known. To compare small things with great, it was very much like having the king of moose, the lord of grizzlies under one's rifle. Only more—infinitely more! In all the broad West, there was no other pair of shoulders like these of Rhiannon; there was no head like his.

And then the voice of Caradac rang across the rocks: "Rhiannon!"

As he cried, he huddled the butt of the rifle into the hollow of his shoulder and shifted his left foot a bit forward. Bad fortune in that move! For he felt the stone turn under his foot and even as he pulled the trigger he knew that he had missed.

Rhiannon bounded sidewise like a startled stag, and whirled as he sprang. The revolver flickered like a flame in his hand, and Caradac for the first time heard the enchanting song of the birds of Rhiannon. A burning rod was thrust through both his legs between knee and hip and he dropped forward.

He knew that he was a dead man and waited for the crushing impact of the second bullet. But it did not come. He himself slipped in a small avalanche down the face of the hill. A sharp-edged boulder rose before him. He struck it, and began to spin head over heels like a child's toy flopping on a floor. All that impetus was used to fling him straight into arms of granite. He felt his life crushed out by the blow, and after that he fell into kindly darkness.

Chapter Two

WHEN LIFE came back to Caradac he lifted his hand and found it so thin that the knuckles and the joints stood out big and red and the light shone through his palm. With that strange hand he touched his face and found it was covered with a beard. He raised himself to his elbows, and his strength was so gone that his whole body shook violently.

Then he saw that he was in a small cave which was not tunneled into the earth by the action of water, but rather it was like cyclopean architecture, a vast slab of stone laid over a square mass on either side. What amazed him more than all was to see at the mouth of the cave his own mule standing, and seated cross-legged on the ground beside him there was a man whose face was covered with a short beard. His beard was as black as night, and his eyes were still blacker. "Steady, steady!" said the man of the black beard, and stretched out a great hand.

"Rhiannon!" said Caradac, and sank back again into his bed. It was a deep, soft bed made of the tips of evergreen branches and, as Caradac sank back in it, it exhaled the fragrance of the pines about him. He lay still. Near by, water was singing; far off, he heard the thunderous trampling of the fall.

"You've come out of it at last, it looks like," said Rhiannon.

Caradac opened his eyes again. He sorted his vague thoughts and said, "You could have let me lie where I fell, Rhiannon."

"I don't kill dead men," said Annan Rhiannon. "Do you feel like eating, now?"

Caradac looked at the ragged ceiling above his head. "If I was big enough to of picked up that stone and laid it yonder for a ceiling," said he, "and if I'd worked for a week and never ate nothing all that time, I'd begin to be about as hungry as I am now."

"What could you take a fancy to?" asked Annan Rhiannon, chuckling a little.

"Good green grass would do me fine," said the sheriff. "Or I'd be pretty partial to the fine tender inside bark of willows. In a pinch, I would chew sagebrush, or swallow pebbles."

"But if you had your pick?" said Rhiannon, chuckling again.

"If I had my pick," said the sheriff, "I would kind of begin with trout, grilled brown. I would float a couple of dozen two-pound trout down my throat to begin with. After that, I'd take to venison. I wouldn't want to be greedy, so I'd stop at a couple. A couple of good, man-sized deer would round me out, maybe, and I'd fill in the niches with a couple of buckets of strong black coffee. After that, I'd aim to begin smoking, and nine or ten pounds of tobacco would be all that I'd need for an after-dinner smoke. Can you fix me up in all them details?"

"Caradac," said the outlaw, "you and me should of met long ago. We got the same sort of ideas about things in general, beginnin' with chuck!"

He built a fire at the mouth of the little cave. The

mule walked in a circle about it, curious as only a mule can be, while Rhiannon walked away and let that fire die down to a great bed of hot coals. And Caradac, lying still, set his teeth and closed his heart against the appetite which began to rage in him. Then he saw Rhiannon come back with shining, silvery fish in his hands, and those fish presently were grilling.

Fiercely Caradac attacked the first portion that was offered to him, but when that small fish was finished, sleep came upon him again.

He slept, and wakened in the middle of the night, and again he was fed.

In another week, he could sit against the rock at the front of the cave, with the southern sun beating against him, warming his thin body to the bone. He saw the river leaping, and the birds flying, and the clouds washing home like waves against the mountains, and he knew that his own strength was welling up in him like a growing fountain.

He saw Rhiannon coming across the mountain side. Large was his stride as he moved among the rocks, and over his shoulders was stretched the burden of a full-grown stag. He came to the mouth of the cave and cast down three hundred pounds of meat before Caradac. The sheriff looked down at the dead eyes and the red tongue which lolled from the mouth of the deer. "Why did you fetch in that little snack, Annan?" said he.

"That's your share for lunch," grinned Annan Rhiannon. "But it's still a couple of hours till midday."

"You're wrong," said the sheriff. "It's past eating time now. It's pretty near night, by the feeling inside of me."

"Start up the fire," said Rhiannon. "I'll go snag some fish for the first course."

Caradac started the fire, and, as it flamed, he turned to the carcass and began to carve it, eyeing the meat with pleasure, for the buck was in his fat prime. He could see Rhiannon down the stream, kneeling on a rock here, a rock there, with a little spear in his hand. It was made of a straight shaft of seasoned ash, slenderly fashioned, and at the end of the shaft there was a little barbed head of steel. It looked like a lance for a pygmy; it was hardly larger than could have been used in fairyland for some gallant elfin knight, armored, on his horse. Rhiannon held

7

the thing between thumb and forefinger. No needle was ever more accurate in the hands of a seamstress than that javelin in the hands of Rhiannon. If a fin winked with the furtive shadows of a pool, the swift death shot down to meet it. If a silver stir thrashed in the white waters, again the spear darted and the dripping prize was drawn out. Caradac himself had tried the same sport. But always he could see nothing. The stream was empty. It was simply a body of water white and black or with eerie streaks of blue in the pools. But always it was empty until Rhiannon came and opened doors and from little glimpses and twinkles of light drew forth living, wriggling, dying trout.

The sheriff watched and marveled as he prepared a spit on which to turn the saddle of the venison. It was not the skill alone, it was the delicacy of touch that amazed him. Rhiannon stood up, at last, and shook back the flood of hair that streamed down over his shoulders. He came to the fire with a string of prizes. These he cleaned, and then he wrapped them in certain grasses and herbs of which he alone knew the secret, unless the red men of the old days had learned it too! He parted the coals. In the hot ashes he buried the fish and then set about making coffee and afterward breaking up cold pone.

Finally they ate. The fish were taken from the charred leaves and laid on clumsy, homemade trenchers of bark. The flesh fell away from the bones; flesh wonderfully fragrant, sweetened by the steam of the herbs.

But the trout were as nothing. The great saddle began to disappear afterwards. Huge drafts of coffee seasoned it. And when the meal had ended, there was no washing of dishes to do for Caradac. His host motioned him into the cave and Caradac went gladly and stretched out his heavy length and slept.

He wakened deep in the afternoon and went forth yawning. He felt as the forest feels in spring, the sap rising, the buds eager to put forth; but still his weakness held him back. Every day he advanced a long stride toward the full, bright summer of his strength, but still there was a time before him.

Now he looked with his fierce, bold eyes over the mountain side, over the shaggy forest, and through the lower mists at the valleys beneath; and beyond the valleys stretched the desert, a gray and pink sea. That thrust of the eyes, far off, gave him a feeling of omniscient divinity. So the Homeric gods glanced down from snowy Olympus to the plains where men lived. So he and Rhiannon lived among the clouds until the winds parted them as with a hand and let their looks go dizzily down. And every day the red blood grew richer in his veins!

Rhiannon, at one side, worked over his guns. Every morning and every afternoon he worked in the same manner. He took them apart, cleaned and oiled them, and reassembled the parts with hands which could have done that work in the darkness. And every morning he practiced with his weapons, patiently, keenly. He made no secret of his skill. He practiced openly before the eyes of Caradac and asked advice, and considered that advice with care. How should a gun be worn, how should it be drawn, how should it be fired? Wherein is speed better than slow certainty, wherein is slow certainty better than speed? He, aspiring greatly, gladly accepted the wisdom of Caradac; and Caradac, aspiring greatly, also looked and learned. They were of one kind; they were of one strength; they were of one skill. Chance would decide, if ever they fought again together. Unless, perhaps, the wilderness was deeper in the blood of Rhiannon, and therefore his eye was a hairsbreadth sharper, his nerves a single twitch swifter in reaction.

Caradac looked upon the man of the mountains and considered him gravely. They did not talk a great deal. There was no need of speech. He had not so much as thanked Rhiannon for the service that had saved his life when that life was clearly forfeit by the law of the West, by the law of the wilderness, by the law of all the beasts and the men who hunt for one another. Then he said: "Rhiannon, come here."

Annan Rhiannon came to him.

"Give me your hand," said the sheriff. The hand was given, and Caradac took out his hunting knife and with the razor edge of it he slit the skin inside the wrist. Then he cut the skin in the wrist of his own right arm, and he placed the two bleeding wounds together and pressed them tight with his left hand.

"Rhiannon," said he, "night or day, mountain or desert, in the law or outside of it, your blood is my blood and my blood is your blood, so help me God!"

9

Annan Rhiannon looked at him with a gleam of his wild black eyes. Then he said, "By God, Caradac, to the end of my life my blood is your blood and your blood is mine!"

Chapter Three

IT WAS a time of blossoming to the sheriff. What ten days do to a garden, when the spring begins, so did ten days work with the sheriff. His lost strength returned. He was robed with it from head to foot, a garment of invincibility like the invulnerable bath of Achilles.

They sat on a fallen log at the edge of the forest and looked across the fire-withered stumps of trees beneath them, and then on to the lofty tops of the spruce beyond. To their right was the river, furiously sweeping, clogged with water from the melted snows.

Then Caradac said, "You have long winters here."

Rhiannon turned his big head and looked at the white heads of the mountains, glittering under the strong sun. Every day the snowline crept higher, but there would be a final cap left on one or two of those lofty heads. "We have long winters," said Rhiannon, finally.

"And you have some wind here, too?"

"It blows," said Rhiannon.

"But you lead a pretty good life," said Caradac. "You're free."

Rhiannon glanced sharply at him. So an eagle looks at an eagle through the soundless sea of air. "I'm free now," said he, and smiled a little.

Caradac smiled in turn. "Ay, you worried a little," he suggested proudly.

"Night and day. I knew we'd have to meet."

"We've met," said the sheriff. He nodded to himself, as though the two words were followed by many others, quietly spoken in his heart of hearts. Then he added, "What'll come in the finish?"

10

"Aw, you can't live outside the pack forever," replied Rhiannon frankly. "I know that."

"But you wouldn't live in it, either?"

"Why, how'n hell could I live in it, Owen? They know me, I guess. They know me pretty well!"

"Of course they know you," said the sheriff.

He stood up and they walked together back across the mountain side. A rabbit leaped from behind a rock and fled wildly before them. Two guns flashed. Two guns exploded. The rabbit turned to a red blur of blood and fur.

"Take us together, we're a mite too strong for such game," said Rhiannon.

They walked on. The smashed flesh of that rabbit was hardly worth salvaging, and therefore they let it remain where it was. A coyote would soon have it, or a passing wolf swallow it; or a bear would give it his attention, perhaps, or a buzzard find it; or the burying beetles, after all, might have the disposition of it, or the flies dissolve it. In so many ways, and many more, nature in the wilderness is able to return flesh to the earth.

They passed on, leisurely, but devouring the ground with their long, tireless striding.

"You have long winters," said Caradac, again.

"Ay, we have some winters," said the other.

"Rheumatism is hell, they tell me," said the sheriff.

"Not my time of life."

"I dunno. You're around forty."

"Am I?"

"Ay, you're about ten years older than me."

"Are you only thirty?"

"That's it."

"I'm twenty-five," said Rhiannon.

The sheriff almost paused in his striding, but then he walked on. He seemed angered, or else he was deeply lost in thought, so black was his frown. "You're twenty-five," he said.

Rhiannon said nothing in answer; his thoughts seemed to be winging far before them.

"You live pretty good," said the sheriff.

"Well, we have long winters," said Rhiannon.

They came the rest of the way to the cave in silence.

"How do you get through the wall?" asked the sheriff.

"I'll show you. I'll take you down that way."

11

"Maybe you better not," said Caradac. "You see how it is. A gent never can tell. Something might happen. It's better to have one secret."

"I'll tell you whenever you want to know," said Rhiannon. "I got no secret from you, Owen. My brain's as plain for you to see as the palm of my hand."

But the sheriff murmured darkly: "No man's soul is so easy to see. My pa and my ma, they never knew me; I never knew them. Nobody knows nobody else. A gent's friends, they're always like Nevada mountains."

"What would you mean by that?" asked the outlaw.

"Nevada mountains always look like they was in your back yard. But you ride fifty miles and die of thirst before you reach the spring that you see on the side of one of 'em. I mean, people are like that. You think you know. You don't know nothin'."

Rhiannon considered this for a time. "You're pretty deep," he said. "Me, I take things the way that I find them!"

"So do most folks," said Caradac. "They take things the way that they find them. They never ask themselves if their eyes can see everything that's worth seeing."

"No," said Rhiannon. "That's true."

"Take you, for instance."

"Well, what about me?"

"Lemme see. When did you start for the mountains?"

"I dunno. Lemme see. Seven years back, I suppose."

"Seven years! Well, that's a spell."

"It is up here, in a way," admitted Rhiannon. He looked across the brutal face of the mountains. "The winters are kind of long," said Rhiannon.

"Bad winds, I guess."

"The ice is hell," said Rhiannon.

They reached the cave. The sun was setting. The valleys were deepened. They were pressed up infinitely higher into the bosom of the flaming sky. Looking down, the desert was on fire too, but the flames were dim as seen through smoke.

"It was an accident, I guess," said the sheriff.

"What?"

"That first trouble you had. It was in Tucson, wasn't it?"

"No, it wasn't no accident. There was a gent from the

12

mines. Him and me had a rough and tumble for fun. He got made and picked up a stone and whanged me on the head with it. I killed him."

"You should of stood trial. They never would of done anything to you for that."

"I knew it. But I seen that I wasn't fit to live around with people. Take when a man hits you; you got no right to get mad. Not when you're like me!" He held out his hands when he spoke and looked down at them curiously, as though they belonged to another man.

"But I get mad," said Rhiannon. "I get hot. My brain, it fills up with smoke. I got no right to live around among people. I seen it, that day in Tucson. I left. Then one thing led to another—"

"That's seven years," said Caradac.

"It seems longer."

"The winters are kind of long, up here," said the sheriff.

"The ice makes the rocks slippery," said Rhiannon. "That's hell!"

They fell silent. The sunset began to die and the mountain tops blossomed with soft rose. The earth beneath them was solid black. No, not solid. The eye could look into it.

After a long time Rhiannon said, "The kids bother me a good deal, too."

The sheriff filled his pipe and waited.

"Once I had an idea," went on the outlaw. "I would go and get me a couple of them. Ones that ain't got no father or mother. I'd get me a boy and a girl and raise them up here pretty good. But—"

He did not finish and the sheriff murmured, "Yes, the winters are pretty long."

"They are," said Rhiannon. "What with the wind. And the ice is hell, too."

"Well," said the sheriff, "I know what you mean. But it ain't the children that you want so much, either."

"Ain't it?"

"You want a woman," said the sheriff.

He remembered he had not lighted his pipe. By the flare of the match he looked askance at Rhiannon, but Rhiannon was staring at the deep darkness of the valleys.

"Yes," said Rhiannon. "I want a woman."

13

Then he added: "Me with a wife! That would be funny!"

"I dunno why," said the sheriff.

"I mean me, the way I am. It would be funny."

"You'd never hurt a woman," said the sheriff.

"Wouldn't I?" said Rhiannon. "I wonder, though. My brain fills up with smoke, kind of. Did I tell you that?"

"Well, you lead a free life up here," said the sheriff. "When you want anything, you can go down to the valleys and get it. You can fade back through the hole-in-the-wall. You got it pretty easy."

"I got it pretty easy," said Rhiannon.

"I guess I'll turn in," said the sheriff.

"I'll sit here awhile. The stars ain't all out, yet."

The sheriff stood in the mouth of the cave. "It ain't the winter and the wind and the ice," he said. "It's you. You're in hell, Annan!"

"Ah, yes," said Rhiannon. "I'm in hell, right enough!"

The sheriff went in and found his bed of the fragrant pine boughs and lay down to sleep.

Chapter Four

FOR ANOTHER day or two it was as though they had not spoken of life in general and the future of Rhiannon in particular. But then a blasting storm struck across the valley on an evening and drove them into the cave. They could not have a fire—the blast would fill the cave with stifling smoke. So they wrapped themselves in copious deerskins, for Rhiannon understood the trick of the Indian in curing those hides. In the deep blackness of the cave they sat and smoked until smoking was no longer interesting.

"Down below, they'll be lighting the lamps," said the sheriff.

Annan answered, "I got to forget what happens down below."

"No," said the sheriff, "you don't." He had been

thinking the matter over for days. His surety was in his voice.

"They'd be waiting for me with open arms, maybe," suggested Rhiannon dryly. "They'd be pretty glad to see me."

He laughed a little, and the sheriff, listening to that voice, wondered at it. There is a touch of roughness in the voice of a youth and only with middle age the throat opens, as it were, and speaks with a resonant sureness. Such was the voice of Rhiannon, rich, mellow, and speaking of middle age.

"You've seen the posters that they put up about you?" asked the sheriff.

"More bear than man, they make me look," said Rhiannon.

"That was Philipson, the artist, that done them. He had a look at you, you know, when you stuck up the Overland!"

"Artist?" sneered Rhiannon. "He done a job for me!"

"Ah, they know you well enough," said the sheriff.

"Of course they do," agreed Rhiannon. "They don't need any photographs of me hanging around."

"They know you by the mane that you wear, blowing around over your shoulders, and by your beard. You know what they call you, some of 'em."

"Blackbeard. I know."

"But supposing, old son, that you clipped your hair and run a razor over your face?"

The wind, at that moment, fell upon the mountain with a human fury. It had the scream of the forests in it, and the raging of the waters, and the mountain trembled before the stroke of that anger. Rhiannon could not make himself heard for a time, so that he had a long moment in which to think. "Well—" he said at last.

The sheriff went on smoothly, very glad that his idea had made any lodgment at all. "You see how it is. If I could hide the scar on my face, I could disguise myself dead easy. Why? Because, suppose people want to describe me? Well, they do like this: 'Big man, got a whacking scar across his face. Looks like a bear had clawed him.' That's how they always describe me. Now, suppose that I could get rid of that scar, I'd never be

15

known very well, if I changed my voice and other things around me!"

"I see what you mean by that," said the other thoughtfully. "I dunno—"

"Or again, supposing that you was to see Mount Laurel with the forest scraped off its face."

"That's true," said Rhiannon.

"And then, you could slip away from this here part of the range—"

"I never could do that."

"The air's as good and the water as pure and the deer as fat in the other parts."

"I'm part of Mount Laurel, and Mount Laurel is a part of me. I'd have to be on it, or else I'd have to have it wedged into my skyline. I couldn't get on, otherwise!"

The sheriff did not try to argue against this. It was not a point of view with which he sympathized, but he was willing to understand when he had reached a wall that could not be scaled. "All right," said he. "Lemme tell you something. People see what they want to see."

"That's true."

"What are you?"

"I'm Rhiannon. I'm the killer. Oh, I know what they say about me!"

"Why? You ride into their minds like this: On a running horse or a racing mule, with a brush of black hair blown over your shoulders and your beard parted by the wind. You been doing that seven years. It seems like seventy to the folks in the valley."

"Yes," said Rhiannon. "They've had their trouble with me. They don't know how to stop me. They don't know about the hole-in-the-wall!"

"Of course they don't," said the sheriff. "You talk about the winters being long, up here. Well, you're like winter to them that are down there. When they look up here, what do they see? Do they see Mount Laurel? No, you damn well bet they don't. They see Annan Rhiannon standing in the middle of the sky with his black beard on his face; and the clouds that blow over the shoulders of Mount Laurel, they're the hair blowing over the back of Rhiannon. You take last month. Sandy Ferguson sold out and quit. He said that Rhiannon was too much for his nerves."

16

"Yes," said Rhiannon without vanity, "it must be kind of bad. Not knowing how I get away every time, I mean. Not knowing about the hole-in-the-mountain. You know there's the fairy yarn about the horse that had wings?"

"Pegasus. I remember hearing that yarn."

"The hole-in-the-mountain is better to me than a horse with wings. No wonder the people get worried."

"And me, I got worried," said the sheriff.

"So you come up to get me. Yes, of course! I was expecting for a long time that I'd see you—"

His voice trailed away. The wind had fallen. But they remained in the cave, looking out at the white dappling of stars that filled the entrance. They were thinking of what might have been; they were thinking of death, of something subtracted from each, instead of something added.

"What's more, I'm gunna take you down," said the sheriff.

"Are you?" asked Rhiannon, curiously, without doubt or challenge in his voice.

"I am! Though nobody will know it. I'm gunna take you down. I'm gunna plant you. And you're gunna grow!"

This he said with deliberation.

Rhiannon made a surprising answer: "To hear the way you talk, it scares me, Owen!"

"Sure it does," replied the sheriff. "You sit tight. You lemme think for you, will you?"

"Of course," said Rhiannon.

At that, Owen Caradac sat up straighter, stiffer; and suddenly he realized that his blood had indeed passed into the blood of Rhiannon, and the blood of Rhiannon had joined that of Owen Caradac more truly than ever it happened in the old days, when the fierce Indians had celebrated that same ceremony. Now he could think for this man, and his thoughts would be accepted. He no longer argued a point; he no longer tried to lead with clever suggestions. He saw that what he must do was simply to satisfy himself; and, when that was accomplished, then he could do as he chose, and dispose of this wild man at his will. So he added up his ideas, one to another, and found a sum total which was far from satisfying.

"I gotta think," said the sheriff, and went out from the cave and stood with his head among the stars. Or so,

17

at least, he seemed to Annan Rhiannon, who remained behind in the blackness. The sheriff remained for a long time without turning his head. Then he came back, went to bed, and spoke no more.

But in the morning, as they stood dripping by the edge of the pool, whipping the icy water from their bodies, he said: "You better shave. I got my razor. You better take that and shave."

"Never shaved in seven years," said Rhiannon. "I'll manage it, though."

"You lose that hair, first," said the sheriff.

He knew something about barbering. There was a sheep shears, useful for many things about camp, and this he carefully ground until the edges were sharp. Then he shore away the heavy black locks of Rhiannon. The story of Samson ran back into his mind, and how the strength of the hero had gone with his hair.

Afterward, he worked more carefully, very precisely, clipping the hair of Rhiannon, rounding it off with caution. And he noticed that the nape of the man's neck was as round as the neck of a boy, and snowy white. "You look lopsided with that stuff left on your face," he said. "Go take a razor and shave, will you?"

Rhiannon went down to the river and shaved. He came back rubbing half a dozen little cuts in the skin, but that skin was white as snow. Only around the eyes and across the nose, like a mask, the skin was sun-blackened.

The sheriff, in amazement, saw that Annan Rhiannon had thrown twenty years over his shoulder. It was impossible for him to believe that this was the formidable man for whom he had come hunting into the mountains. His step was lighter. His shoulders were less broad. The eyes which had glittered from beneath the sweeping masses of his hair were now larger, milder. His very step was more light, and his bulk was stripped away from him.

Caradac knew that this was a miracle, and that, at a touch, the old Rhiannon was dead. However, he merely said: "You rub oil onto that white skin, and you'll get all one piece of color, pretty quick. You gotta lie out in the sun, though, to do that!"

Annan Rhiannon fumbled at his new face with a curious hand. "Feels funny," he remarked.

18

"Sure," said the sheriff. "You got a new name, now. You're what? John Gwynn, say. That's Welsh, too. What do you think of that for a name?"

"It burns like fire!" said Rhiannon.

He was speaking of his newly exposed skin, freshly tormented by the razor's edge.

Chapter Five

BETWEEN Mount Laurel and the desert, looking westward, the foothills roll in pleasant waves. They are too small to look even like stepping-stones to the rigid bulk of Laurel Mountain; they are far too charming to make a border to the desert and verge into it. Instead, they make a narrow region of their own. The clouds which fly over the desert, never letting fall a drop of their moisture, are chilled by the tall head of the mountain, and the rains that fall water these hills so that little streams run everywhere down to the desert, and disappear, after a time, in the hot, smoky pallor of the creosote bushes or in the thin-leaved tangles of mesquite.

Those hills are a sort of Promised Land to the desert dwellers. They drive up their starved cattle to fatten them for market on the fresh slopes; and the lucky ranchers who have settled here and there on the good lands grow fat of purse and jovial of eye, for nature takes care of their property with a careful husbandry. There is never a flood and there is never a drought, and the land yields all that the heart could desire—not grass for cattle, only, but crops of wheat that run fifteen sacks to the acre, and barley that runs forty. It is a kind of soil that gives softly before the plow and that never hardens to tough lumps even when it is summer-fallowed.

Into this region the sheriff brought Annan Rhiannon, alias John Gwynn. They rode a pair of good horses and led a pair of pack mules heavily laden; and so they came through the hills.

19

"What do you think of this lay of the land?" asked Caradac.

"It's a good soft country," said Rhiannon. "You could sleep here." He let his eye lift; far off he saw the head of Mount Laurel splitting apart its hood of clouds.

"Sure you could sleep here," agreed the sheriff. "You could get rich here, too!"

"Sleep is poison," said Rhiannon. "I mean, to me."

Caradac answered: "I've thought it all over. You gotta take a chance."

"All right," said Rhiannon mildly.

"Nothing is safe," argued Caradac with gloomy conviction.

"Sure there's nothing safe," agreed Rhiannon.

"You take a gent and ride herd on him—well, he'll catch measles and die of it, or choke with whooping cough. Being careful ain't always the way to win the game."

"Of course it ain't," said Rhiannon.

"Damn it," said the sheriff, "you gotta do some thinking for yourself!" He wanted to lead the way, and yet he was alarmed when he saw with what docility his friend submitted to all of his judgments.

"Thinking is hard for me," said Rhiannon. "You take the way some people always can figure out things ahead—"

"Man," broke in the sheriff, "you've done your thinking pretty hard and fast, I'd say. Seven years and never snagged!"

Rhiannon half closed his eyes to consider, and this gave Caradac a chance to look keenly at him. Without a beard, Rhiannon was another human being; rather, he was a human being for the first time, instead of a strange ogre. Unshadowed by the masses of hair, his eyes were blue-black, large and mild. There was a patient look in them like the look of the ox in the field, unthinkingly gentle, so that the sheriff continually had to reassure himself and say, "After all, this *is* the great Rhiannon!"

But still he could not believe his eyes. One rarely can. They are the least important feeders of the mind!

"Well," explained Annan Rhiannon, "you take when trouble jumps up under your nose—like when a sheriff pulls down on you with a rifle," he added with a faint

20

smile—"and then you act quick. Not thinking. You think afterward."

"You'd have me feel that that's the way you been living through all of these seven years? Just following your nose?" He added, as the impossibility grew upon him: "Slipping in and out of the towns, taking what you want to take, doing what you want to do? Laughing at me and the rest when we tried to chase you?"

"Look at a wolf," considered Rhiannon—he never seemed to be greatly convinced of anything, but his words were suggestions, merely, to himself as to his companion. "You look at a wolf. It don't think like a man, but sometimes it will fool the shepherds."

The sheriff was so stopped by this suggestion that he could not make an immediate retort, and the other explained more at large: "The wolf he follows his nose, too. But when he's on the trail he's awake. Then besides, I always had the hole-in-the-wall to get through."

Caradac nodded. "You think you'd go to sleep, here?" he asked.

"I dunno," frowned Rhiannon. "Everywhere around and about there is people that would like pretty well to have a knife into me. I don't know them; they know me. There you are!"

"Know you? I don't hardly know you myself!" declared the sheriff. "Rhiannon is a hell-bender. He's about forty or forty-five. You're a sleepy-looking, handsome sort of a lazy kid of twenty-five. They'll never know you!"

Rhiannon did not reply; he merely touched his face lightly with the tips of curious fingers.

"Look here," said the sheriff, "what's that ring?"

"I picked it up, once," said Rhiannon.

He held out his hand. It was a flat-faced lump of lapis lazuli.

"When you stuck up somebody?" asked the sheriff.

"I found it on the floor in the hole-in-the-wall."

The sheriff whistled. "Then other people go there, too?"

"I dunno. I don't think so. This must of been left long ago."

"There ain't much sparkle to it," observed Caradac, critically. He was thinking that for his part he would not care to wear so cheap a stone. No stones at all, or else diamonds. He could remember Sam Larkin selling a thousand calves for the price of a single diamond. A thousand calves stuck into your necktie. That's something!

"There ain't much sparkle," said the outlaw, "but you look pretty close. There's a hand with an iron glove on it, and there's a heart with the blood dripping out of it. It's carved pretty neat and exact, I'd say!"

The sheriff gave the thing a glance. He was incurious. All that interested him was that Rhiannon should have cared to wear so large and dull a stone on his hand.

"Have other folks seen this?" he asked.

"I never wore it when I was working," said Rhiannon. "It might get in the way of a draw."

"Of course."

"But now I only pack one gun," said Rhiannon, "and the left hand don't matter much."

For they had agreed between them that it would be better for him to use only one Colt. He who carries two is apt to be put down as a gunman—and this was a train of thought to be avoided.

"There's a pretty good little place," said Rhiannon, presently.

"That?" scoffed the sheriff. "That's only a shack."

"It's got a look about it," said Rhiannon.

He actually drew rein to stare. It was, to be sure, a very small house, but a tide of green climbing vines washed up the front of it, and the white honeysuckle blossoms dropped from the eaves and over the windows. The picket fence in front of it needed repairing; it ran in a staggering wave. And the front gate hung by one hinge. A patch of orchard stood behind it—say, ten acres of apples and prunes. There were two small pastures. And through the place ran a little creek with an embowering of willows and oaks near the banks. The house itself was somewhat obscured by a great fig tree in the front yard, and the yard itself was a mass of tangled alfalfa which needed cutting. There were a small barn and a diminutive shed, both opening upon a little corral.

"It's got a sort of a look," repeated Rhiannon.

"Come on," said the sheriff. "We ain't gunna waste the whole day here, are we? We gotta travel, don't we?"

But when they came just opposite the place and the

broken gate, Rhiannon stopped his horse again. "Listen!" he said inaccurately. "You can smell the honeysuckle. Sort of sweetish, I'd say."

"Doggone me," remarked the sheriff; "it sure beats me, though. A man-sized man like you interested in a doll's house like that!"

"Sure," said Rhiannon. "It sounds funny, all right. You know how it is. It sort of fits into my mind. Like I had seen it before!"

"How would you like that place for your own?" asked the sheriff, yawning.

"Me?" Rhiannon looked on it with a smile. "It ain't much," he said, "but I never would ask God for nothin' more—"

"Except a woman to put into it, maybe?"

"You always got to ride on ahead, don't you?" smiled Rhiannon.

"Couple of years back," remarked the sheriff, "gent needed some money and I loaned it. He went bad; couldn't pay. I got his place. And this is it."

"The hell you say!"

"The hell I don't. You go in and hang up your hat, kid. I brought you all the way to show you this. Now it belongs to you!"

Chapter Six

THEY LOOKED it over from top to bottom. There were two small attic rooms—an old, battered trunk in one of them. On the ground floor were a kitchen, a bedroom with the honeysuckle showering through a broken windowpane, a dining room that opened upon a back porch, and a living room whose door stepped upon the front veranda. It was furnished cheerfully, without expense.

In the barn lay three or four tons of loose hay. When they entered the mow, pigeons flew from the loft with whistling wings, and Rhiannon looked up at them and laughed softly. There was stall room for five horses on each side of the barn.

In the shed they found the sagging remnants of a buggy, a two-ton wagon, two rusty plows, a harrow, and a jumble of odds and ends—broken harness, broken chains, collars, pads for the shoulders, a forge and dusty bellows, and a litter of tools for blacksmithing.

Rhiannon hung over these items with a fascinated eye. "You could make things, here," said he.

They went back to the yard of the house and walked beneath the trees. The figs were not ripe, but the tree was loaded heavily. The alfalfa crunched beneath their feet.

"We better keep to the path," said Rhiannon. "There's no use spoiling things!"

The sheriff smiled.

They went out to the broken gate.

"It only needs a new back and a couple of bolts," said Rhiannon.

"You know about such things?" asked the sheriff.

"I done blacksmithing when I was a kid," said Rhiannon.

"Think of that!" said Caradac.

"The blacksmith is the only gent that's free," explained Rhiannon. "The others, they gotta have tools. The blacksmith, he makes his own tools!"

"Guns, even?" grinned the sheriff.

Rhiannon brushed a long, blue-barreled Colt into his hand. "I dunno. You gimme time, even a gun, maybe," said he. And his eyes sharpened with an ambitious eagerness. "I'd even make a bet," he said.

Caradac shrugged his shoulders. "I never bet," said he.

"Now," said Rhiannon, "I'll run this here place for you. I don't know orcharding, but I'll learn."

"You'll run this here place for yourself," said the sheriff.

He looked about him and sighed a little. He had saved more money than this represented. Still—it was a tidy item, and a rare stroke to have gained it. And the sheriff was a thrifty man!

He looked back to Rhiannon and found that he had turned a dark red and was staring at Mount Laurel's head of iron and white.

"Me, speaking personal," said Caradac carelessly, "I'm kind of glad to be alive to give anything to anybody."

Rhiannon made no answer. He was a darker red than ever.

"Look here," explained the sheriff, "I'll tell you how it is. He was no good, the fellow that had this. He was a skunk. Got the place from his old man and let it run to hell. When I foreclosed nobody would bid in. I got the place for the mortgage. It was worth five times as much, I guess. It was luck, that was all! Luck—like me being alive this minute!"

A glitter came into the eyes of Rhiannon and changed them so suddenly that the sheriff backed up half a step, instinctively on his guard.

"You gimme a chance to work for this place. I'll do the work for you until I can make something out of it. Maybe, someday, I can buy it off of you."

"Man, man—" began the sheriff.

But Rhiannon raised his hand. "Nobody can give a man happiness," said he. "You don't pick happiness out of the dirt. You gotta work for it. I used to sit up on Mount Laurel. The winters are kind of long up there, and the ice is hell. I used to sit and think. I used to say, 'I'd work, for happiness!' Well, now I got a chance to work. You couldn't give me anything, Owen. You could loan me things for a start. That's all that you could do!"

The heart of the sheriff grew warmer and it grew larger. After all, he was a thrifty man. Besides, he told himself that he understood what was in the mind of Rhiannon.

"We'll start any way that you say," he said. "Afterward we can make terms. Shall we go in and write it on paper?"

Rhiannon rarely expressed an emotion, but now he reached out and laid his hand on the shoulder of his friend. "You'll remember," said he. "So will I." Then he explained, "Papers and things, they don't leave a man free!"

It was seen that Caradac had planned all exactly. The loads which he had bought for the mules made an ample stock of provisions and odds and ends such as a new ax, a brace and bits, and such oddments of tools and nails and screws as might be needed. He even had brought a sack of coke for the forge. The two pack mules could be worked to the plow. The horse remained with Rhiannon as a means of conveyance, whether under the saddle or hitched to the buggy.

"It's up to your two hands," said the sheriff. "Funny thing. I knew you'd want it. I knew what you'd want to do!"

They looked upon each other, each striving to veil from his eyes the affection and the understanding.

"Suppose that something rare turned up," said the sheriff. "Suppose that there was a way of falling into some money quick. You know what I mean. They come through here, pretty often. Up from the south, down from the north, heading for one border or another. They got thousands on their heads, sometimes. What would you say if I sent over word to you? You could come in on it. Me and you on one trail—God help the crook!"

The eyes of Rhiannon blazed again like—the sheriff could think of no other thing—the eyes of a cat in the dusk.

But at last the outlaw said: "Maybe I better keep quiet. After you been sick, it's better to be quiet, maybe?"

Caradac understood, and he said no more.

That evening he started back down the road, and, turning at the first fork, he looked back and made out the pale blue-white column of smoke which arose over the roof of the cottage. He felt that a dead thing had come to life. He had another feeling, too. As though he had planted strange seed, and wondered what sort of plant it would bring forth in due season—blossom or grain, food or poison.

Chapter Seven

Now Rhiannon loved beyond all things the noble head and the broad bosom and the outstretched, muscular arms of Mount Laurel; but whenever he grew tired, he remembered the long winter nights, and the wind, and the ice which dripped over the rocks and turned them to glass. By lantern light he worked in the morning; he used up the sun like a precious candle; and at night he worked by lantern light again.

Every evening the forge fire glowed and cast its rosy light into the gathering dusk. Every night his hammer clattered in the house or in the barn. So, from the battered harness, strong, serviceable suits appeared; the shares for the plow were tapped and retempered to sharpness; the fences stood up straight; the sagging buggy drew in its sprawling knees and glistened with new paint; the tall, rank grass in the orchard fell before the plow, and then the harrow crunched through the clods and made them soft, thick, moist dust. A scythe felled the tangled alfalfa in the front yard. The ground was flooded and the new crop began to arise.

Also, over the well in the back yard, the skeleton of a windmill stood up, higher and higher. It was finished. The ruined wheel of the fallen mill was repaired and set in place. It began to spin with a cheerful, reassuring clank, night and day.

There was a slight rise of ground behind the house. In the top of it was a natural hollow, and around this Rhiannon carried a stout wall, plastered with coats of mud on the inside, and heaped with earth on the outside. It grew up foot by foot until it was four yards high. Into this reservoir he turned the overplus of water drawn up by the windmill, and from the reservoir he conducted lines to the eastern pasture land. All that pasture he leveled and checked, and then he flooded it in time to plant a last crop of alfalfa for that year.

Neither were these things done slowly. In his hands was the power of two strong men. In his heart was the deep impatience which comes of wasted time. He was flooding the little farm with the wasted hours of seven years. And he nerved himself constantly for greater and greater efforts.

The sheriff rode over once or twice a week and perhaps helped in the placing of the heavier timbers. Once he came cursing and red-faced, but driving three cows before him.

"I could feed that alfalfa instead of selling it," Rhiannon had said the week before. So after that he added to his other duties the milking of the cows, and their feeding,

27

and the making of butter which Caradac brought back to the town and sold. It was the first earned money. A thin trickle, but more than diamonds to Rhiannon.

He leveled the second pasture, all but a narrow strip, and flooded that also, to plow, and then seed for the crops of the following year.

And so all the face of the little farm turned green and began even in that fertile district to look like a rich emerald among green glass beads. So he worked with fervor and with violence and always with his eye cast forward to a future when perfection on the little estate would become still more perfect.

He allowed himself two pauses in the fury of his work. One was after the evening meal, when he sat for a cool half-hour, smoking one cigarette after another, and watching the dusk grow to night; the other pause was when, finally, he flung himself into his bed and slept like a sailor gone below from his watch off the pitch of the Horn.

There was only one moment of enjoyment and leisure, therefore, and that was the half-hour during which he sat on his veranda after his supper, letting his aching muscles relax, letting his brain drop away from the strenuous realities of the day.

In that time, he was fond of looking toward Mount Laurel, since even in the half-light he could see it clearly, and when the plain was dusk, the mountain still glowed with a vague illumination. He knew it so well that he could identify every polished knob of granite and every shadowed indentation. What looked like slight depressions were, he knew, ragged-lipped gorges, thronged with mighty trees, and what appeared as a deep scratch scoring the cheek of the monster was a great ravine through which the mountain winds billowed and thundered.

And as he sat in the peace of his veranda and looked up to this veteran of the range, he tasted the quiet, the relaxation—and furthermore he tasted the sweat of labor! Pain of exhaustion, pain of monotony, pain of constant effort, he knew now. Yonder on the mountain there had been the winter, like a devouring wolf. But also there had been the wolf's liberty—a savage and a constant joy. Yet he could shake his head at that grim and splendid existence and turn away to the trailing vines which swept down from the eaves before him; and the whisper of the breeze and the swaying top of the fig tree were in place of the screaming hurricane which would be blowing now over Mount Laurel. Witness the stiff-standing flag of clouds that whipped and snapped toward the south, hanging from the neck of the giant!

So, turning his eyes and his mind down from such larger emotions and such larger speculations, he looked across the hills and marked a rider jogging up the road. The man came nearer, paused, turned his horse to the gate of Rhiannon, and waved a hand in greeting.

Through the stillness of the evening his voice came gently and clearly: "Evening, stranger."

"Evening," said Rhiannon.

He went on rolling a cigarette, dimly wondering why the other was there—a young, trimly made man.

"I guess I ain't invited in?" asked the other.

"Hey? Sure. Get down and come in," said Rhiannon. He began to frown. His smoking time almost was ended. And in the forge there was waiting for him—and waiting for fire—a shapeless lump of iron, to be turned white hot and then drawn out long and long under the terrific blows of a twelve-pound hammer, wielded in the single hand of Rhiannon.

The stranger came up the path. He paused under the fig tree. The figs were ripe now and, bending down a branch, he picked a few. "Good plump figs," he declared. "Never seen such off of this tree for five years. The old tree is thankin' you for water, I guess!"

He came on up the path to the veranda. "I'm Charlie Dee," said he. "I come from the Dee place. My father owns it. You look across the hills there. You see the top of the roof of the big barn? No, you can't see it now."

"I've seen it in the day," said Rhiannon.

"And what's your name?"

"My name's John Gwynn."

"Hello, John Gwynn. I'm glad to know you. Shall I sit down? Thanks. We been aching to have a look at you. We been watching what you've done to the old place here, of course. My father used to own this place. He used to own all this land around here, pretty near!"

He seemed a vacuous young man. He made Rhiannon feel even older than toil had made him feel. "You smoke?" asked Rhiannon by way of comment and reply.

"Thanks. I don't mind if I do. I run out of papers coming out from town. You like it here, Gwynn?"

"Pretty well," said Rhiannon.

"You bought the place from Sheriff Caradac, didn't you?"

"I'm just his hired man," said Rhiannon. He laughed shortly, a little embarrassed. "How would I be buying a place like this?"

"The sheriff says that it's your place," said the other with his bright and cheerful inquisitiveness.

He seemed to Rhiannon to have the manner of a bird on a branch, twittering senselessly, picking up seeds of information. "He says that. He wants to make me happy," explained Rhiannon.

"Because you've done so much to the place, eh? Funny, though," commented Charlie Dee. "You take Caradac, I never knew him to talk like he was chucking away a claim to a place. Kind of tight, I've always found him. No?"

Rhiannon said nothing. He did not like this conversation. He did not like this visitor. The iron waited for him in the forge. Midnight before he could finish the rough outlining of that task!

"Got a light?"

Rhiannon with growing distaste struck a match and held it out. The other leaned forward and drew for some time at the cigarette before he seemed able to light it, and finally jerked his head away as though he were afraid that the flame would catch his nose. Rhiannon almost wished that it had!

"How many acres you got here?" asked the youth.

"Sixty-three," said Rhiannon.

"Nothin' careless about that," said Charlie Dee. "You must of measured it, eh?"

Rhiannon was silent again.

"Hard job, too," said Charlie Dee. "You gotta understand geometry and everything like that before you can measure out land. I stuck at mathematics. I never could get through it. Algebra—that was what broke my heart!"

He laughed loudly, as young men laugh, appreciating his pointless remark.

"I'm pretty busy," said Rhiannon. "I gotta get to work pretty soon."

"Gotta get to work!" cried Charlie Dee. "This time of night? Say, how d'you stand it?"

"Starting up a place—you gotta put in hours," explained Rhiannon, rising to his feet.

He waited for the other to leave, but instead, though he rose, Charlie Dee queried with exhaustless curiosity, "What could you be doing at this time of the night?"

"Out at the forge," said Rhiannon, shorter than ever. "I'll have to be getting along."

"I'll go along," said Charlie Dee, "and watch you what you're doing. Always took to forge-work, myself."

"It's smoky out there. Maybe you better be getting back home. It's late," said Rhiannon.

"Lateness doesn't matter in my house. There's always a handout of chuck, if you're hungry. Besides, I wouldn't go back home this quick. The old man told me to see you and talk to you. He wants to be friendly with all the new settlers. He's a friendly fellow, my father. He ain't proud. You know the way some people are. They make their money. Then they hold up their chins."

He continued to chatter as they went out toward the blacksmith shop. "He just goes out and rides range the same as anybody," said the youngster. "There ain't a calf foaled on the whole ranch that he don't know about it. There ain't a twig that sprouts in the spring, hardly. He sees everything. He told me to come over here and see you."

Rhiannon smiled to himself. But he determined to endure. It might be the mere garrulousness of youth, or again it might be that Charlie Dee was a little weak in the brain. At any rate, he must accustom himself to having strangers about, now and then. The West is not a country where one can play hermit and prosper. The weight of public opinion insists on knocking down even the most private walls, from time to time.

The family of Dee, it appeared, once had possessed most of this district, and still it looked upon itself as a sort of overlord. And though that attitude was sufficiently irritating, still it was far better for an outlaw to have no enemies, even the most humble ones—to say nothing of lords of the land. So he looked upon young Charlie Dee—perforce—more cheerfully, and took him into the gloomy shed.

It was not gloomy long. The first cloud of smoke from the wisp of paper and the kindling was soon billowing out the door or curling in the rafters, while the fierce little jet of red fire stabbed up in pulses. It was covered over. Thick coal smoke, foul with gas, rose in turn, but the heavy strokes on the bellows soon increased the field of the fire. It grew broader, it grew deeper, with a sullen roaring, and at last Rhiannon could take up the mass of iron and place it in the flame.

"Stand over here and get rested," said Charlie Dee. "I'll work the bellows. I'll hold the iron for you, too, if you want. I can hold and turn. I've done it a lot. I like it."

Rhiannon said nothing, but he went over to his hammers. He had been unable to get exactly what he wanted. He had a twelve-pounder for his own striking, when he had to hold as well. Something more had been needed for both his mighty hands. He had taken a sixteen-pound sledge and forced two or more pounds of lead into the head.

This heavy engine he now took from the rack and swung it lightly a few times to accustom himself to the balance. After that he shifted the lantern so that its light fell more strongly upon the anvil.

In the meantime, with a cautious eye, he observed Charlie Dee at the bellows and saw that he worked it properly, and that he kept feeding the coal properly, too. In a long rectangle, the fire was working, and presently Charlie scraped aside the top layer of coal and called: "She's ripe as a well-hung steak, old-timer. Shall I take her out?"

Rhiannon nodded, and Charlie Dee, with a strong pincers, lifted out a great mass of metal, white hot, snapping out sparks like tiny diamonds lighted from within.

Rhiannon bared his own arms to the elbows, spat on his hands, and braced his feet. Then he began to work. The terrific blows of the big hammer, dropping in a ceaseless hail, smashed the iron lump, flattened it, then drew it out. And at every stroke the sparks spurted out in showers—straight to the sides and down toward the floor. At every stroke it was as though strong lights had been turned on. The uppermost reaches of the rafters were revealed, blackened by soot, and now with dense smoke

32

masses settling on them. Still the blows fell, and spark showers turned to red. The metal mass darkened.

"Let the fire work," said Charlie Dee. "Fire's cheaper than men!"

He replaced the bar in the flames. Then he dusted his hands. "Like a lot to stop here and help you through with that job," he declared. "But as a matter of fact, I suppose I gotta get home sometime."

He paused by the door and lifted the sledge, swayed it with a grunt, and let it fall heavily. Then he whistled softly. "So long," said Charlie Dee.

"So long, and thanks," said Rhiannon. He even stepped to the door and watched his cheerful visitor disappear into the dark. He looked up with a half-sigh at the stars —like other sparks dancing in the sky. Then he went back to his labor.

Chapter Eight

CARADAC CAME in the morning through the brown autumn fields to the green little farm and found Rhiannon working in the creamery—he had repaired a small shed behind the house and installed his pans there for the setting of the milk.

He had finished dropping the skimmings of the morning into the churn as Caradac entered, and the sheriff, with a grin, sat down to work the churn handle.

"All right," said Rhiannon. "I'll get back to the mules—"

"Hey, wait a minute," said the sheriff. "If you work like hell all the time, you ain't never going to be Rockefeller, are you? And you ain't gunna have any glory, either, are you?"

Rhiannon hesitated.

"Sit down," said Caradac.

Rhiannon sat down obediently.

"I wanted to tell you something, old son. About this place. Sixty-five or seventy acres—"

"Sixty-three," said Rhiannon.

"Hey? Well, let it go at that. I loaned twenty dollars an acre on the ground. I got it for that. Twelve hundred bucks I laid out. A month after I foreclosed I could of sold it for seventy-five. Then you come along. Yesterday I got another offer in town. You guess. I'll hold the sack."

"We've worked it up a bit," said Rhiannon. Then, anxiously. "You want to sell, Owen?"

"Well, I got an offer. You guess."

"A hundred an acre," said Rhiannon, more anxious than ever.

"Look here, son," said the other. "Next winter we'll be selling hay, won't we?"

"Yes."

"What's a good winter price?"

"I dunno, exactly."

"I don't mean for volunteer weeds like they cut here and there on the range, but for good, first quality alfalfa?"

"I dunno."

"Around about twenty dollars a ton, I can get—if I sell at the right time."

"Well, that's money."

"Money don't interest you none, you'd say. Wait a minute. How many acres we got under water?"

"Fifty-one."

"All right. How many tons an acre in a season?"

"Six, if we have any luck."

"That's five crops?"

"Yes."

"Six times fifty is three hundred. Times twenty is six thousand dollars a whack. Six thousand every year!"

"Yes," said Rhiannon. "You got to count out expenses. And resowing every few years. And such things. You'll have to have an extra man out here, too!"

"I hired him today," said the sheriff. "Now, we got a good apple orchard, too, haven't we?"

"Yes. It looks good."

"It *is* good. You tried the apples?"

"Yes."

"Table, not cider, eh?"

"Yes, good table apples."

"Now, son, will those ten acres pay the taxes and the

improvements and the fertilizer and the cost of the extra hired man?"

"I don't know," said the cautious Rhiannon.

"I do," said the sheriff. "It'll pay all of that and more. Now, look here. Six thousand is gunna be clear every year."

"Don't count the chickens," urged the other, worried.

"Shut up, Annan. I'm talking, now! Six thousand is a good fat interest on a hundred thousand. People are beginning to get their eyes open. I ask you what I got offered to me for this little farm that folks laughed when I swallowed it. What did I get offered? A hundred an acre, you say? Four hundred bucks an acre, my boy!" He paused.

"That's more than twenty thousand dollars," said Rhiannon slowly.

"That's a lot more. And what did I say? Nothing doing, I said!"

Rhiannon rolled and lighted a cigarette. He waited, pleasure in his eyes.

"You're glad?"

Rhiannon nodded.

"Now, boy. Suppose I write off my seventy-five dollars an acre. Suppose that I even make it a hundred dollars an acre. You can pay me in your first year. Is that right?"

Rhiannon held up a hand. "We do this as partners, Owen," he protested.

Rhythmically the sheriff drove the plunger up and down through the sweet cream which crashed and slushed inside the tin churn. "You talk like a damn fool, son," said he.

Rhiannon shook his head.

"Is that all?" said the sheriff.

"Yes."

"Then," said the sheriff, "suppose that we take it fifty-fifty?"

"That's generous, Owen. You could of hired men to fix up this place the way I have."

"Hired them? They never would have had the sense. Nobody would of had the sense. Not old Dee, even, when he owned the land. He never thought of making that draw into a reservoir. He let the old windmill fall down!"

So Rhiannon turned, full of his thoughts, and saw

35

Mount Laurel standing bald and shining in the bright morning sun of that autumn day, and he knew that he had made his place among men, the workers. Other things might come, after that. He had his hands on the way to comfort, to wealth, even!

But he merely said: "Dee? You know them?"

"Like a book."

"There's a young one. There's one named Charlie."

"You spotted him, have you?"

Rhiannon shrugged his shoulders. "What about him?" he asked.

"All got brains," said the sheriff. "Every Dee has got brains. You'd think, to know about them, that they all had an extra share. But then you come to Charlie. He's different."

"I thought he was," agreed Rhiannon, remembering the aimless chatter of that youth.

"There's brains and brains," declared the sheriff. "There's good hard wits, and there's something a strike above 'em. There's genius! By God, that's Charlie Dee."

Rhiannon forgot to smoke. He listened in bewilderment.

"You ever play chess?" went on the sheriff.

"A little when I was a kid."

"You know most people play bad; some study and work hard and have good heads for the game besides, and they're hard to beat."

"That's right."

"But beyond them, there's the ones with genius. They chuck away a rook, a couple of bishops, and three or four pawns. And then, when you think you're winning, they slip through and checkmate you in a couple of moves."

"True," sighed Rhiannon, remembering from the dim past.

"They're the real experts. And that's the way with Charlie Dee. He's always working five moves ahead of you. You block him here, you block him there. But before you know it, he's won. Genius, Annan, my boy!"

Rhiannon frowned. He was trying to fit this description with his estimate of the youth. It failed completely. "He was over here last night," he said.

"He was?"

"What's wrong about that?"

"Nothing—nothing—" sighed the sheriff.

He let the handle of the churn stand idle. "Only," he said, "I'd rather that anybody else had come through. He sees too much!"

"About me?" asked Rhiannon, his face turning to iron.

"Hey, Annan. It ain't as bad as that. Most likely he didn't see anything, or suspect anything. You ain't throwing away any tricks!"

"I pray and hope to God," said Rhiannon, "that he didn't suspect anything about me. Because if any man tries to part me from this—this new life, Owen—I'll—I'll—"

He paused. The sheriff said nothing, but sweat stood suddenly on his forehead.

Chapter Nine

THE BROWN autumn continued drier and more brown all over the hills, but the green farm of Rhiannon seemed more fresh than ever, more like a rich emerald. And when he sat out, this evening, to smoke his pipe, he allowed his eyes to close. He was so weary from long effort that when he closed his eyes, almost immediately he would fall asleep, and waken with the heavy nodding of his head. Again, through a moment of wakefulness, he breathed the scent of the alfalfa, sweeter to him than the fragrance of roses, and vaguely noted the dropping of the daylight in the west. From the blacksmith shop he was soothed by the chiming of a hammer on iron. His hired man, Richards, already was at work, and Rhiannon smiled with a fierce satisfaction.

The sheriff had brought out Richards without recommendation. In some respects he needed none. He was a Hercules—almost as strong as Rhiannon himself. He cared nothing how much work was demanded of him. He spent the day in utter silence. All of these things were agreeable to Rhiannon. But Richards was a surly fellow with a dark brow and a sneering lip, so that he seemed continually to be meditating mischief. He had maintained that contemptuous attitude until, on the third morning after his arrival, a mountain grouse rose from a bush on heavy wings, and Rhiannon dropped the bird with a quick shot from his Colt. After that the hired man altered his ways and grew respectful, watchful to please. Now he was laboring almost as hard as Rhiannon himself. He was, in fact, a treasure, and slumber stole back on the tired outlaw as he heard the tinkle of the hammer again.

Then he stirred and sat up, wide awake. It was like the passage of a hoot owl, a low shadow sweeping across the ground; but, at that distance, it was more than an owl. He sharpened his glance; it was a rider, cutting steadily through the evening, and now out of sight.

Excited, he hardly knew why, Rhiannon stood up from his chair. Then he could remember. Other times, three or four at least, he had been aware, at just this hour, of the same shadow flying across the fields.

He walked down the veranda steps and went out to the gate. It swung open without a sound under the pressure of his hand; that was due to Richards, who shrank from the noise of screeching, rusty hinges.

The rider no longer was in sight, but he could remember the course. The road ran at a different angle; and who would care to go cross-country, jumping the dangerous fences, when the road would bring one almost as quickly in the same general direction?

He pondered this problem. What had taken his sleepy eye, each evening in the dusk, was the sweep of the horse as it rose to fence after fence.

Wherefore?

He was no longer sleepy. Every vestige of fatigue was gone from him; in the morning he would examine this question more at length! So he went hastily to the blacksmith shop and joined the silent Richards. Their two pairs of clever, mighty hands worked iron like wax.

It was late when they left the shop and went to the house. There Rhiannon dropped into his bed and slept heavily, but roused again with the gray morning.

Out he went, through the dew-drenched fields and presently he reached a line of scrub oaks along a draw. Those oaks had been the background against which he had seen the horse rising.

And in a moment he found what he wanted—the trail of a horse at a gallop. He followed it to the next fence. It disappeared and was in sight again on the farther side at such a distance as proved a powerful and practiced jumper.

He followed the trail. Now another set of hoof marks joined the first. He examined the new ones with care and found they were identical, and fresher; simply another of the trail which the same horse had laid down—on a later evening! He followed on until he came to a knoll the top of which was thick with rocks. Here the trail went out. He searched with the utmost care over all the ground at the base of the little hill, but there was no sign to be observed there. On the other front, however, he found half a dozen points at which the same horse had been turned back. This, then, was the goal to which the shadowy horseman went in the dusk of every day. But why should it be a goal at all?

He looked at the rocks carefully. There was nothing mysterious about them. Weather-blackened, they jutted from the ground, a heavy outcropping, and could not be stirred by all the weight of his lifting power.

He sat down to consider.

If the rider came here for some distinct purpose—and who would ride the same course half a dozen times in the half-light except under the impulsion of some almost desperate necessity?—then it was clear that the purpose lay not in the knoll itself but in something beyond it. And what could that something be?

Before the knoll lay a gentle valley, and in the center of the valley arose the tall house of Dee, its roof loftier than the lofty trees which surrounded it, but the outlying barns and sheds were only dimly revealed. To the left was the wandering course of a creek, outlined by a heavy growth of trees. As for the valley itself, it was checked across by many fences into fields whose richness was shown by the shrubs that continually sprouted wherever the plowshare did not reach—under the fence lines. For perfect innocence and absence of anything suspicious, Rhiannon could not have imagined a more perfect scene. And yet something was wrong!

He resumed his search of the ground before the knoll, looking not for the sign of horses, this time, but for even the faint imprint of a human foot. Even then he had no reward!

He turned to the rear of the knoll and carried on his search among the shrubs until, in a small drift of leaves, he saw a hint of white. From the leaves he drew forth a handkerchief. No great trophy, but interesting to Rhiannon for several reasons. In the first place, it was of the thinnest, most transparent linen. In the second place, it was ridiculously small. In the third place, it was worked around with dainty hemstitching.

No man since the beginning of time ever carried such a handkerchief. No woman of the West would carry such a one, unless to a party occasion. But it was such a thing as a woman of some wealth would carry in her palm, held up by a slim finger, a very symbol and symptom of idle hands. There was furthermore a monogram, and this, though extremely elaborate and obscure, he made out to be "N. M."

He laughed softly, with pleasure. Then he restored the handkerchief with care to its former hiding place in the leaves and went back to his day's work as though he never had known fatigue.

A woman, then, was in the habit of riding recklessly across the fields every day—most recklessly unless her horse were a very fine one. Reckless still, because the best of horses might make a mistake in jumping fences by a half-light. Reckless—therefore young. Desperate, certainly, for some cause or other.

He would follow the back trail, on his way to the farm. But the back trail gave him no information. Straightway it joined the road not two hundred yards above his house, and in the thousand signs of the road it was lost completely.

So he went back to his labor of the day. In the middle afternoon, as he and Richards worked opposite one another in the making of a bed for a hay rack, he found that his hired man was staring at him, bewildered; and

40

then he was aware that he, Rhiannon, the outlaw, had been singing loudly as he worked.

It cast a shadow over him. So much was meant to him by merely the hint of a mystery; and if that were true, how long would he maintain his quiet, home-abiding life? It made big Rhiannon sweat with fear, the worst fear, fear of himself! He had thought, before, that so long as he could avoid the law, he would live here content, but now he found that he was wrong. He could see, looking to the past and the future, that the first glamor was stolen from this new life. The moment he had made the farm successful, he was half weary of it! And here came a touch of adventure, stinging him with joy to the very soul!

Full of this trouble, he determined, in the first place, that he would pay no more attention to the night-rider. He would fix his mind carefully on his work. Let the future come as the future might!

In this frame of mind, Rhiannon came to the end of what seemed a very long day. After supper he was half of a mind to go straight to the shop to work again, but it seemed a cowardly turning of the back upon temptation!

He went out to the veranda. Even there he did not pause. He went on to the garden gate and saw a shadow swoop across the field—

His heart jumped; then a long, melancholy note floated to his ears. A hoot owl indeed, this time! But the strange rider would be coming before many moments. Already the line of the trees was thickening the twilight!

Rhiannon left the gate and crossed the road, and, coming to the fence on the farther side, he laid a hand on a post and hesitated. But he knew that he was lost even while he stood fast, striving to deliberate, striving to fight back the temptation.

Of course it was not a large matter, said the heart of Rhiannon. All seeming mysteries have simple explanations! And yet, the voice of common sense told him, it would be better by far to leave well enough alone. He who had been burned by fire should never again handle flames.

Common sense had ruled him too long. For too many months it had exercised a rigorous sway. And now he needed a change. The weariness of monotony and physical labor was burned from him. He was left light, strong, and keen as a trained dog, running on a trail.

He vaulted over the fence, and, putting good resolutions behind him, he walked rapidly forward, straight for the rocky knoll which he had visited the day before.

Chapter Ten

IT WAS not utter dark as he came to the knoll. The ground was dim enough, but to the northeast the upper cliffs of Mount Laurel still took a mysterous light. That uppermost section of the big mountain seemed to float in the mid-sky, like a cloud.

Very cautiously Rhiannon approached the hillock. There was such a joy in his breast that he hardly could keep from laughing aloud as he slipped from bush to bush, bending low, making sure that he never for a moment showed himself against the skyline. This was the old, familiar labor. This was the field in which all his faculties had been trained. And the first lessons are those which last.

He came close up to the hillock and then placed himself among several shrubs, for he found a place perfectly fitted to accommodate him. There he remained at ease, attuning his ears for the beating hoofs of a horse. It came at last, though a little later than the night before. Straight through the darkness sped a galloping horse, its shod hoofs ringing loudly now and again upon the rocks.

And at last the rider loomed before Rhiannon and came to a halt, the horse prancing uneasily on the rocks, then settling down as though it recognized the place and stretching out its head toward the grass.

The rider let it have its head freely. With hands crossed on the pommel, she seemed to stare before her. At last she took out a pair of glasses and fixed them at her eyes.

Night glasses, then!

The curiosity of Rhiannon became fairly feverish! He

slipped a little closer. At a new angle, he could see that she was fixing the glasses straight at the distant house of Dee, whose upper windows gleamed through the trees. Five or ten minutes that careful scrutiny continued. Then the glasses were slipped back into their case and the girl dismounted. She sat on one of the larger rocks, still with her head turned toward the far-off house, and for a time the silence continued, troubled only by the breathing of the horse, which grew less and less violent, and the rattling of the bit against his teeth as he cropped the grass and stamped with content.

She sighed. And at that, Rhiannon stood up and moved closer, softly. The horse tossed its head with a loud snort.

"Evening," said Rhiannon cheerfully.

A wild scream answered him. She sprang from the rock and reached the horse with a bound. But then, seeing Rhiannon towering above her, she shrank back against the shoulder of her mount and cowered in mortal fear.

"Hold on," said Rhiannon. "I'm not here to harm you."

It was as though she could not understand. A torrent of frightened words came from her, stumbling, incoherent. He could barely make out what she meant. But she knew, she said, that "they" had sent him. She had done nothing wrong. She begged him to let her go. If she were allowed to go, she never would come back again. They would be free from her—

And then tears and heavy sobbing.

Rhiannon stood above her and laughed to himself. This was the shadow which had floated across the field like a hoot owl. This trembling girl was she who had jumped the dangerous fences in the half-light of the evening!

Then a mild pity for her came over him. Out of the largeness of his own past, out of the height of a thousand grim dangers, he looked down upon her, he spoke. "And who are 'they' that have sent me here, ma'am?"

"The Dees sent you. Oh, they sent you, I know!"

She mastered her weeping; still her voice was shaken. "But you could tell them you didn't find me, perhaps that you saw me coming, and that I saw you and rode away again—and they'll never know. And here is money. Here is more than a hundred dollars—I haven't any more—"

He made no effort to take it. She caught up his big

43

hand and pressed the money into his limp fingers. "I'll send you more, too!" said she. "On my honor—I'll—"

"Look here," said Rhiannon, "I don't belong to the Dees. I don't know anything about them, much, except that their house is over yonder. And I don't want your money!"

"You don't—you—" she began. And then, in a long breath of relief: "Thank God! I thought it was the end!"

She hooked her arm over the pommel of the saddle and leaned back against the horse, almost fainting, as it seemed.

"Now, steady up," said Rhiannon. "I'm a quiet, peaceable sort of a man, but I don't like to see a girl done in. Suppose that you was to need help out of a little trouble, maybe—" He paused, unsure of himself; he was glad that the sheriff was not there to hear his words.

"Help?" said the girl, with a hollow ring in her voice. "Help! Oh, there's no one in the world can help me."

"That's a large saying," said Rhiannon. "There's men and men in the world. And it's a hard thing that can't be managed by someone. You know your business. I ain't inquiring. Only, the way that I was raised, a man's a man, and a woman's a woman, and not to be left to carry the heaviest pail."

This homely bit of philosophy made her raise her head, and she even left the horse and came a hesitant step nearer to Rhiannon. "Will you tell me who you are?" she asked.

"By name of—John Gwynn," said he, hesitating an instant before he recalled the name which he must use. "And you, ma'am?"

"I'm Nancy Morgan," said she. Then, with a world of bitterness in her voice, she added: "And if I could have another name, I'd never have to be here! I'd never have to be here!"

It was too dark for him to see the gesture, but he heard her hands struck together.

"I've seen you," he said gently, "half a dozen times coming riding your hoss across the evening, taking the fences. I live in the little house, back yonder. That's how I happened to see. You been coming here the last half dozen evenings."

"I had to come and wait," she said, with a sob in her

throat again. "I had to come and wait, but no one came to me. No soul would come to me. I've waited every evening, for hours, and still no one would come to me! And tomorrow night—"

He listened eagerly, frowning, straining all his mind to come at some meaning behind her words or between them.

"Well," said Rhiannon, "I'm sorry for you, and that's straight. And supposing that you could use a farmer—with a pair of hands to help you—"

"What could one man do? What could one man do against all of them? Even if I could have Rhiannon down from the mountain to fight for me, what could even Rhiannon do?"

He started violently. "Rhiannon!" breathed he. "Rhiannon! What do you know about Rhiannon?"

"Only what the world knows," she answered, "that he's cruel and strong and terrible—but that he's never cruel to women."

"Ay," said Rhiannon, breathing deeply, "it's true! He—he never done harm to a woman. I dunno that he ever would! But what would you be needing a red-handed outlaw like him for?"

"Who but an outlaw would break the law for me?" she asked. "And who but Rhiannon would dare to face the Dees?"

"I dunno," said the other slowly. "It ain't always the tall house that makes the tall man! What claim have the Dees agin you?"

"They have no right!" said the girl bitterly. "They have no claim and no right against me. But they hate me, they hate me! They hate every Morgan and they always have. And I'll have to be there tomorrow night—I—I—"

She broke off with a moan of despair. Rhiannon, his brain spinning, strove to follow, but found his wits enmeshed.

"They hate you. You know it. But you got to be there—where?"

"In their house! In their house!" she cried. "Oh, God help my wretched soul! Helpless in their hands! And what will they do with me?"

Sweat poured out upon Rhiannon. "You gotta go to them? How are they pullin' you? By money? By men? Oh— Hold on! Maybe I understand! Yonder in the Dee house there's one different from the rest. You been waiting for him here—and, since he ain't come, you gotta go to him—because you're mighty fond of him—and I've guessed the truth, haven't I?"

"Fond of a Dee?" she asked with a voice between tears and anger. "Wait here for my lover to come out of that house? If a Dee found any love in his heart for a Morgan, he'd cut out his own heart and throw it away! If a Morgan found love in her heart for a Dee, she'd cut out her own heart, too! Wait here for one of them because I care for him?"

Her voice changed again. It was all anger, all fierceness now. "If I had a pack and they were in the hills, I'd trail them down like wolves. I'd hunt them. I'd put a bounty on their heads!"

He had been waiting for his opportunity, and, to make an excuse, he had rolled a cigarette as he talked to her. Now he struck a match, and as he lighted the cigarette he could see her.

The flame burned the calloused tips of his fingers with a blistering heat. He dropped it in a thin streak of fluttering light to the ground. But though the darkness washed back across them, still he could see her, brown-faced and rosy-cheeked and lovely with a dewy freshness. Very young. Slender and strong. And all that youth, that tenderness, now strained and desperate with a great anger, and a great fear.

Suddenly she was in the saddle. "Go back to them, John Gwynn," she cried down at him fiercely, "and tell them everything that I've told to you. And tell them most of all that I hate them, and hate them, and hate them! And that I'll never give up to them while there's breath in me!"

He called out to her, but she was gone. The whip cracked against the flank of the willing horse. They rose at the first fence, and floated away into the darkness.

Chapter Eleven

RHIANNON sat till midnight on the veranda. He was oppressed with the lowness of the roof above his head and
by a sudden sense of the smallness of this life which he
was leading. He dreaded the necessity of turning into the
small, dark, hot room where he must sleep. Out here on
the veranda he still could keep his eye upon the cold and
distant faces of the stars—very far away they were, but
on Mount Laurel they had been as near to him as the
faces of friends!

He could not pity this girl too much. For she, tor-
tured though she were, still lived. He had lived, too, in
the rare old days. He had been a man with something
that filled all his soul and both his hands. His hands were
filled now—but only with material weights to be lifted.

Yonder on the mountain which wedged itself so
loftily among the lights of heaven—ay, yonder he had
been able to touch the eagles with his hands, as it were.
Here he was lost in the sod. He was no more than a plant
which puts down roots and lifts up a fixed head, unable to
move. How base seemed that life—so rooted like a very
plant, or like a beast unable to move beyond a definite
little range! So the thoughts of Rhiannon roamed fiercely
back and forth and always struck against bars, like a
tiger pacing in its cage. In the morning the sheriff would
come. He would give the place into his hands and ride for
Mount Laurel once more!

With that decision made, he was light of mind again.
He went to his bed and slept with happy dreams and did
not waken until he heard the saw of Richards biting into
hard wood behind the house. Then he got up and dressed
and cooked the breakfast for the two of them. It was
hardly finished before Caradac came in whistling, and
leaned loftily in the rear doorway, his eyes dim with the
music he was making.

"You been doing something, Owen," said Rhiannon.

"I been and got me a man, John Gwynn," said the sheriff.

Richards stood up and went out on the back porch. He lingered there, perhaps to make a cigarette. But the sheriff jerked a thumb over his shoulder and nodded back toward the hired man. Then he continued, "I been an' got me a real expensive man, old son."

"For this place? I don't need another man out here," said Rhiannon. "Unless——" he added.

For, after his departure, of course the sheriff would need more help!

"He ain't for this place. He's for jail," said the sheriff. "A real little high-priced jewel of a man, he is! He tried to hang himself with a sheet, last night, and was pretty near strangled when we seen him this morning. A real high-class crook, he is."

"What might his name be?" asked Rhiannon.

"Stew Moffet."

"Ah, him!"

The feet of Richards were heard descending the steps to the yard. Then they sounded on the board walk leading to the corral gate.

"Him!" went on the sheriff. "I got him! Where's the coffee? Hospitable as hell, you are not! I'm hungry, old son!"

He sat down to black coffee from a tin cup. His long arms reached here and there—after fragments of fried bacon, after cold pone, and then a helping of strawberry jam. He ate vastly, bolting his food like a hungry wolf.

"When you eat last?" asked Rhiannon, dimly interested.

"I dunno. Sometime yesterday. Been too doggone amused to eat, son. Been havin' a fine party!"

He chuckled, his mouth full.

The last of the coffee disappeared and he went on, "How much you think?"

Rhiannon frowned.

"Three thousand," he suggested.

"Five, me son," said the sheriff. "Five thousand, to plant in the bank and let it roll downhill and get bigger and bigger! Five thousand iron men for two days' work. It ain't such a bad line I'm in."

48

"No," said Rhiannon dryly, "and when they plant you, maybe you'll grow a couple more like yourself."

"How'd you mean that?" asked the sheriff.

"Nothin'!" said the other. "Only who'll enjoy the coin you've saved? You got no kids. You ain't close to havin' no kids, Owen, you hard-headed, iron-brained, stone-hearted clod of a man, you!"

"Me?" said the sheriff with easy good-nature, tapping his empty cup with contented fingers. "Me? I'm a lamb. A woolly lamb!"

"Damn long wool," said the outlaw.

"I got a heart," said the sheriff, "like a doggone blatting sheep, Annan me boy. All I been missing was the right woman to come along and knock me off my hoss, and when I find her, I'm gunna put her in my pocket and take her home, and we'll raise more little Caradacs than would fill a county. Lemme tell you about how I nailed him, this—"

"I don't want to hear," said Rhiannon darkly.

"It riles you a good deal, don't it?" asked the sheriff. "Always riles you when you hear about me picking up one of those gold-plated skunks?"

"They're no good. I know that," explained Rhiannon, "only it feeds me up hearing you talk about—blood money, Owen."

"Blood money!" exclaimed the sheriff hotly.

He pushed back his chair from the table. "Blood money?" he echoed more furiously.

"Blood money!" said Annan Rhiannon, and his jaw thrust out.

For a moment they eyed each other like two savage wolves. Then the sheriff rose with a snarl and walked to the door. When he turned, he had lighted a cigarette. "I get used to being respected," he said dryly, his self-control in command again. "But then I come on out here, and I see that I don't amount to much."

Rhiannon said nothing to meet this advance. His anger was too deep-seated, and he explained his position more at large. "What bought this here farm? Blood money! No good'll ever come out of it! Blood money!"

The sheriff said calmly: "Of course I ain't surprised. Take a peaceable, quiet living gent like you—even think-

49

ing about blood must pretty near make your head swim, don't it?"

"I never made a penny off a dead man," said Rhiannon.

"You killed the guard in the Shallop bank!" said the sheriff.

"A sneaking murderer!" said Rhiannon. "And I never touched a penny of the money in the bank after killing him!"

"Because they give you the run too fast!"

"The cashier's safe I already had open. It was take and go. But I wouldn't have blood in my pocketbook, Caradac!"

"Damn my heart!" cried the tormented sheriff. "I dunno what you want out of this line of talk. Trouble?"

The other did not wince. "I'm telling you the straight of it. Quit your line of business, Caradac, or else don't come out here and blow about the coin that you got out of a—"

"He ain't a man. It's a yaller little rat that's been gnawing out the hearts of men and cutting the throats of drunks and sleepers."

"All right," said Rhiannon, as one who disdains further argument.

"And where would you be?" The sheriff could not help breaking out in justification, for he was sweating with confusion and anger, and no little sense of guilt. "Where would you be if you hadn't found this place and I hadn't been able to give it to you?"

"Oh, shut up!" said Rhiannon absently. He made a cigarette and rolled it and drummed on the table.

"You always hold everything agin me," complained the sheriff. "Damned if I ain't tired of it! Nobody else minds. The papers are full of what I done to him. Nobody grudges me what I get out of that sort of work. But *you* grudge me! Why? Because you been on the other side of the fence! Is that it?"

"Choke it off, will you? Let the dog die!" said Rhiannon.

He was more absent than ever. The sheriff subsided, but he writhed in his chair with suppressed speech.

"Speaking of the Morgans," went on Rhiannon, unable to bring up his intention of quitting the farm.

"Well—speaking of the Morgans, you know about them?"

"You mean the bankers?" said the sheriff. "Sure I know them. Who else could handle my funds, the scale that I invest on? The last time I was in dear old New York I walked into their doggone office and sunk to my spurs in their carpets, and I went into the office of the old man and asked him for the makings and says to him—"

"Shut up," answered Rhiannon wearily.

"You was asking me about the Morgans," said the sheriff, grinning.

"Out here. This hill breed of Morgans I asked you about, and you begun to think you was at a party entertaining a crowd, you poor sap!"

"You look to me like a crowd," replied Caradac. "Damned if I ever know how to take you. You got more faces to you than any crowd I ever was in. Morgans? There ain't any Morgans."

"You sure?"

"Not one. Not since the cattle war."

"Killed?"

"All planted in a row. Go out to the cemetery and see them. They boasted that they had to be buried in their boots."

"Who killed them?"

"The Dees. Who else?"

"The Dees, eh? Now, what kind are the Dees? Respectable, you was saying the other day."

"Ain't it respectable to kill a man now and then?" asked the sheriff. "My God, you're a hard man, Annan!"

He rose suddenly and walked to the door.

Then he came back. "Soft step, that Richards has," he murmured.

"What about him?"

"In the back yard again. Seen me coming and seemed to be just drifting by."

"Is *he* wrong?" asked Rhiannon without heat.

"Him? Of course he is!"

Rhiannon looked at his friend with grave observance. "So you sent him out to me?"

"Sure. Why not? The honest men are mostly soft. The crooks sometimes are tough. All one knot. I knew that you'd make him work. And so of course I sent him along out!"

"Of course," said Rhiannon sourly.

"But," went on the sheriff, "after I got this gent I found out that he'd been asked by other folks if he wanted to go to work. And some of them offered him higher pay than I would give him out here. But he didn't take it."

"Ah?" murmured Rhiannon. "Liked the sheriff so well that he'd pretty near go to work for you for nothing, eh?"

"In fact, Annan, he had some good reason for wanting to come out here. Now, what was it?"

Rhiannon shrugged his shoulders.

"And just now, he was soft-shoeing it into the back yard, where our talk was floating out pretty free. What's he after?"

"I dunno," remarked Rhiannon. "Of course there ain't anything about me that would make anybody curious. I ain't ever done anything that would make questions be asked. I always been an honest working man!"

"Is that it?" the sheriff demanded softly of himself. "If it is—if it is—!"

He looked askance at his friend, but Rhiannon was yawning broadly.

Chapter Twelve

"SPEAKING about the Morgans," said Rhiannon.

"What's fixed them in your head?"

"I'm asking questions. I'm too tired in the head to answer," said Rhiannon. "You go on and do the talking."

"The Morgans," declared the sheriff, "was the kind of people that was best stayed away from. Shooting, cussing, hell-raising birds, they were!"

"Yes, yes!" said Rhiannon, half-closing his eyes. He was trying to fit that description with the shrinking, frightened, lovely girl he had met in the darkness. He tried to make a liberal allowance for the difference between men and women, but still she hardly seemed to go with the sheriff's description.

"They kept a sheriff busy?" he suggested.

"There was a marshal, a sheriff, and a deputy taken off by the Morgans, from time to time," said Caradac.

"Go on. How'd they look?"

"Oh, fine set up! When I was a kid I used to know a few of them. That was before the Dees rode in and cleaned them all up."

"Good looking?"

"Sure. The finest that you ever seen."

"Big men, I guess?"

"No. Smallish. All blue eyes. All yaller hair. All the Morgans was the same. They all looked like twins in one family! They all could do the same thing, too. They could all ride a hoss and shoot straight and tell a lie—"

"What?"

"Kind of shocking, ain't it? I mean that. They all could ride like hell, and shoot like hell, and lie like hell. They lied from having a taste for it. They lied for they had a liking for it. They lied because they had a talent for it, too. All of them reasons is good reasons, old son, and they excelled! They couldn't tell you the truth about the state of the weather. And everything they said, they smiled a little at you out of the corner of their eyes!"

Rhiannon asked softly, "All gone?"

"Yep."

"Man, woman, and child?"

"Children they didn't go in for much," said the other. "They mostly didn't have much time. About the time that one of the boys got to be fourteen of fifteen, he went out to get him a man. Like the Injuns, they didn't feel that they had ought to claim long trousers until they had up and collected a couple of scalps. They was a real charming lot, the Morgans of the good old days."

"I'd admire to meet some or them," said Rhiannon. "And they all died out?"

"You dunno the Dees, kid?"

"I met Charlie."

"Charlie. Yes. But nobody knows Charlie, except that he's wonderful smart. But you dunno the Dees. Lemme tell you, then. The Dees are thorough. They start at the top and they go right on down to the bottom!"

"Yep. I understand that."

"When the Morgans started in, they was numerous and

rich and had a lot of friends. If you didn't like the Morgans and said so, you'd have to have a stomach that could digest lead a couple of times a day. Well, the Dees, they come along out here and they right away started in saying how little that they liked the Morgans. We all hung around and waited for the Morgans to sweep 'em off of the face of the earth. And the Morgans tried to. They made a mass attack. The Dees had piled up sandbags inside the walls of their house. When the Morgans come, the Dees they just blowed them out of their saddles. After that, they went around in little gangs, and those little gangs hung onto the trail of any Morgan that they come across, and finally they had them all gone except a handful, and them they rounded up one night behind the schoolhouse on the edge of the woods, and they dropped 'em all and went up and shot 'em through the head as they lay there. And that was the finish of the Morgans."

The sheriff told this story with a certain amount of emotion, and now he could not help adding: "Them was the days to be living in, kid. I just seen the sunset of 'em. I seen the afterglow. But they had the real fun, then. You didn't have to be a sheriff!" He laughed as he said it, but there was a trace of something more than mirth in his tone.

"And so all the Morgans dropped off of the face of the earth?"

"Just the way that I been telling you about. Why do you smile to yourself?"

Rhiannon did not answer. But he could have told the sheriff of a blue-eyed girl with "yaller" hair, by the name of Nancy Morgan. He thought of something other than the verity of her identity, however. It was odd that the sheriff did not know of her. She was not the sort of a girl that was kept hidden under a bushel measure. She was a light to be set on a hill and known to the cities of man afar off. And yet the wise Caradac had not the slightest idea of her existence. It simply meant that she had traveled secretly from some distant place and come here to the hill country for the sake of some purpose known only to herself and, apparently, to the Dees.

The mystery of the attraction which drew her to the house of her enemies—that he would not allow his mind to dwell upon. He could only realize that, in some manner, danger threatened her, and he, Rhiannon, would never see her again. Never see her again, not even for an instant by the flare of a match! He said this thing to himself several times, but it had no meaning, no more than if he had declared to his heart of hearts that he would never again see the blue of the sky, the yellow of ripe autumn fields!

He brooded about another thing, too. How should he tell the sheriff that he was weary of this manner of living?

Caradac reached out and touched his shoulder.

"Ay," said Rhiannon dreamily.

"You take a vacation," said Caradac.

"Me?"

"When a man gets off his feed enough to sass the sheriff of the county—and him with a criminal record," grinned Caradac, "it's time for him to take a rest—before he goes behind the bars!"

"You want me to take a leave of absence, Owen?"

"Shake loose from all of this, and when you come back, you start in at this farm not like a crazy man with one idea, but like a human being that wants to live some, and work some, and laugh some, too!"

"I'm wondering about it," said Rhiannon.

"I'll do your thinking for you, son."

"Ay, ay," said Rhiannon. "If you could do my thinking for me I might pull through. Only—only—"

His voice trailed away. The clever sheriff waited and said not a word. His patience was the patience of a fox— or a cat.

"I'm in bad trouble, Owen."

"Ay," said the sheriff.

"And nobody but you and God to help me through with it!"

"Ay," said the sheriff, in the same quiet voice.

Rhiannon parted his lips to speak. He shut them again.

"Woman," said the sheriff, at last.

"Ay, woman."

"What of it?" asked big Caradac with an expansive gesture. "Here you got the neatest little farm in the hills. You can make this house twice as big. No trouble at all. You can show a woman as fine a place as ever made a girl's heart jump. What need for you to be scared at the idea of a woman?"

"Aw, shut up," said Rhiannon.

"You're John Gwynn. You're the strongest man in the county. You got the best little farm."

"My name is Annan Rhiannon," said the outlaw.

"Hey? Look here, son, you wouldn't be that much fool!"

"Would I lie to a woman I loved?" asked the outlaw, with a curious smile.

"Lie? It ain't a lie. You're being a new man. And you got a right to a new name!"

"There is lies and lies," said Rhiannon, "but the worst kind is those that you tell to a woman. No, son, I'm gunna be as straight as the edge of a sharp knife with her."

"She'll have you hanged, most like," remarked the sheriff.

"Most like," said Rhiannon. "But I wasn't thinking about that!"

Chapter Thirteen

DUSK FOUND Rhiannon on the hill of the rocks. He waited until midnight, coldly patient. She did not come. And then he stood up and looked across the valley at the house of Dee. Only one light shone from it, but it seemed to Rhiannon like a strong eye which could see him through the darkness and make sure of him. It was aware of him, as he was aware of it. It knew and scorned his hatred!

Then Rhiannon went home and forced himself to sleep, for a man can do that much and more if his nerve is like steel and his will remorselessly great. He was up in the first of the morning and went out to milk the cows before even the restless and hard-working Richards was awake.

He saw Mount Laurel throned above the mists and he

looked upon it with a strange envy in his eye. It had seemed to him, not long before, as a strenuous field of pain—a sort of place of mortal glory; but now it appeared like a region of calm peace, and a refuge from the sad world which lay at its feet.

He milked the cows, resting his head against their flanks, stilling them with curses if they stirred or lifted foot against the iron gripping of his hands. His herd had increased. So much had it increased that, though it was the falling season of the year when the dry, dead grass diminished the supply of milk, yet twice he filled a pair of five-gallon cans and carried them to the creamery behind the house before Richards came out. He did not apologize for a late start that morning. In fact, the sky in the east only now was beginning to turn pink. And Richards simply set himself about straining the milk into the setting pans and then skimming the old pans which were ranged within the sackcloth coolers. A thin, sour smell pervaded the creamery. In spite of much scrubbing with hot water, the floor was dark and ingrained and slippery under foot; the working table was greasy to the touch; the very walls were unclean. And Rhiannon suddenly was aware of this. It seemed to him that his whole life had been flavored with sour cream. He was glad when he had rushed into the house and begun to make the fire with a huge clattering of the iron lids of the stove.

He cooked what was always cooked—oatmeal mush, coffee, fat bacon, underdone and served swimming in its own grease, then potatoes fried in lard, and either pone or crackers.

They ate enormously of this food. Richards rivaled even the master of the house in the greatness of his appetite. He surpassed him this morning because he was filled with the zest of hunger, whereas Rhiannon ate only because of habit.

After breakfast, Richards washed and Rhiannon dried the few tins. They made this the work of only an instant. Sometimes they referred with brief scorn to that inferior creature, woman, who complained of household labors and who dragged out feeble hours in small tasks. Then, when the washrag had been wrung out and spread over the faucet to dry, and after the dishtowel had been hung behind the stove for the same purpose, Rhiannon suddenly announced:

"I'm gunna get us a change of chuck for lunch. I'm gunna go bag something for us."

Richards said nothing. He never answered unless an answer was necessary, and now he turned his back and sauntered outdoors, the screen door banging loudly at his heels. Rhiannon looked down at the floor, one hand resting on the wet, greasy edge of the sink.

Our great moments do not always find us in the most dignified attitude or periods of existence. So Rhiannon beside the sink considered himself vaguely. He knew well that if he took that rifle, he was surrendering to a great weakness; but he compromised by refusing to carry on the inquiry. Usually he was frank enough with himself, but now he submitted to that most usual form of cowardice in which men neither fight nor flee, but draw a veil and walk past the crisis. He said to himself resolutely and repeatedly, as though he were striving to hypnotize himself by the repetition: "I'm gunna go get something. I'm gunna go and shoot something!"

He took down his rifle from its rack. It was a good Winchester, typical of the famous type of that weapon which fires fifteen shots without reloading—the same gun which stopped Indian charges in older times.

He looked it over with a familiar but vague eye, jerked a shapeless felt hat on his head, and went out with the gun. Besides, comfortingly close to his heart, a Colt hung under the pit of his left arm.

He almost closed his eyes. "I ain't gunna go in any particular direction!" said Rhiannon to his beating heart. So he told himself that he was looking eagerly for rabbits or birds or above all for one of those deer whose fawn-colored legs often were seen twinkling through brush or across the open among the hills.

Then he found himself at the hill of the rocks! At this he drew a long breath and looked about him sternly. He was like one who has emerged from the sea and stands on a strange coast.

He saw the valley, he saw the thickets along the creek, and finally he saw the house of Dee in the distance, with its windows twinkling at him with a purely human malice.

Then he said to himself: "I sort of have happened to

come along here! I might as well go on farther!" For still he would not admit the truth to himself. And he went on with his jaw set and his eyes narrowed, so vastly was he using his will to close the truth away from his sight. And if for a single instant he had allowed the curtain to flicker to one side, he would have known that he was inevitably bound for the house of Dee! So the strong accept or deny God with passion, but the weak are afraid of facing the sky and the problems that lie beyond it.

He went down the valley, rather forcing himself to the left, off the straight line to the house, and as he came toward the creek a deer stepped out and looked him in the face with mild, astonished eyes. Then it whirled and sprang for the brush.

He had his rifle under his arm and he did not raise it to the shoulder to fire. He did not have to. Hunting through the tangles of Mount Laurel, he had learned to fire by guess with both rifle and revolver.

He who guesses right will eat and he who guesses wrong will die! The stag leaped into the air and fell on his back, crushing a thorn bush with a loud crackling. So Rhiannon, astonished at this hunting luck and not really pleased, drew forth his prize and to cut it up.

When you have had to cut up an elk on an icy morning, and you have learned to move fast enough to keep your fingers from freezing, it is simple beyond words to prepare a deer. He took off the skin of that stag as a careless man takes off his coat on a warm day. Not that he needed the pelt, but on Mount Laurel he had formed the habit of wasting no more of a kill than a hungry bear wastes, or a wolf pack. Hardly the bones escaped, on Mount Laurel!

The skin was off, and the quartering was in rapid progress when something snapped, as under foot.

Those with very keen ears can tell the slight difference between the natural crackling which is constantly occurring in woods, as the wind presses trees and shrubs back and forth, and that other half-stifled sound which a twig makes under foot, the foot itself choking the noise a little.

It made Rhiannon whirl. His rifle was down and his revolver in his hand. He was for the moment standing again on the hard breast of Mount Laurel, where so many men had chased him, where he had chased so many men!

A form came toward him through the brush—a horseman revealed almost as through a brown mist. And then Charles Dee came out before him. Rhiannon slipped the revolver back into its hidden holster.

"Poaching, eh?" said Charlie Dee amiably.

Rhiannon looked him over with more attention than he had used on that night by the forge. In the meantime, the sheriff had had something to say about the youth.

In every respect, seen a second time, Charlie Dee looked the part of a true Western man of action, lean of body, strong of shoulders. He had his rifle in a long holster under his right knee. He had a pair of Colts in saddle holsters, also. His horse was a good one, with blood telling in its reach of skinny, muscular neck. Rhiannon made no mistake; this rider could handle both horse and weapons with expert ease.

"Poaching?" he echoed. "Poaching?"

"This is our land," said Charlie Dee, waving toward a distant fence line. But he added hospitably: "I was joking about the poaching, though. We keep out everybody but friends and neighbors. And you're one of the nearest, I guess! You got a fine one, there!"

He rode over toward the spoils, until his horse balked, putting its head down and sniffing at the remains with fear.

"Quick work," said Charlie Dee, leaning a little from the saddle. "I heard your gun about a half a minute ago, and the job's about finished already! How you gunna get the meat home?"

"Why," said Rhiannon, surprised in turn, "carry it. It won't carry itself, hardly." He was rather angry. The appearance of young Dee definitely turned him back from his way.

"I'll load you up," suggested the boy. He dismounted, threw his reins, and helped tie the burden on the back of Rhiannon. The latter shrugged the load into place and started off.

"But hold on!" said Charlie Dee. "What am I thinking about? Come on with it to our house, and we'll give you a hoss to ride it back to your place!"

Rhiannon turned, irresolute. The huge side of the Dee house loomed not far off among the trees. But this was manifest destiny, and he nodded his head with inward joy.

"Thanks," said he. "I don't mind if I do!"

Chapter Fourteen

WHEN THEY came up through the trees, it seemed to Rhiannon that they were coming full crash against the very wall of Mount Laurel, for though the precipitous side of the peak was at least a mile away, yet it jumped from the plain so suddenly that it seemed infinitely nearer, and to either side the long arms reached from the base of the peak and half surrounded the Dee house. But Rhiannon looked with affectionate interest on the ragged cliff. The hole-in-the-wall to which he had owed his life so many times lay straight before him—and in all the world no other man knew it! It was almost as if he understood the art of flying by merely stretching out his arms. This was his ready way of escape from all possible perils!

"It's kind of lucky that I ran into you," said Charlie Dee. "Dad wants to talk to you."

"About what?" asked Rhiannon roughly. And he looked earnestly at this clever young man of whom the sheriff had not been able to say too much.

Charlie Dee opened his eyes in surprise at this excessive curtness. "Why," said he, "about the way you run your place, I guess!" Then he added: "There's the meat house. We could leave the venison there and go in and see if Dad's around."

It was almost mysteriously exactly what Rhiannon wished, and when the load had been taken from his thick shoulders by Dee, he followed the latter toward the house.

He could see now why it appeared so huge at a distance. At its back the ground dropped down sharply, and the trees were struggling up a most difficult slope. As a matter of fact, it was simply a two-storied ranch house—rambling like all ranch houses of the old days, and built in Spanish fashion around a patio.

All the windows of the western wing were rudely boarded up—plain sign that the head of the Dee establishment did not care to occupy more rooms than the family needed. And there were other signs that this was not kept as the home of a rich man. The patio, for instance, looked almost more like a stable yard than a house court. There were a few climbing vines which struggled wanly up the face of the house, to be sure, and there was even a strip of roses, but it could be seen that some animal had recently browsed on them. Once all the surface had been flagged, but half the flags were gone and dusty holes left instead, and of the remaining half, the majority were chipped or smashed. At least one room of the western wing was occupied, and opened upon the patio. It was apparently a junk shop and saddle room. A saddle lay at that moment upon the threshold, and a confusion of dusty straps and stirrups and battered chaps and rusty spurs and a litter of ironwork cluttered up the interior, which was partially revealed through the door and partially through a window of which one pane was gone, and its place taken by a flap of canvas tacked over the opening.

In the eastern wing of the house all was apparently much different. Potted flowers appeared in the windows. A shoe mat lay before the door, and the brass knob of that door was actually polished so that it shone with a jewel-like brilliance.

In the door of the saddle room, seated beside the saddle, was a man of fifty with a face red with heat and labor, now working at some repair upon the saddle flap. His misshapen sombrero was pushed far back on his head, and his nose was ornamented by a pair of spectacles with which he was constantly at war. For the sweat ran down his forehead and down his nose, and, combined with the touch of his spectacles, it kept him continually snorting with such violence that at every snort the glasses almost fell from place, sliding half way to the tip of the nose. He damned them without ceasing, but stuck to his work.

"There's Dad now," said Charlie Dee.

Rhiannon was well armed against most strange appearances in this life. He had seen his share of oddities. But he thought that Oliver Dee, the richest man among the hills, deserved to be set apart in a new class, away from other men.

He wore a pair of overalls which washing and wearing alternately had faded almost white across the knees, and these overalls were kept up neither by belt nor by braces, but by taking a roll in the top of the trousers, much after the fashion of some Italian laborers. He wore old cowhide boots that would have served a prospector much better than a horseman. His shirt was an ancient one of red flannel, but the red had faded across the shoulders and the back to a pale brown. His neck was girt by a bandanna which excessive perspiration had lodged in flat wrinkles and folds.

In person, he was one of those fat men who once have been slenderly made. Even the rough make of his boots could not disguise overmuch the smallness of his foot, and his hips were still slim in spite of the bulk of his body. His ways, too, were still quick, so that it was plain his spirit remained nervously athletic, although it was encumbered by so much gross flesh.

"I got a poacher, Dad," said the son.

"I'll throw the son-of-a-gun into the jail for half his life," said the violent parent. "Who the hell is he?"

He blinked behind his glasses as he raised his head.

"It's John Gwynn," said Charlie Dee. "He got a whacking big fat buck down on the creek."

"Why don't you stay on your own land?" asked Oliver Dee. "If you ain't got enough land to raise your own deer, why don't you buy some more? *I* ain't gunna raise cattle for the whole damn county to come here and slaughter. I got a pantry that needs filling myself, and a meat house, too."

"Don't pay no attention to him," advised Charlie. "He carries on like that."

"Who you talkin' about carryin' on?" asked Oliver Dee. "When did you grow up and get brains, you spindle-shafted, knock-kneed half-man, you?"

"I've introduced you," said Charlie patiently. "This is John Gwynn. My father, Oliver Dee."

"You oughta raise your own deer," said Oliver Dee by way of acknowledgment. "It ain't fair. A deer costs me more than a cow to raise. The way they range around and cut down the grass with their sharp hoofs. Then you come and shoot them. Where do I come out?"

He added, in the same breath: "Glad to see you, Gwynn. Sit down and rest your feet!"

"Where'll he sit? On the ground?" asked Charlie.

"Ain't there room beside me?" asked the other. "And you could go and fetch me a couple of chairs for him, too," went on the father. "You won't grow a chair by wishing for one!"

"Where'll I get a chair?" asked Charlie Dee.

"Hell, boy, ain't the house full of 'em?"

"Sure it is," answered Charlie, carelessly resting a hand against the wall of the house. "But will I get one of them away from Mother?"

Oliver Dee exploded with great oath. "Go *make* a chair, then," said he.

His son disappeared.

"They gotta run everything," said Oliver Dee. "They gotta hang a bit of lip onto everything that a man wants, and everything that a man does! The women, I mean. Look yonder! Who owns this house? Who pays the bills? I do! But the minute that I get inside that door I gotta have clean feet and a washed face and combed hair, and I gotta talk soft, I do. I gotta watch where I step, and if I leave a dust mark on a chair, there's all hell poppin' for a month afterward!"

Partly in wrath and partly in humble sorrow he made these remarks, and then Charlie Dee was seen approaching bearing a pair of cracker boxes. On one of these Rhiannon sat down, amused and watchful. He never had seen a family exactly like the Dees.

"G'wan away," said the father to his son. "I don't need you and I ain't asked for you. Gwynn, I'm glad to see you. I admire how you done up the old place, over there. I been by and admired to see it. I wanta buy that place. What you sell for?"

"It ain't mine," replied Rhiannon. "The sheriff, he owns it, Mr. Dee."

"Ha?" exclaimed Oliver Dee. "How old am I?"

"Fifty," guessed Rhiannon, surrendering himself to the oddities of this conversation.

"Is that old enough to be mistered?" asked Mr. Dee.

"Maybe not," said Rhiannon, and smiled. He rarely smiled!

"Maybe not? Of course not. Now, I asked you what you gunna sell that place for—"

"I said the sheriff—"

"Oh, damn the sheriff!" said Oliver Dee. "He owned that place a couple a years. Never done nothin' with it. Rented it out. Got nothin'. You come along. Now look at the like of it. Nothin' around the hills to match with it!"

Rhiannon smiled again, faintly. Praise from this rich old eccentric was surprisingly sweet.

"Few months!" said the cattleman. "Water and manure are the gods of the doggone farmers, like you. Water and manure! Takin' chances and shootin' at long odds and ridin' like hell was the way that the cattlemen always got on!" He looked almost fiercely at Rhiannon as though he dared him to deny his statement, but Rhiannon nodded slightly, and held his peace. He felt a great, vague satisfaction, looking at this battered millionaire. There was a reality about him. He was not at all prepared to say that the man was good or bad, but certainly he was not dull. He had had wit enough to strip life of all except what was to him the essential principle. Hence this cartoon of a patio. Hence those clothes, perfectly ragged and perfectly comfortable. A house was a place to be used, according to the philosophy of Oliver Dee. And clothes were made to be worn—to keep out the heat and the cold!

"Well?" snapped the rancher.

"You don't believe me," said Rhiannon. "I tell you, the sheriff owns that place. I only got an interest in it."

"How big an interest?" asked the other.

"Half, I suppose."

"Half! He let you do that job and then he only gave you a half interest? He's a skinflint! By God, every Welshman is a skinflint! Are you Welsh?"

"Yes," said Rhiannon.

"The hell you are!" admired the other. "I don't believe it. Not pure blooded."

65

"No."

"I knew that. You got something foolish mixed up with it. Something soft-headed. You let him beat you out! I tell you what. You ought to take a gun and go for him. He's robbed you!"

"I don't use a gun," said Rhiannon, "if I don't have to kill game. I'm not a good hand with one."

"Ain't you?" asked the rancher, looking fixedly at him.

"No," said Rhiannon, and found that it required an amazing amount of resolution to meet those old eyes, looking brightly out at him from under wrinkled lids, like the eyes of a parrot.

"You can kill a deer," said Dee. "That's good enough, nowadays. There was a time when a man needed to know how to shoot straight. You don't need to now. The world has gone to hell! There ain't any men any more. Me, I still can shoot, thank God. You see that bit of flagging that's sticking up on end?" He pointed to it, not with his hand, but with a revolver which came suddenly into view. The gun spoke. The standing bit of flagging shuddered but did not fall. A white streak appeared on the pavement beside it.

"Missed!" said the old rancher, putting up his gun. "Could you better that?"

"No," said Rhiannon. "That's good shooting. You wouldn't have missed a man!"

"No," chuckled the other. "I wouldn't have missed a man. Not me." And he began to rub his hands together and nod to himself.

Chapter Fifteen

RHIANNON was fitting facts and surmises together. It had appeared to him, after his talk with Nancy Morgan, that it would be hard indeed to find white men capable of tormenting such a woman and such a beauty. But now he was beginning to change his mind. There was sufficient eccentricity in Oliver Dee to place him rather outside the range of other humans. He seemed to follow laws peculiar to himself, and of his own making. So Rhiannon grew even a shade more watchful, behind the enforced calmness of his eyes. He watched every nook and corner of the court, every shadow behind every window that stirred in the interior.

The door of the house was jerked open. "Oliver!" called a shrill woman's voice. "O—li—ve-r-r!"

"Here I am," answered Oliver Dee.

"You been shooting?"

"Aw, I dunno," said Oliver Dee.

"You stop it right away. I got a headache!" The door slammed.

Oliver Dee stared at that door, fascinated, for a long moment. Then he said, but with a stealthy softness: "Can't call my name my own, around here. Got no place any more. Gettin' old. They don't want an old man. No woman wants an old man around! Reminds her too much of everything. A dog wouldn't want my life. Not even a dog wouldn't want it!"

He said this with an earnestness that made Rhiannon look curiously at him, but with a shrug of his shoulders, the other continued: "Now about that sale? You own half. Well, you sell me half, then!"

"You got a lot of land," replied Rhiannon. "What you want with that snack of a place up yonder?"

"It ain't up. It's down," Dee corrected him. "I want it because I want it. I want to take folks over there when they come to visit me. The Easterners, they look around, superior. 'What kind of crops you raise?' they say to me. 'Cows,' say I. 'No grain?' says they. 'Cows,' say I. 'Isn't it good land?' they ask me. 'Hell, yes,' say I, 'but I ain't got time to develop all of it. Cows is good enough for me.'

"But they don't believe me. I want to take them over and show them your alfalfa. 'That's what I can make this land produce,' I'd tell them. Understand, kid?"

"I understand," said Rhiannon, but he knew that it was only a sham. No motives as simple as this controlled the life of Oliver Dee and his reactions. There was no one in the world to whom the opinions of others mattered so little, he suspected.

"Now, you tell me how much you want, and I'll tell you what I'll pay."

"I won't sell," said Rhiannon.

"You want to stick me, I see," said the other. "You want to boost the price right up into the sky. You want to make a sucker out of me. But I'll fool you. Go on and name your price, though. Always tell by the price that a man asks how big a fool he thinks I am."

"I won't name a price, because I'm not selling," Rhiannon assured him.

The rancher smiled. "Son," said he, "I admire to hear you talk. I like to hear a man that knows how to make a bargain. But I tell you what. I been livin' for fifty years. Everybody sells everything. Men sell their best hosses. Hosses that of saved their lives. Sell their dogs that of saved 'em, too. Sell their sons, sell their daughters. Women sell themselves, too. So do men. Everybody sells everything. All for a price. Right price you gotta find. That's all. Sometimes it's a smile. Sometimes it's a bunch of flowers. Mostly it's hard cash. Everybody sells. Now, you talk to me, John Gwynn."

"I've finished," said Rhiannon.

"Don't you go on wastin' my time," said Oliver Dee in complaint. "I've stuck this here needle into my finger three times since you came. You're spoilin' my work, and you're wastin' my time. You've raised your price enough, by now. Go on, name a top figger."

"There's no figger," answered Rhiannon. "I'm not aiming to draw you out. You keep your money. I keep that land. We're happy, then."

The rancher looked at him again, with eyes like the eyes of a bird. "I pretty near believe you," said he.

After that, he looked down to his work. Sewing vigorously—for he was repairing a flap which had been torn almost from the body of the saddle—he said, after a time: "The sheriff. What about him? Would he sell?"

"You wouldn't like his bargain," suggested Rhiannon.

"Damn what you think," said the rude Oliver Dee. "You tell me—would he sell?"

"Not if I don't want him to. And I don't," answered Rhiannon.

"You got him under your thumb, have you?" scowled

Oliver Dee. "He's gotta do what you want, eh? I don't believe it!"

"You try," said Rhiannon.

He stood up. "I gotta be going back," said he.

"You do? you don't. Why you gotta go back?"

"I gotta work."

"Work? No, you're takin' a vacation. You're ramblin' round and shootin' deer."

"I'm not," said Rhiannon. "I just went out to get some venison, or something. We're tired of bacon, over there."

"Sit down!" commanded the other.

Rhiannon submitted weakly. He by no means had accomplished the purpose of his visit to the house of Dee.

"Now, you go on talkin'," said the rancher, "and I'll work. I want to know about you. I raise cows. I can tell you about cows. You raise alfalfa. You tell me about alfalfa. Is that right?"

"I'm not a good talker," said Rhiannon.

"I'll tell you if you ain't," said the other. "I'll stop you and tell you. Now go ahead. Tell me how you started. Tell me everything you done!"

Rhiannon obeyed. He had no great will to talk about what he had done. But he wanted to remain as long as possible in the house of Dee.

"They'll have me down there!" Nancy Morgan had said.

He drew a breath, and then he began his talk. He found his words stumbling, at first. He forgot a great deal. For he had been working from day to day, without much planning, doing the next thing that came to hand. Now, however, as he began to sketch the details, he could see the thing like a narrative stretching before him, and a most interesting narrative it seemed to Rhiannon.

He began with the blacksmith shop, for that was the heart of the farm, to him. And he told in detail exactly how he had rearranged it, and how he had worked up the old, rusted iron into new forms, and how he had made his own hammers and chisels, and nearly everything that he needed on the farm.

"You made your tools!" broke in the other.

"Nearly all of them. Not the brace and bit."

"No. You couldn't make that!"

69

"I could, but it would take me a terribly long time. Then it wouldn't be as good as what you can buy."

"That's a lie," said the terrible Oliver Dee. "Anything that you make yourself is a lot better than anything that you can buy. Nothing that you buy belongs to you. You pay money. You get a hoss. You don't own that hoss. The man that raised and bred his dam is the owner of that hoss, and you know it."

Rhiannon actually smiled again. "You're right," said he.

"You go home and make your own brace and bit," said the rancher.

"I got half a mind to try," said Rhiannon.

"You better. Him that can make his own tools, he can make his own world, he can make his own life. He can make everything except his own women."

"Yes," said Rhiannon, with a sudden warmth of agreement.

"Don't say yes to me," said Dee. "I know I'm right, I'm never wrong. I've lived fifty years. You ain't lived at all. Except in a blacksmith shop. However, you got the beginnin's of sense! Go on and talk some more to me. I don't half mind listenin' to you!"

So Rhiannon talked on and on, and with an increased interest, as he saw the sun climbing high and higher in the sky. Noon was coming. He wanted with all his heart to be asked to lunch. He wanted to see Mrs. Dee. He wanted to see the rest of the family, and the inside of the house which, for all he knew, at that moment might be sheltering Nancy Morgan! Perhaps he would walk in and find her at the lunch table! So he talked steadily enough until a bell clanged.

"Chuck!" said the rancher, and rose to his feet with agility. "Come along to the washroom. You got blood on your hands. Maggie would raise hell if you come into the house like that."

"I better be sloping home," said Rhiannon.

"Shut up," said Oliver Dee. "You talk like nothin' at all." So he took Rhiannon into a laundry room where Charlie Dee already had his face and neck covered with suds as he leaned above a granite basin. Rhiannon followed the example. And when they had washed thoroughly and combed their hair at a cracked, fly-specked mirror, Oliver Dee brushed off his clothes with a whisk-broom and then actually turned around and around under inspection of his son.

"You'll do pretty well," said Charlie. "But you better put on a fresh bandana."

"I'm damned if I will!" exclaimed Oliver Dee. "I put this one on Monday. If two bandanas a week ain't enough for me, I'm damned if I ain't gunna go and get me a new house and a new woman. I'm tired of foolin' around!"

Chapter Sixteen

THEY WERE met at the door of the house by a rather pretty woman of forty years and a little more. She had an eye as clear as crystal, and a wonderfully youthful mouth and throat such as some women preserve almost to the end, by the grace of God.

"Mother," said Charlie, "I want you to know a neighbor of ours that you've heard me talking about lately. This is—"

"Oliver Dee!" said Mrs. Dee.

"Well, Maggie?" said the husband with a scowl.

"You gunna expect to come in to lunch with that dirty bandana around your neck?"

"What's wrong with it, hey?" asked Oliver Dee. "I put it on Monday."

"I don't care when you put it on. It's a filthy thing. I wouldn't sit at the table with it."

"You don't have to. I'm the one that's got to wear it. If it don't bother me none I don't see why it should bother you and—"

"Oliver Dee," said his wife in a deeper tone, "you go right up to your room as fast as you can and get yourself another bandana on."

Mr. Dee groaned, but he obeyed.

"This is John Gwynn," said Charlie.

71

"Hello," said Mrs. Dee. "Come on in. I hope it wasn't you that started Dad shooting, a while ago?"

"I don't know," said Rhiannon.

"You better know," said she grimly. "I don't have no guns around this house. The day's gone by for that non-sense. Now come along in and have some lunch. I don't suppose you got any appetite, though, just sitting and idling, all morning!"

"He killed a deer," said Charlie in defense of his guest.

"Is that work?" snapped his mother. "The red Injuns did *that* kind of work."

"Don't mind her any," murmured Charlie.

"What's that?" she snapped. *"You'd* be a sight better off, young man, if you begun and minded me more! Come along in, John Gwynn. You come along and tell me about the place you been making. It's the prettiest place on the road from town. It does my heart good when I come by and see that greenness and that windmill clank-ing."

"Ay," said Rhiannon. "It's a good sound."

"It is," said Mrs. Dee. "We won't wait for Dad. He's always late. He's always got to fix himself or something at the last minute. God knows how I've lived with that man for so many years!"

They went into a dining room where a red plush carpet covered the floor, worn so that the seams showed as easily defined streaks of gray. There were red plush curtains, too, with most of the tassels missing. Upon the wall hung enlarged photographs of men who appeared to be wearing stiff white collars for the first time; they had frozen faces of despair. And there were equivalent ladies with bustles arching behind and sleeked hair, knotted on top of their heads, and curls like grace notes hanging down, one on either side.

Rhiannon observed this grandeur and found it oppres-sive, and most of all a tremendous candelabrum which hung from the ceiling and threatened to crash upon the table.

"Isabella!" called the mistress of the house. "Where are you?"

Feet tapped on a stairway and then came with a rustling of skirts to the door. Rhiannon found himself looking at the obvious sister of Charlie Dee, slender and

72

dark, and pretty. A flash came in her eyes at the sight of a stranger.

"This is John Gwynn that has the alfalfa and the milk cows," said Mrs. Dee. "I been thanking God for those cows of yours, John Gwynn," she added. "I can get decent butter from town, now. Suppose I was to send right over to your place, I could get it fresher, too, maybe. It's apt to sort of melt down on the way out from town."

Rhiannon assented.

Isabella Dee had given him a cool, slender little hand and had smiled upon him openly, with approval. "You sit here beside me," she said. "No, you sit opposite, so we can talk better."

They sat down.

"Isabella's just home from school. She's been getting finished off a bit."

"Learning to smoke," commented Charlie.

"Shut up and let your sister be, will you?" said Mrs. Dee.

"I don't mind a bit," said Isabella, smiling again at Rhiannon, "I'm modern. Charlie thinks he likes girls to be old-fashioned, but—"

"I only think, do I?" said Charlie darkly.

The father entered the room and took his place at the head of the table. "What we got, Ma?" he said. "I got an appetite with me, today." He rested the hilt of an expectant knife on the table beside his plate.

"We got enough," said Margaret Dee sternly. "Put your knife down on the table, and sit up and keep your hands in your lap. You've had one meal today."

"Never allowed to forget that I get food in my own house," said Oliver Dee to Rhiannon.

A Chinese cook in white came in with a steaming tray.

"By jiminy, it smells good. What is it, Wong?"

"It ain't polite to talk about your food," said Mrs. Dee.

"Let poor Dad alone," said Isabella.

"He'd be getting out of hand right away," replied the mother.

"I want to talk to John Gwynn," said Isabella. "Let's be peaceful, Mother, please!" She added: "I want to come and see your beautiful place some day!"

"You come along any time," invited Rhiannon.

"When you're not working?" she asked.

"He works all the time," said Charlie.

"He'll knock off when Bella comes," declared Oliver Dee.

"Isabella is the name, please," said Mrs. Dee fiercely.

"Now what do you know about that," demanded Oliver Dee. "Can't call my daughter by her own name!"

"It *ain't* her name!" said Mrs. Dee.

"Am I gunna make a whole speech every time I want to speak to her? I hesitated between Isa and Bella, but Bella won out. And the proof of the puddin' is the eatin'. She answers to it!"

"You talk of your own daughter like she was a common cook," declared Mrs. Dee.

"What's a finer thing for a woman than to be a cook?" demanded the irrepressible Oliver Dee. "Never seen you more becomin' than when you was in the kitchen dressed up in white and with the steam goin' up from the stove into your face!"

"Will you leave me be?" said Mrs. Dee without pleasure in this compliment.

"I tell you what," said Oliver Dee, unchecked, "I used to come in and go into the kitchen and slip up when she wasn't lookin' and kiss her. 'Get away,' says she. 'Honey,' says I, 'I love you!' You can't help but lovin' a good cook, Gwynn!"

"Oliver!" came the ringing voice of Mrs. Dee.

Isabella laughed frankly across the table to Rhiannon. "Poor dear old Dad!" said she.

"You just encourage him, Isabella," complained the mother. "What'll John Gwynn be thinking of us?"

"John Gwynn ain't thinkin' of you and me at all," declared the father of the family. "He's thinkin' about Isabella. Ain't you, Gwynn?"

"Good gracious!" cried the badgered Mrs. Dee. "I never heard such talk. It's plain disgraceful, Oliver Dee!"

"Now, why not call a spade a spade?" said Oliver Dee. "Isabella's young. Isabella's pretty, ain't she?"

"Has the looks of our child anything to do with the kind of language that you been using?"

"Not to you. But they has to John Gwynn. Here he is, young and handsome—"

74

"Oliver!" cried the infuriated wife. "I'm gunna leave the table!"

"Finish your soup first," said Oliver Dee. "Ain't he handsome, Bella?"

"Of course he is," said Isabella, and her smile invited Rhiannon to pay no attention to this badgering.

"Young and handsome, and set up in the world already with a bang-up farm! What more could a girl want than him? What more could a boy want than her, if only she'd learn cookin'. And what's the good of closin' your eyes to the fact that they're gunna be interested in each other?"

Charlie Dee leaned back in his chair, chuckling.

"Oliver," cried Mrs. Dee, "of all the outrageous—"

"Oh, Mother," said Isabella, "do let poor Dad ramble on. I don't care a whit. Neither does John Gwynn!"

"Isabella, there's something kind of immodest about the way that you talk."

"Hell, Maggie," said Oliver Dee, "why not call a spade a spade?"

"Why not?" said the dauntless Isabella. "I don't see young men every day on the ranch, do I? And you don't see girls, either, John Gwynn, do you?"

"I never see anything but cows," grinned Rhiannon.

"I give up," said Mrs. Dee. "When I was young, young people was raised to have manners and learn how to talk."

"About weather, Mother dear," said Isabella. "But they never really cared a whit about the weather, you know. I'm thankful to Dad, really."

"Because I break the ice, eh? Of course. You got some sense, Bella. You and Gwynn will be like old friends, before I been with you for a half hour."

"Of course we will," said Isabella. "Won't we, John Gwynn?"

Chapter Seventeen

THERE WAS so much perfectly cheerful camaraderie in the manner of Isabella, and Charlie Dee listened to the talk with such a careless smile that what might have been an embarrassing moment under the bold tongue of Oliver Dee passed off well enough. But when the lunch ended and the men started to leave the house, Mrs. Dee said coldly, "I gotta speak to you for a minute, Oliver."

"All right, later on," said he. "Busy out yonder for a time. See you later, Maggie."

He confided to Rhiannon: "I'm gunna collect some thunder and lightnin' later on, for what I been doin'. But I gotta be nacheral once in a while. I'd choke, if I didn't. You come down in the hollow and tell me about how I could try irrigatin' that low ground. I got some ground down there, Gwynn—if you was to scratch it with your heel it would grow you stacks of watermelons; if you was to plow it, you'd raise double eagles, ten sacks to the acre. I wanta know how to get the water onto it, that's all. If you won't sell your land to me, sell me some advice!"

"For how much, Dad?" asked Charlie. "You can't ask him something for nothing!"

"I'll tie this knot. You leave your hand out of it, will you?" asked the father.

"I'll tell you what I know. It ain't much," admitted Rhiannon. "Lemme come over some other day. I gotta get back to work, now."

"Never keep a man from his work," agreed the rancher. "Mind you, Gwynn, you're gunna be welcome over here. You slide over whenever you like. I like you. And maybe Bella does, too!"

He said it with a broad, significant grin, and Rhiannon chuckled in turn as he walked away with Charlie Dee.

"Dad's a rare one, eh?" commented Charlie. "They

don't grow two of a kind like him—not in one place. But don't you be fooled. He's got a head, too!"

"You don't have to explain him," said Rhiannon. "I've known some men in my day!"

They went back to the stable, beside which half a dozen men were building a stack, one forking a load off a big wagon, and one driving the derrick horse, and the rest squaring and trampling on the stack.

"Have a horse or a mule?" said Charlie Dee.

"Mule," said Rhiannon without hesitation. "Hosses apt to cut up when they smell fresh meat."

They brought out a mule from the barn with a packsaddle strapped on its back. "This is pretty kind of you," acknowledged Rhiannon. "I'll fetch the mule back tomorrow!"

"Oh, any time, and—hey, Chuck, watch yourself or that—hey!"

The derrick driver had been giving only a portion of his attention to the guiding of his horse, walking out with head turned back, of necessity, to regard the progress of the big Jackson fork. The tines of this, deeply buried in the hay, now tugged and worked at their burden and finally wrenched loose a great bite from the load. The released strain sent the derrick horse lurching ahead. At the same time the rope tripped the driver. He floundered, then fell forward with his arm caught in the singletree.

And the horse bolted! The Jackson fork crashed against the top of the derrick with such force that it tripped, and the load it had been lifting showered back upon the head of the forker. The whole derrick staggered, and then began to lift its farther leg, the pins screeching briefly against the foot of the big beams.

It could not help but fall on the helpless derrick driver. There was a wild chorus of yells, which were chopped in the middle by the bark of a revolver. The derrick horse swayed and pitched upon its side, shot fairly through the head, and a little wreath of pungent smoke was visible near the person of Rhiannon. Even then the anxiety was not entirely ended. The derrick, tilted well over to the right side, was balancing and seeming to pause in order to aim itself with more surety at the unlucky Chuck, who lay sprawled and helpless in its path.

Charlie Dee sped to the rescue, but a larger form shot past him—Rhiannon, stooping with hardly a pause to scoop up Chuck. The sleeve of Chuck's strong, flannel shirt was ripped away and he himself borne off to safety just as the derrick came down with a crash.

Charlie Dee had to leap backward to avoid the whirring peril.

Chuck, placed upright on his feet once more, staggered a little, and then was calm. "Doggone my heart if he wasn't a first cuttin' hoss," he commented. "It wasn't his fault. He wouldn't of made a wrong step, if I'd kept onto my feet. But I flopped. It scared him. Poor little devil!"

He went over to the fallen horse and looked down at him in bewilderment rather than in grief. "Eight years, colt and hoss, I've knowed him," said Chuck. "Don't seem possible that he's finished. Only this morning he tried to kick the head off of my shoulders. Only yesterday he crawled into the manger to get at me. Things is gunna be different, now that Mike is gone!"

The stack builders had assembled, not nervously, but with a calm curiosity.

"Very neat," said a big fellow with a scraggly pair of mustaches and a voice that rumbled deep in his stomach. "Neat and exact. That was a shot. Who done the shooting?"

"Charlie, I suppose."

"It was Gwynn," said Charlie Dee. "This is John Gwynn, boys. He's the farmer over on the windmill place—the alfalfa man, you know."

"Alfalfa, hell!" said Chuck with much earnestness. "If he's a farmer, I'm King Solomon and no mistake. Farmers, they don't shoot like that!"

The little side glance which Rhiannon gave to this speaker was no more than a flicker of the eye, but if Chuck could have read the emotion which inspired it, he would have turned and fled and never again come into that region of the world.

"Patch up the derrick," Charlie Dee was directing. "And get four mules to help lift it. We gotta have that stack topped off before three days. May rain any day. Shake a leg, you boys. Chuck, I'm sorry that you lost your cutting horse. I'll make that good to you."

"Pay me for the hoss," said that honest philosopher,

"when I can pay you for the derrick. I got my head on my shoulders—I ain't mashed to a red jam—I can thank God and John Gwynn for that!"

It was the nearest he came to any direct expression of gratitude and, as a matter of fact, he actually avoided the eye of Rhiannon. The others of the haying crew, unoppressed by any such diffidence or sense of debt, looked upon the stranger with a sort of grim admiration. Such speed of gun and hand, such readiness to leap into peril's way—and then a perfect indifference afterward such as Rhiannon showed were all qualities which moved them. Their very eyes said that here was a man!

"That's finished," said Charlie Dee to Rhiannon. "Come along and we'll load up the mule with that deer."

"I'm sorry about the hoss," said Rhiannon in apology as they went along. "As a matter of fact, didn't dream that he was a cutting hoss!"

"What else could you do, Gwynn? What else, man? Chuck was dead, otherwise. Do you think I grudge the price of that horse? Not a bit! It was a grand piece of work. A grand piece of work!"

Rhiannon watched him askance, very interested, for Charlie Dee plainly was greatly excited. However, it had been enough to excite many a man—the derrick's fall, the dropping of the horse, the imminent danger of Chuck. And yet there was something unexplained by all of these considerations, for Charlie Dee, as Rhiannon was coming to see, was not an ordinary man. Behind his eyes there was ever present thought, and such a fellow was not apt to be thrown off balance as he appeared to be now!

He showed, indeed, a tense preoccupation all during the process of loading the mule. Then he shook hands with almost too much earnestness. "Here you've been right at our elbows all these months," said he to Rhiannon, "and we've missed knowing you. But we'll make up time from now on, old fellow. Drop in when you can, will you? So long—good luck!"

Rhiannon led off the mule and its load of meat, and as he went, he stumbled and involuntarily looked back. Charlie Dee had remained on the spot of the farewell without moving, still looking after his departing guest, and still with the same fixed look in his face as though he were seeing distant thoughts.

It gave Rhiannon so much to ponder on that the way back to the alfalfa farm seemed extraordinarily short. Something had entered the mind of young Charlie Dee. And what that thing could be, he would have given a great deal to know.

When he reached the house he unloaded the meat and put it in the cooler. Then he banged the big gong, and Richards came in from the field, where he had been putting phosphorus poison down gopher holes. "Richard's," said Rhiannon, "you jump on a hoss and ride in to the town. Get hold of the sheriff if he's there and tell him that I'd like a lot to see him out here. Make it pronto, will you?"

Richards made his usual reply—a wave of the hand which was half a salute and half a mere assent. He went off down the board walk to the corral, but when he came to the gate, he paused there, with the gate half open.

"If we had any chickens, you'd be letting them into the yard," Rhiannon called after him in sarcasm.

Richards jerked his head around with a start. It was an ugly look even at that distance, an ugly gesture. Then he went on toward the barn with his head dropped between his heavy shoulders.

His employer looked after him and began to rub his massive knuckles across his chin.

Chapter Eighteen

THROUGH the soft evening colors the sheriff came jogging, a stately form on a stately horse, and he sat with Rhiannon on the veranda and watched the golden head of Mount Laurel turn dim again with the coming of the night. They talked or were silent in turns for a casual hour, at least, and Rhiannon had not told why he had sent for the man of the law.

At last Caradac muttered: "I been thinking, old son."

"Kinda hard to believe that," answered Rhiannon with disrespect.

"About a yarn that my ma read to me when I was a kid. About the wolf that dressed itself up like a sheep. You remember?"

"I've heard of it."

"When he showed his foot under the door—that was the give-away. It was a wolf's foot, with a wolf's claws!"

He became impressively silent.

"Aw, go on," urged Rhiannon. "I'm not gunna ask questions. What d'you mean?"

"You been over to the Dee place, ain't you?"

"Yes."

"What you been doing there?"

"Aw, nothing much."

"Who introduced you to 'em?"

"My Winchester. I killed a deer, and Charlie Dee happened to be there."

"Happened? It wasn't just happening. He's where he wants to be!"

"Maybe."

"Anything else doing?"

"Nope. Oh, we went in and had lunch. The old man wanted to buy this place. That was about all."

"Nothing else?"

"Nothing. I heard them yapping at each other a good deal—Oliver Dee and his wife. There was a girl there, too. A fair beauty, Owen."

"All the Dee girls always are beauties."

"All of 'em? I only seen one."

"In that house. But they only gotta whistle, and they can fill that house with men and girls. There's a lot of Dees around this neck of the woods. Nothing else happened?"

"Not worth talking about. Derrick took a tumble. Had to shoot the derrick hoss."

"For what?"

"Keep him from dragging the derrick onto the derrick driver. By name of Chuck. A proper looking gent, at that."

"Chuck Maple?"

"He didn't say."

"Chuck Maple and me has played games together," mused Caradac. "He's been a sort of active boy. Counterfeiting and pushing the queer. Rustling a few cows now and then to keep his hand in. Salting mines. Faking

81

brands. Never seen a prettier hand with a running iron than Chuck Maple is!" He fairly whistled in his admiration.

"What you driving at?" asked Rhiannon.

"Where did you shoot the horse?"

"Through the head. Couldn't chance the body. He had to be stopped quick."

"You shot him through the head?" asked the sheriff in disgust.

"Why not?"

"Was he running?"

"Yes. Starting a gallop."

"How far away from you?"

"Aw, thirty yards. Not more than that. Why?"

"And you shot him through the head!" groaned the sheriff.

"Damn it," murmured Rhiannon, "you don't understand! You see, Owen, then the derrick was beginning to—"

"Leave the derrick be. It's you! You shot a running hoss through the head at thirty yards. What'll people be saying?"

"What could they say?"

"That a man that can shoot like that never was raised on no farm, and don't belong on no farm! You've started them talking already. The town's full of it!"

Rhiannon sat up. "You've heard about today?"

"Heard about it? I never heard nothing else. All this afternoon, they been saying: 'Where'd you pick up that gunman, Caradac? You opening up a bad boys' asylum? You starting a reform school? Who is he? What's he done? Why's he laying low on that dinky farm?' That's all I been hearing. It made a pretty fine afternoon for me," concluded the sarcastic Caradac.

"I didn't want to do it," said Rhiannon. "Matter of fact—"

"Shut up!" barked Caradac. "Shut up. Don't talk. Just answer questions. When you come here, what was you to do with your guns?"

"Leave them alone," murmured Rhiannon meekly.

"Have you done it?"

"I had to have a little practice with the old Colt," said Rhiannon with a sigh. "I couldn't just leave the door open for the first thug to come and drop me. I had to keep my hand in."

"Who's seen you practice?"

"Nobody."

"What?"

"Nobody but Richards. All he seen was me shooting a bird."

"A what?"

"A grouse," said Rhiannon faintly. "Come out of a bush. I was hungering for a change of meat, that day."

"You shot it on the wing," said the sheriff, his voice husky with anger and with disgust.

"It wouldn't sit still for me," said Rhiannon, fairly cringing.

"And Richards there to look on! The whole county knows about that too, by this time!"

"Richards wouldn't talk. He don't know anybody to talk to!"

"Don't he? I seen him talking to Charlie Dee this same afternoon! Whadya think about that?"

"My God, man," pleaded Rhiannon, "I ain't the only man west of the Rockies that can use a Colt!"

"No. You ain't," admitted the other thoughtfully. "There's about four or five others. That's why they're hesitating about recognizing you."

The outlaw gasped.

"Where's Richards now?" asked the sheriff.

"Out feeding the cows alfalfa. Why?"

"Nothing, only I like best to know where he is when I'm talking private business. Annan, I'm telling you straight. They're all sitting around like crows on a roost, there in town. 'Who can it be?' they say to one another. 'Some wild man,' they say. They're pretty near to getting you spotted. I heard one man say: 'He's as big as Rhiannon!' "

"Good God!" breathed Rhiannon. "What did they say to that?"

" 'Twenty years too young for Rhiannon,' says another.

" 'Who knows what lies under Rhiannon's beard?' pipes up a doggone old croaking graybeard. But they ain't sure."

"I've proved that I ain't Rhiannon. I've laid low here

83

for months! I've proved that I'm just a hard-working farmer with a good—"

"And after all those months, you step out, and inside of one day you shoot, skin and cut up a deer in five minutes, and then you shoot a hoss through the head when it's on the run, and then you pick up a man and jump with him out of the way of a falling derrick!"

"Of course," said Rhiannon, "I mightn't of stepped out quite so far."

"You've stepped right into the shadow of the gallows," said the stern sheriff, "and damned if I care if you finally get there. You're a fool! Why'd you send for me this evening? I'm a busy man. I can't go traipsing out of town to this rotten little farm every day!"

The wrath of the sheriff was as great as his disgust. Rhiannon waited for that disgust to abate, and then he ventured: "I seen a thing go riding over the fences, yonder, like an owl floating over the ground, looking for field mice and squirrels. Six nights I seen it go riding past. And then I follered it. It was a woman!"

"Don't say the word that way," groaned Caradac. "You make me feel weak and foolish, when you say it that way. You only seen her by night, anyway."

"I lit a match and started a cigarette, and seen her. And if I'd looked at her with the eyes of a doggone parboiled, wrapped-in-lead Egyptian mummy, Caradac, I would of busted the wrappings and done a war dance, when I seen her!"

"Go on," said Caradac. "I might of knowed. Always a woman. Every crook dies because of a woman. No brains! No sense!"

"Yaller and blue!" signed Rhiannon.

"What you talkin' about?"

"Yaller, yaller hair like sunset on a wheat field, and—"

"And blue, blue eyes, eh? You make me sick, Rhiannon!"

"I'm sunk, Owen. I'm fair sunk. I been mourning for her like a calf for its ma. But the point was that she was aimed for the Dee house, and didn't want to be. But if I didn't find her on the hill next night, she'd be gone to the Dees—and she's a Morgan. What you said there wasn't none left! And God help her soul. And God help my soul, too. What am I gunna do?"

"Shut up," warned the sheriff. "I gotta think."

Rhiannon rose from his chair and paced the veranda like a heavy cat, without sound. Then he paused by the parlor window, laid hold on the lower sash, and plucked out the under half of that window as a boy would pluck off the rind of an orange. He tore it away, and dived into the black of the room like a swimmer into water. A gun flashed and boomed mightly. There was a great impact, a struggle, silence and panting.

"All right," said the sheriff, who had not risen from his chair. "Bring him out here, old son. We'll have a look!"

Chapter Nineteen

THERE WAS a brief continuance of the struggling in the dark of the room, and then, justifying the confidence of the sheriff, Rhiannon led forth his captive and presented him to the man of the law.

Caradac regarded him with calm pleasure by the light of the stars. It was Richards, his breath coming in great gasps, and his body shaken by the violence of the struggle; for the loser is always the wearier of two combatants.

"Listen to me, old son," said the sheriff to Rhiannon, "I told you that I didn't like the way of him. Now he's been standing around and eavesdropping! What're we gunna do with him?"

"Go fetch a lantern out of the kitchen," said Rhiannon.

The sheriff obeyed and, when he brought it out, Rhiannon directed him to hang it on a nail from one of the pillars of the veranda.

"Now stand out here, Richards!" he commanded.

Richards submitted to his master. He was made to face Rhiannon, and the latter straightway released him.

The struggle had been of some violence in spite of its shortness. Richards' coat was half ripped from his back and a huge red spot was swelling along one side of his face.

Rhiannon stepped back from him. "Now, you sneaking traitor," said the master, "you got your hands free and your chance for yourself. Go for your gun and fill your hand!"

Richards did not move, except to brace his legs a little farther apart, and drop his head a shade more between his shoulders.

"He's gunna show yaller," said the sheriff calmly. "He don't want none of your game, old son. He's had his share this evening, I suppose."

"He got me when I was more'n half down," growled Richards. "I didn't have a half-chance at him."

"You put a bullet right through the hair of my head, you damn rat," declared Rhiannon. "Is that a chance? Go for your gun, or I'll drop you where you stand!"

"Drop me, then," Richards defied him. "I seen you work with a gun, and I ain't gunna take any chances against Rhiannon. If you want me dead, shoot me. I ain't gunna shoot back!"

"He knows me," said Rhiannon, calmly to the sheriff. "I dunno what I'm gunna do about this."

"Suggest something, kid."

"I'll chuck my gun, Richards," said Annan Rhiannon. "Here I'll stand to you man to man with bare hands, and—"

Richards snarled, without waiting for the sentence to be finished: "And your partner, Caradac, standing by to put a slug through me if I looked like winning!"

"It's true," said Rhiannon, "that you can't expect a sneak to act like a man or to think like a man. D'you imagine that Owen Caradac would take any advantage of you?"

"I won't fight you," said Richards, sullenly, as before. "I've had my neck pretty near twisted off of my shoulders, my jaw is out of joint so's I can hardly talk, and I think I got a couple of busted ribs when you landed on me. Otherwise I would of broke you in two!"

"He's brave like a woman," said the sheriff. "He ain't gunna take no chances, except with his tongue."

"What'll I do?" asked Rhiannon. "I dunno how to handle this kind of a fish!"

"Find out who put him on your track, then."

"Richards, will you talk up? Will you tell me who sent you here?"

Richards merely sneered. "I sent myself," said he.

"You lie," answered the sheriff, rolling a cigarette. He added, "Tie him to a post, Annan."

The outlaw obeyed, with a bit of rope securing his man to one of the pillars of the porch.

It happened that Caradac had brought his riding quirt with him, and now he threw it to Rhiannon, a heavy whip of snaky slenderness. "Give him a couple a tastes of this and maybe he'll open his face."

"I give you warning," said Rhiannon. "You gunna talk out, man?"

"I'll see you damned first," growled Richards, who seemed to be fortifying himself with a passive courage.

The whip was made to whistle sharply through the air. It fanned the very skin of Richards, without touching him.

"The next lick, I'll cut you in two," said Rhiannon. "Will you say who sent you here?"

The answer was silence.

"Let him have it!" said the sheriff.

"I will," answered Rhiannon, and whirled the whip again. "Talk up, Richards."

The latter cursed, but said no other word, and Rhiannon threw the whip aside. Its loaded butt landed heavily on the veranda flooring.

"I can't do it," said Rhiannon.

"You can't? I can, and it'll be a pleasure to me to do it, what's more!"

"Leave him be," broke in Rhiannon. "I couldn't stand it. Turning a man into a dog or a hoss, I mean."

"No dog or hoss was ever low enough to do what he's been doing!"

"Never mind," answered Rhiannon. "I've said my say."

He loosed Richards. "Get out of here, Richards," said he. "Now I'm gunna tell you one thing before you go. I ain't gonna cut and run, in spite of the fact that you've spotted me. But if I'm hunted, I'll start for you, and I'll find you if you're as far away as the bottom of the sea, and when I find you, I'll feed you to foxes, a bite at a time. You hear me?"

Richards said nothing. He kept his head down, looking up at Rhiannon like a pugilist about to rush in.

"Mind you, Richards, I'm gunna turn you loose. But I wanta know how you spotted me. Will you tell me that? It was tonight, listening, wasn't it?"

Richards was strangely charmed into speech by this appeal to his vanity. He could pose here as a clever fellow, and who can avoid such a temptation? "I knew that there was something in you the minute I came out here," he declared. "When I seen you swing a twenty-pound sledge like it was a tack hammer, that made me think. When you dropped that bird with a Colt, I knew that you was something pretty rare. Inside of that same minute I guessed at the truth—that you was Rhiannon. Rhiannon could shoot like that. Nobody else around these parts except one or two, and they didn't have your shoulders. I never could of told by your face. But I guessed by the shooting, and the look of your shoulders, walking away from me."

Rhiannon sighed. "Where'd you ever see me before?"

"I was on the Overland, that day when you stuck it up!"

"What did I take from you?"

"My watch. But you chucked it back to me. It wasn't good enough for you!" There was not gratitude, but only ugly complaint in that voice of his, and malice. As though he would rather have had his watch stolen than to be shamed by having it tossed back to him before so many witnesses.

"Get out then," said Rhiannon. "I don't want to see any more of you!"

"Do I get my blanket roll?"

"Take it and be damned!" said Rhiannon.

Richards went off with a long, quick step, entered the house, and was heard striding down the hall.

"Suppose that he comes around on the sneak and picks you off from the veranda?" asked the sheriff with great curiosity. "You gunna let him prowl around the house, here, without watching him?"

"I am."

"How you figger it, Rhiannon?"

"I couldn't die by that kind of a man," declared the outlaw simply. "I ain't made that way."

To this calm statement of creed, the sheriff listened with no doubt in his face, but biting his lips a little. He could see the viewpoint of Rhiannon. He could see it at a distance, like the glimmer of a star, seen, but not at all comprehended. It might be a few short billions of miles away, and again the ray might travel from another universe.

But he knew that this superstitious feeling prevailed to a certain extent in all successful criminals. It enabled them to turn their backs on rooms filled with armed men, and escape, no one daring to try a shot even at the back of the gunman. So the sheriff pondered for a while. Then a step was heard over the leaves. Richards came around the side of the house with a bundle at his back.

"Remember," said Rhiannon. "If you try to give me a lead toward jail, I'll just nacherally find you and break your neck, Richards."

The latter went on a few more steps, until he was deep in the darkness beneath the fig tree. Then he turned. His voice was hard and chisel-edged with malice: "I've heard you talk. Now you hear me. The boss that I work for, he don't want you in jail. He wants you out of jail. He's gunna use you—like an ox in a yoke. He's gunna work you to a line and plow his field with you. That's you, Annan Rhiannon!"

He went on. The gate at the end of the path clanged shut behind him, and he turned down the road toward town.

The sheriff stood up. "I'm off," he murmured.

"Sit down!" commanded Rhiannon. "There's no use trying to follow him. There's too much autumn stubble in the fields. Too much noise under your foot and too much starlight to see by. Let him go. You never could foller him!"

Chapter Twenty

"I'D GIVE the inside lining of my heart to be tanned for saddle leather," sighed the sheriff, "if I could track him down to his boss!"

To this remark Rhiannon returned total silence for a long time. Then he declared with the quiet of conviction: "I tell you what, old boy; it's been a good try. It didn't work. Now I gotta beat it."

"You gunna chuck this?"

"What's the good of me staying here?" asked Rhiannon. "Jail for me; jail for you!"

"Listen to me," murmured the sheriff." "You heard him yap just as he started off. D'you think that he was talking for fun or did he mean what he said?"

"I dunno," said Rhiannon.

"He meant what he said," replied Caradac. "I dunno what the game may be, but whatever it is, it's deep. You're gunna be used by somebody. For what, I can't guess. Neither can you. If you would have let me do it, it would of done a lot of good to me to flog the secret out of him."

"No use in that," replied the outlaw. "You could never keep your head up, I tell you, after using a white man like a dog! You think," he added, "that there's a chance they won't simply try to run me into jail?"

"I know it," answered the sheriff bravely.

"I can't stay," persisted Rhiannon. "No matter what the trick is that's in the air, it would wind up with ruin for you, old-timer. I gotta go my own way!"

"Your way is my way," said Caradac quietly. "Your life is my life, and the trail you travel is the trail that I ride."

To this announcement Rhiannon could not make a rejoinder. Once or twice, in the moments that followed, his lips parted. Then he got up and began to pace the veranda in his usual restless way when his mind was full. At last he paused behind the sheriff's chair and rested his big hand for a single instant upon the wide shoulder of Caradac. That was all. Then he resumed his pacing, but whole volumes had been communicated from one to the other by a sort of nervous wireless that traversed the air in silence.

"It ain't jail," repeated Caradac. "They don't mean that. The minute that they had a suspicion about who you were, they'd of run you in, if that had been what they was driving at. But it was something different. Richards said so himself. And he meant what he said."

"I'll trust him tomorrow—not today," answered Rhiannon dryly.

"Lemme do your thinking," replied Caradac.

"And get yourself hanged," said Rhiannon.

"About the girl—" began Caradac.

"Leave her be. I've forgotten her," said Rhiannon.

"About the girl—what're you gonna do?"

"Go to the Dee house."

"And shoot up the Dees and take her away. Ain't that the program?" asked the sheriff sarcastically.

"Guns have got me where talk never would of," replied Rhiannon.

At this the sheriff rejoined. "You sit tight. Tomorrow I'll send out another man. He'll take the place of Richards. You show him the ropes. Take things slowly. There ain't any hand for you to force, just now, and there ain't any bluff that you can work. The other side sees your cards. They know that you're Rhiannon. They're outside in the dark, and you're sitting inside reading beside a lamp. You're in their hands. Just sit tight and wait. That's all you can do! The girl—leave her be. Keep shut of the Dees. They're poison. So long, Annan. I'm gunna jog back to town."

He departed at once, and Rhiannon sat gloomily on the veranda and listened until the hoof beat had died away, heard its strangely loud and hollow knocking as Caradac rode over the bridge half a mile distant, and then the muffling dust stole all the sound away once more.

The dark grew more black; the stars at one stride were drawn to a farther remove; and a mysterious whisper of danger stole under the fig tree. Rhiannon felt the sweat start on his great body, felt his muscles turn to brittle hardness.

Then he forced himself to stand up and walk out into the quiet. There he stood, conquering his weakness, looking calmly about him, and at length the horror departed from the air. He came back into the house, went to bed, and forced from his brain every thought except that of sleep.

Sleep indeed came in a dark wave, and he stood up the next morning, ready for work, though not within such narrow limits as the sheriff had assigned him.

He had not finished milking, the sun had barely finished turning the eastern sky from rose to pale yellow fire, when the new man came. He was an Italian with a prize fighter's jaw and a sailor's bowed legs; but his eye was as open and mild as his native skies. He did not smile when he introduced himself and learned what his work would be, but he went off to the first task at once, and in half an hour his voice was floating from the barn in cheerful song.

Rhiannon, listening, was depressed, as one who on a winter night passes lighted windows and the swinging music of the dance. But he worked on through that day, taking Joe Caracci over the place and pointing out details of irrigation, the weak places in the checks which would have to be repaired before the next flooding, the management of the milk in the creamery, and a score of other things.

He came to the late afternoon, with the sun a step above the skyline. "You cook your own chuck," said he to Caracci.

"Easy," said Caracci. "Spaghetti, boss?"

"Who'n hell ever heard of spaghetti on a ranch?" asked Rhiannon. "You get bacon, corn pone, coffee, mush, potatoes. Mix those cards however you please. But if you want some spaghetti, I'll send for some tomorrow."

So, relenting at the end of his hardness, he grinned at Joe Caracci, and the latter ducked his head and grinned back in a perfect understanding. Rhiannon felt that he had gained an ally of the first importance.

Then he mounted the mule of the Dees and jogged across country toward the rancher's house, taking his way, not as a bird flies, but around the road way. So he came up to the barn and Chuck Maple in person came out to receive him. He took the head of the mule.

"I'll put him up, chief," said Chuck with an ugly scowl.

But the scowl meant nothing, as Rhiannon could understand. It was merely the habitual expression upon the face of the man. No doubt his past had been black enough, as the sheriff had pointed out; but something told Rhiannon that here was another ally, and the discovery meant much to him. The night before he had been a lone man, badgered by sad doubts of himself and the future. And now he was enriched! He had had the strength of the sheriff, to be sure; but what are two against many? Now he had behind him cheerful Joe Caracci; and he was sufficiently assured of this Chuck Maple, as well.

When he sauntered toward the patio, it was almost dusk. He came unobserved around the corner of the house and heard hot dispute. Oliver Dee was in the midst of talk.

"I give you a harness, too," said Oliver Dee. "I throw that in. Now you come yappin'!"

"The harness was no good," said the other disputant. "It busted the first pull. The tugs busted right out of the hames at the first good pull, goin' up hill. The hame straps was rotten as cheese. They broke when you tried to pull them up. What kind of a harness was that, I ask you?"

"How could I read the mind of a set of harness?" argued Oliver Dee shrewdly. "I seen it hangin' there all fine and slicked up and black and greasy lookin', like the day that it come out of the store! That was pretty near as good as new, I should of said."

"You had it greased up," said the other, "and you had it blacked up good, too. But grease and blackin' ain't good leather. Oliver, you can't put it over on me! There's the harness back in your shed. And I've put up your mule in your barn, too. Now I want the right to go and catch my hoss out of your pasture!"

"And how do you think that stands with me?" asked Oliver Dee. "You make a bargain. You got your eyes open. You ain't a baby. You get a mule and a harness in exchange for a hoss that I had to buy because that doggone wasteful John Gwynn shot one of mine through the head

93

the other day. Now you take that fine good-lookin' harness and bust it all to bits, and you want your bargain back. Is that good sense, Jimmy?"

"I dunno. I dunno," said Jimmy. "I ain't any hand at talk, and it's your long suit. I leave it somebody else. Charlie, you say!"

Charlie Dee appeared from the shadow near the house. "If he was a stranger," said Charlie, "a bargain is a bargain. Particular in a horse trade. But if he ain't a stranger and he's a Dee, he's gotta have more than a square deal."

"Bah!" growled old Oliver. "If ever you get your hands on this ranch, I see where my few dollars that I've saved are chucked right away inside of six months! You're wasteful—nacherally just plain wasteful, Charlie!"

The youth replied calmly: "Besides, I seen you polishing up that old harness. It had been hanging up in the loft for years. It was dry and dead as a bone and—"

"Shut up!" snapped Oliver Dee. "You talk like a fool! You—"

He choked with wrath, and Jimmy chuckled. "You settle it anyway that you want, Oliver," said he. "Only, you think it over, and I think that you'll see that Charlie has the right of it."

"Charlie has the right of nothin'!" said Oliver Dee. "Stay over for dinner, and afterward you can catch up your damn hoss and go home with it or to hell with it, for all that I care! All you folks are hard on me. Everybody! Beginnin' with my own boy. Hey, who's that? It's John Gwynn, damn if it ain't! Come here, Gwynn. Lemme tell you what they're doin' to me!"

Chapter Twenty-One

THE TALE of the rancher was sad indeed, and Rhiannon smiled as he listened.

"That's the way it goes," said he in irony. "You take a man that's down and out—no land, no money, hardly a pair of boots to his feet—and everybody jumps on him.

I'm sorry for you, Dee, with your own son against you!"

"You're another of them," answered Oliver Dee. "Smart! Too damn smart! Young kids was taught how to keep their tongues in order, when I was a boy. This is James Dee. Jimmy, shake hands with John Gwynn."

James Dee was tall, broad, strong, and good-natured. He took the hand of Rhiannon with a vigorous grasp. "I heard about you, Gwynn," said he. "I suppose that everybody in this neck of the woods has heard about you, lately. Mighty fine shooting you done the other day. I'm glad to know you!"

Rhiannon smiled grimly to himself. Very odd it would be if James Dee could have guessed how little his polite speech was pleasing to Rhiannon.

The supper bell rang with a heavy, booming note that beat across the patio and sent an echo humming back from the farther walls.

"By jiminy!" exclaimed Oliver Dee. "There's supper ready, and me not washed, and the old woman will give me hell. Hurry up, boys. We gotta rush!"

There was a stampede to the wash room. And then they filed into the house, their faces still glistening with water about the ears and the backs of their necks. They came into the dining room, where Mrs. Dee looked them over with her relentless eye. When her glance came to Rhiannon, it measured him with a measure of steel, and seemed to find him not altogether wanting.

"Come up here and set down beside me, John Gwynn," said she. "I gotta talk with you a little."

"Wait a minute, Ma," said Oliver Dee. "You better ask Bella where she wants him to sit."

Mrs. Dee turned upon her spouse a glance of such dreadful wrath that even the loquacious tongue of Oliver Dee was silenced for a time. Isabella came in. She went up to Rhiannon and shook hands with him with the brightest of smiles—a starry brightness, as it seemed to Rhiannon, so that he felt that her greeting would have slipped into his heart like a shaft of light, had it not been that his heart was filled with another image. She went to James Dee and lingered a moment, asking him little questions about his family.

"Aw, sit down," said her father. "You're keepin' us all on edge."

"Leave the child be!" commanded Mrs. Dee. "Thank God that there's one person in the house that has got some manners!"

She added: "Come up here, Isabella darling. Here's your place on this side of me, tonight. John Gwynn has the other place."

"We hoped that you'd come tonight," said Isabella. "We all wanted to talk to you about that fall of the derrick, and the saving of poor Chuck Maple."

"It comes of hiring crooks and worthless folks," said Mrs. Dee, directing her head toward Rhiannon and her eyes toward her husband.

"Worthless?" barked Oliver Dee. "Chuck Maple can do more cuttin' in one day than three ordinary punchers would dream of doin'!"

"It was his hoss, not him," declared Mrs. Dee.

"Ma'am," said her husband, "lemme ask you a question, will you?"

"Go right on, Oliver," she replied. "I dunno but it's the first time in my life that ever you've asked me a question. You always been telling me things before!"

He flushed a little. "Answer me this!" said he. "Are my cows rounded up in your kitchen?"

Mrs. Dee glared.

"Are they rounded up in your parlor, then?" asked her husband.

She snorted with contemptuous anger.

"Are they rounded up in your dinin' room, or your bedroom? And if they ain't rounded up in any of those places, what d'you know about the work of the men and the hosses?"

Mrs. Dee grew pale, not with confusion, not with fear, but with terrible fury, because, strive as she might, she could not find a way of warding this terrible thrust from her, she could not find a single word with which to answer.

And her husband, at a success so overwhelming, so complete, sat upright in his chair and balanced his table knife on its hilt, and rolled himself slightly from side to side in his chair.

Rhiannon gave only a glance to either of them. He noted the broad, satisfied grin of James Dee, who looked down at his plate, as though trying vainly to conceal his satisfaction at this victory of his sex.

The answering volley therefore fell upon him. "Hold up your head, James Dee," said Mrs. Dee. "Hold up your head and laugh right out loud, or you'll be strangling! Hold up your head and laugh! It's a right and fitting thing for the men of the Dee family to sit by and laugh when a woman is insulted—in her own house—at her own table —by her own husband!"

Jimmy Dee raised his head as though a gun had been held under his nose. And his face, brightly crimsoned, showed not a sign of mirth upon it.

"And as for you, Oliver Dee," said his wife, regarding her paralyzed power of speech after this first slight effort, "as for you—"

"Let's forget Chuck Maple and his work," said Isabella gravely.

"What has Chuck Maple got to do with it?" snapped her mother.

"That's where the argument started," said Isabella.

Rhiannon waited for a volley to blast the girl, but not a syllable was directed at her. Suddenly silenced, her father and mother stared at each other for an instant, and then Rhiannon dragged in a little talk about his new man, and his odd Italian face, and his strong hands, and his cheerful ways.

That restored the peace at this stormy table, which seemed to be looked upon as a scene of battle rather than as a family point of reunion. And Rhiannon's reward for his effort was the brightest of smiles from Isabella. She surprised him—there was such a difference between her and the rest of her family. She had their olive skin, their dark eyes; and yet she differed from them. They themselves seemed to feel it keenly. With a word she had stopped the brawling at the table—that usual occupation of her father and mother.

There was nothing else of importance said during the dinner except one thing which, afterward, Rhiannon understood.

That was when Mrs. Dee said: "How's Will and Mort?"

"I thought they were comin' over," replied James with surprise.

"Did you?" answered Oliver Dee, and with a shrug

the matter of Will and Mortimer Dee was dropped. Afterward, Rhiannon remembered.

Then he became interested in Charlie Dee. He never had been able to see in that young man any tokens of the powers which the sheriff attributed to him, but this evening he began to notice that Charlie, even when he talked least, was most keenly occupied with all the people around him. He kept them perpetually under observation, with side glances. He seemed to have an electric apprehension of everything that was going on around him.

They went into the patio after the supper was over, for the night was warm and still, with all the stars out shimmering and trembling in the sky. The Square of Pegasus stood in the zenith; Boötes was setting; Orion, with bright Betelgeuse, was beginning to climb from the eastern horizon.

They sat in a loosely formed semicircle.

"I better be going," said Rhiannon.

"You stay around," answered Oliver Dee. "Bella, you fetch out your guitar and entertain your young man, will you?"

She went obediently into the house.

"Hello," said James Dee. "Is Gwynn Isabella's—"

"Not him!" broke in Mrs. Dee. "Dad's just making a fool of himself again. You'd think that he was aching and burning to get rid of my girl from the house."

"Give a girl rope, give a girl rope," said the quiet voice of Charlie Dee. "Otherwise she may hang herself."

"What might you mean by that, Charlie?" asked the mother sharply.

"Charlie's right," said the father.

To Rhiannon Mrs. Dee said, but quite gently: "You'll be plumb embarrassed, the shameful way that Oliver carries on about poor Isabella!"

He assured her that he was not a bit embarrassed. Then Isabella returned carrying the guitar. She curled up in a chair and strummed it. "What'll I play?" asked Isabella.

"Sumpn simple and easy," said her father. "After the sharp way that Jimmy here has been bargainin' with me, my brain has been all wore out and it needs a lot of soothin'!"

At this, Jimmy laughed with a perfect good-nature. Rhiannon began to understand that, in spite of wranglings, there was an enormous kindness existing among all the Dees. The spirit of the clan drew them together and held them with strong bonds. For that very reason they took liberties with one another. But their hearts were really untouched by all the jangling.

Isabella, in accordance with her father's wish, plucked the strings softly and began to sing:

"When Israel was in Pharaohs' land—
Come down, Moses!—
Oppressed so hard they could not stand—"

A door crashed in the unused wing of the house. There was a sound like the screech of a window thrust violently up, and then a scream rang terribly across the patio!

Chapter Twenty-Two

THERE IS neither sex nor word in a scream of fear. So it was now, as that wild cry burst across the night air and brought all in the patio to their feet.

"What's up?" cried Charlie Dee, and he started running toward the old wing.

Rhiannon was at his heels. James and Oliver Dee followed.

"Oliver! Oliver!" called Mrs. Dee. "You stay here with us. We don't want to be alone!"

Oliver Dee did not turn back. Charlie had opened a door in the lower story of the old wing. He had opened it by the weight of his shoulder, driven relentlessly home against it so that the bolt was torn away. They poured up a dark flight of steps, still with Oliver in the lead and Rhiannon, gun in hand, behind.

At the top there was a shout from Charlie Dee. "Halt, there, or I'll fire!"

"Hello! Hello!" called a pair of voices. "We've halted! Damn it, Charlie—it's me and Mort. Don't shoot!"

Matches flared, spurting blue flames. Rhiannon saw two young men in the upper hall. In their fright, they had thrown their hands above their heads.

"It's Will and Mortimer," said James Dee. "What you doing here, you two, anyway?"

"Last time I'll ever come to the damn place," said one of the two. "Very last time! I've had the hide scared off of me. And then I've pretty near been shot by Charlie. You oughta handle your gun a mite more careful, Charlie!"

"Sure you should!" put in the second captive.

"I thought—I dunno what I thought!" said Charlie Dee. "I heard a screech up here."

"It was me," said Mortimer, laughing shakily. "I was exploring around. Me and Will, we thought that we'd just slide around the old house and take a look at things. Always has a sort of ghostly look up here. While I was in the room over the patio, there, I thought that Will was downstairs still. But he got it into his fool head to play a joke on me. I heard a sigh behind me. I turned around and seen a man standing with a face that was just a white blank. Scared me to death. I whooped the window up and yelled—then my ghost said that he was Will! My hair's gunna turn gray."

"You oughta be horsewhipped!" said Oliver Dee. "That's what ought to happen to you, young man!"

"I'd put my handkerchief over my face," chuckled Will Dee. "It was a fool trick. I'm sorry. Wasn't that a holler that Mort let out, though?"

"If you've done enough exploring," said Charlie Dee dryly, "you better come on down with us. You must of aged Ma ten years with your fool trick!"

They went clattering down the stairs. The place had been unused so long that this disturbance raised a thin, pungent dust which set everyone sneezing. Rhiannon, if he had been one of the first to advance, was the last to leave, coming down slowly. He was filled with thought. No matter what explanation was offered, he had fitted that wild scream to the thought of Nancy Morgan, and he could not get rid of the idea.

As they stepped into the patio he heard Charlie Dee saying: "Sounded more like the yell of a woman, I thought!"

"Sure," said Mortimer Dee. "I still got an ache behind the eyes. You scare a man enough and it throws his voice up the scale a ways, seems like. I feel pretty sick, Charlie. Got a shot of something for me?"

100

"Go ask Wong. He'll give you a glass of moonshine."
Mortimer disappeared into the house.

A scattering conversation began in the patio, dominated by the loud voice of Mrs. Dee as she berated Will Dee for his prank. "They oughta be jailed for such a crazy monkey trick as that!" she declared. "Scaring a woman out of her skin!"

Rhiannon said good night. He was hardly noticed in the confusion of talk, except by Isabella Dee. "Sorry it happened," said she. "You seem worried, John Gwynn."

"Not a bit. But it's getting late. I have to start work early."

"We're a wild lot. Too wild to understand easily. But do come and try us again. I hope there'll be no screams the next time!"

He thanked her and took her proffered hand, and through the starlight he could see that her eyes were fixed steadily and gravely upon him.

Then he left her and started home.

He circled the side of the old wing, but instead of going on across the fields in a straight line for his farm, he turned in behind the building to look at it again. No matter how easily the others could dismiss the subject, that cry still ran through his mind.

He had barely turned the last corner when he heard the lightest of scratching sounds, and then he saw the dim silhouette of a man who was climbing down the back of the old wing of the Dee house—climbing with great agility, making finger and footholds where there seemed no possible purchase, and so descending gradually to the ground.

Rhiannon dropped behind a bush and watched earnestly. Once or twice he noted that the climber paused and looked carefully around beneath him, as though to make sure that he was not observed. But then he went on and finally, thrusting himself back with both hands to clear the wall, he dropped lightly to his feet—and into the arms of Rhiannon! Lost in that mighty grasp, arms and hands paralyzed, the stranger shuddered with one impotent struggle and then gasped, "God!"

"It's you, Maple, is it?" demanded Rhiannon.

"The chief!" said Maple. "Are you mixed up in this dirty business, too?"

Rhiannon slipped down his hands until he found the

101

wrists of his captive. Securing those in this manner, he turned Maple to face him. "What business, Maple?" he asked.

"Why ask me?" said the other. "I climbed up to see what I could see, but the shutters was fastened too strong for me, this trip."

Rhiannon sighed. Whoever he touched, with whomever he talked on the Dee place, he felt that he was baffled and held off at arm's length by some mystery. "You heard that yell?" he asked.

"Heard it? It would of been heard in hell, I tell you!"

There was an honest emotion in this speech, at the least. "Who called out?"

"Would I of climbed the wall of the house to find out, if I'd known? Slipped, up there, and hung by one hand for a couple of seconds. I thought I was done!" He cursed softly at the memory of his peril.

"How did that call sound to you?" asked Rhiannon. "What did you make of it?"

"Call? It wasn't no call!" said Maple. "It was just a yell!"

"What d'you mean by that?"

"Just a yip. Somebody up there was scared stiff!"

"It was Mortimer Dee," said Rhiannon.

"Him? Whatcha givin' me?" sneered Maple. "Don't I know the screech of a woman from the screech of a man?"

"I listened. I couldn't tell," said Rhiannon, his heart quickening with both fear and hope as he saw a suggestion that his first suspicion might be fortified by the testimony of another man.

"You couldn't tell? Well, I could. It was a woman that yelled out, old son, and don't you be forgettin' it! A woman that yelled! There's a difference. D'you hear the sob at the end of that yip?"

Rhiannon remembered.

"Men don't cry when they screech. They groan. Women and children, they cry."

"How d'you know that?"

"I worked in a nut factory, once."

"What's that?"

"Lunie asylum, I mean. You hear all kinds of hollerin' there, among the bad ones. I tell you what, I know all about it. I was there for pretty near a year. I was lyin' low

102

that year," he admitted frankly. Then he added with an oath, "Are you gunna bust my two wrists?"

Rhiannon released them, and Chuck Maple began to chafe and rub the bruised flesh. "You gotta grip," he declared. "Damned if it ain't like an iron clamp laid on a man! Y'oughta be a wrestler, chief. You'd make your thousand dead easy, in that game! Just the layin' on of hands would be enough to make those Rooshian and Dago saps curl up and lie down and yell for help!"

Rhiannon said nothing.

"And you ain't in this?" asked Chuck Maple.

Still Rhiannon did not reply. His brain was too busy.

"If you're in, I'm out," said Chuck. "I ain't blockin' your game. Wherever you stand, chief, I stand with you. You're my boss—that's all!"

"Thanks," said Rhiannon, for he believed that the criminal meant what he said. "But I'm not in it, Chuck. I'm not in any 'game' that may be going on. What sort of a game could it be?"

"The holding of a woman in a damn cemetery like the old wing of that house. That's what the game is!"

Rhiannon set his teeth to keep from an outbreak of excitement. It was true, then, and Nancy Morgan was actually in the hands of these most mysterious people!

"A queer game," said Rhiannon huskily.

"Queer?" said Chuck Maple. "Queer is the middle name of these folks."

"Can you tell me?"

"Tell you, chief? I could tell you a whole book!"

Chapter Twenty-Three

Now, for a time, the mind of the outlaw balanced between two doubts—of himself and his right to pry into the affairs of the house of Dee—of Chuck Maple, and the possibility of that worthy telling a truthful story.

But the temptation to listen was too strong. In a way, he felt that Chuck Maple had been thrown in his path

103

almost by a divine coincidence to assist him in his search. "Will you walk on toward my place with me?" he asked.

"Whatever you want," said Maple. "Come along. It's better to talk on the wing than anywhere near that hound, Charlie Dee."

They started on together, therefore, leaving the barn to their left with a wide detour. "Nobody's showed up from the stables and the bunk house," said Rhiannon. "Don't they hear anything—as close as that to the house?"

Chuck Maple snorted. "Wait a minute. I'll talk!" said he.

They went on across the bridge which spanned the creek, and so came up the slope beyond. And at last, still without speech, they came to the rocky little hill where Rhiannon, that dark and strange night, had met Nancy Morgan.

Then Chuck Maple turned and looked back at the lighted rear wall of the Dee house. Once more, small as it was close up, it looked huge as a barracks from the distance, looming among the great trees which surrounded it.

Chuck took up the conversation exactly where it had been terminated before. "Of course they heard it!" said he. "How could they help? It was as loud as the blast of a factory whistle. Where was I at the time? I was sittin' right there in the bunk house doin' a patch on the seat of me old pair of trousers. Porky Smith was a-lyin' on his bunk readin' a magazine. The rest of the boys was sort of littered around. When we heard that yap did we jump and start like a fire brigade, I ask you?"

"Well?" asked Rhiannon curiously. "You didn't budge, eh?"

"No, chief, we didn't!"

"And you didn't say anything?"

"What good is there to say anything?" asked Maple with a sort of angry scorn. "Porky just growled: 'More hell!' Then he went on with his magazine.

"I wanted to ask: 'What sort of hell?'

"But I'm the new man out here, and I don't ask no more questions than I gotta."

"How long you been here on the Dee place?"

"Me? Year and a half about."

"How many men they got?"

"Nine, all told."

"And out of nine, you're the latest?"

"Sure."

"How do they keep them? Big wages? Good chuck?"

"Average—average!" said Chuck Maple. "We feed pretty good and we get fair pay. That ain't what keeps us!"

"What does?"

"They got the low-down on us all!" said Maple beneath his breath.

"What's that?"

"Look how they got me!" said Chuck with emotion. "I was in a little trouble in town. Sure, I was guilty. 'A couple of years will about suit you, my friend,' the judge began to say, and before he could continue his sentence, a note was handed to him. He read the note. Then he frowned at me. He declared a recess and left the room. Pretty soon I was called into his chambers. I went in and there was the judge sittin' lookin' me up and down, and there was young Charlie Dee, smooth and cool, like he always is, damn him!

"The judge says to me: 'Look here, Maple, I have your record. I know that you ought to go behind the bars. But I'm goin' to give you another chance. My friend Charlie Dee says that he thinks he could keep you straight. You stay here and talk it over with him. I'm goin' to have a cup of coffee. Can you take charge of him, Charlie?'

"Charlie says that he thinks he can—me bein' in a pair of handcuffs. The judge went out. Charlie says to me: 'Maple, this is the way that things stand. I got a ranch up the valley under Mount Laurel. You could come up there and work for me and get your pay the same as any straight ranch hand gets his. You get a good place, good bunk house, good chuck, and everything fine for you. Or if you don't like that, you can stay here and go to the penitentiary for two or three years. What do you say, Maple?'

"What could I say? I looked him over. He seemed all right. I says: 'How long do I stay?'

"'Five years,' says he.

"I think it over. Two years in the pen; five years on a ranch. I know ranch work and I ain't a slouch at it, but I hate it. But I think it over.

105

"I says, 'Suppose that I meet up with a girl and want to travel double?'

" 'We'll always provide for a married man,' says he. 'Give you a shack, some ground to raise vegetables on, fix you up with a cow, even, and make your life easy—after you've been with us a year, say, and show that you're the right stuff.'

"Nacherally, I was surprised, hearin' that sort of talk. I busted right out: 'Look here, Mr. Dee, how d'you know that I won't blow as soon as you get me out there? What makes you think that I'll stick it out?'

"That's what I said to him. And he leans forward and puts his elbows on his knees and he says to me—"

Here Maple became silent, and Rhiannon could hear his hard breathing. "I ain't been a saint," said Maple finally. "I been around the world, and I've stepped in the tar, too. I've raised my share of hell. And once—well, I raised more than my share! This Dee, he know about it. I dunno where he found out. I thought it was off the books—never been on them. But he knew about it. And he says to me exactly what I done one night in New Orleans.

" 'That's why you'll stay with me for five years,' says he.

"I begun to hate the sight of him. But what could I do?

"He goes on: 'Mind you, I'm not makin' you do this. You take it or leave it. But if once you come out to me, you'll stay put!'

"I thought it over some more. I was almost on the point of sayin' that I'd rather stay in jail for two years than work for him for five, but I didn't. I gave him my promise and I came out here. That's my story!"

He waited for comments, but Rhiannon made none. Outside of the sheriff's testimony, he could have spotted Chuck Maple at a great distance as a professional criminal. He had nothing to say. What had his own life been?

"Now," said Maple, "when I come out here, I looked over the rest of the boys, and I seen what they were. Every one of them like me. I knew three of them already pretty well, and one of them—well, him and me done a job in Denver, once, on a damn tough safe. The rest was all the same—long-riders, yeggs, crooks of all kinds that have to live with a gun on the hip and an eye over one shoulder.

" 'What sort of a game is this?' I says to one of them.

" 'I dunno,' says he, and walks away from me.

" 'What are you held for?' I says to another.

" 'Stick around and find out if you can,' says he.

"And so I stuck around and waited. I been waitin' ever since, and I never found out. I got some ideas, but that was all!"

"What ideas, then?"

"You've heard about the Morgans?"

"A little. Not much."

"They run this whole section of the hills, once. The Morgans was a little wild, I take it. But they was white. The Dees wiped 'em out. How did they do it? Why, by buildin' up an organization that was something worth while, if you want to know. What I mean to say: There ain't many honest men that shoot straight. Some of 'em do pretty good, but most of them that shoot straight do it because their life depends on it. Who'd practice an hour a day? Nobody but a fellow that had to. And a crook has to. I'm a crook," said Maple frankly. "That's why I took to guns. You shoot straight yourself, Gwynn," he added tersely, "but I don't ask you no questions!"

After this near hit, he went on rapidly: "Of course old man Dee had a brain in his head, and he got together a bunch of boys like myself, that had traveled wide and loose and took what they wanted—not by work! The Morgans was fine, upstandin' men with guns, but they never had the accuracy that the Dees had. They made a good fight, but they always lost, and old Dee, gradually, he wiped them out. He beat them here and he beat them there. He had fellers that knew how to lay traps! And how to keep out of the traps themselves. I've talked to some of the old-timers that was in the fightin'. They've told me some things that would make the hair stand up on your head. Anyway, the Morgans went down, and the Dees, they went up. And there you are!"

"He got together a band of hard-shooting boys," said Rhiannon.

"He done just that," said Chuck Maple. "There ain't one of the boys in that bunk house that ain't got at least a couple of rifles and a couple of pairs of revolvers. Don't

107

have to put the coin out of your pocket. Just say to Charlie Dee that you feel that your old gat is gettin' burned out. 'All right,' says he, and the next day he brings you out half a dozen. Well, you can up and take your pick of the whole lot. Or then again, suppose that you want to have a lot of ammunition. Ask Charlie Dee. He'll give you a barrel full of it. All he wants to know is that it's burned up! He don't care at what! I've seen a puncher sit on the back steps of the bunk house and burn up forty shots out of a revolver tryin' to make a tin can roll across the yard. That's the way that they manage it! Money's no object with them, so long as the money goes into powder and lead. And of course, how could the Morgans stand up agin that sort of fightin' men?"

"That's simple to understand," said Rhiannon. "That's easy to see. But I don't foller it all. Not all the way. Look here. When the Morgans was around, I could understand that, of course. But what about the time when the Morgans was cleaned out? After the back of the Morgans was broke, what then, I say?"

"Sure," answered Chuck. "I've wondered about the same thing. A gent would! But I figger it out this way. You get used to havin' a fast hoss because you need to cover miles with him. And after you get used to him, even if you don't have much ridin' to do, still you want the same kind of a hoss in your stables. Ain't that right?"

"That's right," agreed Rhiannon.

"They got used to havin' their little old army around them, and they couldn't any ways give it up, you see."

"Exactly. But I have an idea, from the talk of them, that the Dees wouldn't spend so much money on a hobby. They'd want to have some use of it, too!"

"Aye," said Chuck Maple, "they would, and they got a reason for what they want. I never could quite guess at it until the other day. I always thought it was just because this was a handy country for rustlers to work—so near under Mount Laurel. But the other night I got the answer!"

"Go on," said Rhiannon, controlling his impatience with an effort. "What is the reason, then?"

"Reason? The best in the world. All of the Morgans ain't dead!"

Chapter Twenty-Four

A TOTAL surprise is never a very great shock. The unprepared mind does not grasp its full meaning. It is what we more than half expect that strikes us dumb, as Rhiannon was struck dumb, now.

"Morgans still alive!" said he.

"Seems to kind of stir you up, hearin' that?" asked Chuck curiously. "D'you know any of them in the old days?"

"No," said Rhiannon truthfully. "I never knew any of them in the old days. What made you think some of them were still alive?"

"I'll tell you. I heard it the other night. And I'll tell you how it come about. I was lyin' in my bunk, sort of sore and stiff. And while I was lyin' there, word comes in that Charlie wants me.

" 'Tell him to go to hell,' says I, polite. 'I'm busted up where Gwynn grabbed me and jerked me from under that derrick.'

"Because, as a matter of fact, you pretty near tore my arm out of my shoulder when you grabbed me and yanked me clear from that singletree. But word come in again that I had to come. So I went along. Charlie was waitin' for me by the stable. He says to me, right off: 'Chuck, I been watchin' you for a long time. I have gents on the ranch that have worked for me a longer time. And I have a lot of them that I'd trust with pretty near anything, but not quite with the job that I got on my hands tonight.'

"He ain't the kind of a man that throws out compliments like he was sowin' wheat. I was flattered. It swelled me up a good deal, and I told him that I was glad to know that I'd pleased them. 'Chuck,' says he, 'I'll tell you something more. Sometimes you wish that you could be through with this work on the ranch.'

" 'I get that wish pretty frequent,' I admitted to him.

" 'Now take time, and go careful, and do the job that I'm gunna have lined out for you, and *keep your mouth shut all the time!* If you'll do that, I got an idea that I can shorten down the rest of your five years to les'n five weeks!'

"It took my breath to hear that. I want to be a free man. Good chuck and easy work ain't enough. A man wants to have his own way about things, as maybe you know! Well, I told him to lead me to the job.

" 'You don't mind if it's—something extra?' he asked me.

" 'You know me, Charlie,' I told him. 'You know that I sometimes gotta wear gloves when I'm doin' my own work!'

"He laughed a little at that. Then he told me to get my hoss—my new one—and ride down the valley road about a half mile.

"I done that, and pretty soon along he comes and somebody else along with him, small as a boy. When they got closer, I seen the flappin' of divided skirts. It was a girl! Well, I pricked up my ears at that. It took the heart out of me. I don't mind rough work, and I don't mind dirty work, but I keep my hands off of decent women.

"Anyway, Charlie comes up to me and he says, 'Ride down the road ahead of us. Don't go fast. Let your hoss walk. Ride over the top of that hill and look around you. On the way, if a man comes out of the brush—foot or horseback—you sing out, "What's the time?" If he answers, "Dark!" then you say: "All right. Stand by, here." And you sit your hoss beside him and wait for us!'

"When he got through sayin' this, the girl sings out in a sort of flutterin' voice: 'Oh, d'you think that he'll come? D'you think that he'll come?'

" 'I got his word for it,' says Charlie. 'Go ahead, Chuck.'

"This looked like funny business to me. I went ahead, at a slow walk, and I went up over that hill, and I watched all around me, but there wasn't any sign of any man ridin' out of the brush. Finally Charlie and the girl come up to me.

" 'It's funny!' says Charlie. 'He swore that he'd be here. Maybe something has delayed him.'

110

" 'Nothin' would delay him,' says the girl. 'No Morgan ever broke his word!'

" 'Of course not,' says Charlie, very smooth and gentle, 'but you know how it is, Nancy. Things will happen, now and then and—' "

"What did he call her?" broke in Rhiannon.

"Nancy was the name that he gave to her."

"Nancy!" said Rhiannon. It was spoken half to himself.

"You know her?" asked Chuck.

"Me? How should I know her?" asked Rhiannon tartly. "Go on with your story!"

"Well, don't get sore if I ask you a simple question. We waited around there on the hill for quite a spell, and finally the girl says: 'He won't come! He won't come! Oh, you haven't told me the truth!'

" 'Look here,' says Charlie, 'why shouldn't I tell you the truth? The fact is, Nancy, that something must have stopped him.'

" 'What could have stopped him?' says the girl.

" 'A thousand things,' says Charlie.

" 'Well, he hasn't come,' says she. 'I won't wait any longer. I'll ride on, Charlie.'

" 'Where would you go to?' says he.

" 'I don't care, I just want to go away,' says she.

" 'Nan,' says he, 'how could I turn you loose to go wanderin' at night—and through the hills!'

"She made a little stop, then. She turned her face toward him, and there was enough starlight for me to see the glistenin' of her eyes. She was scared. I could tell that. It didn't please me none. It never pleases me none to see a woman scared half to death. I says to her: 'It's all right, ma'am. Don't you worry!'

" 'Certainly there's nothin' to worry about,' says Charlie. 'But of course I couldn't let you go away on a night like this!'

" 'Are you goin' to take me back?' she says in a dull, sad sort of a voice.

" 'I gotta,' says Charlie. 'What would Dad say if he knew that I let you go without takin' any care of you?'

"Then she busted out in a laugh—it only lasted about half a second, that laugh, and there was no fun in it.

"She says: 'He always took such care of the Morgans!

Of course he wouldn't want to stop lookin' after them now!'

"But she turned back down the road, ridin' with Charlie, while he had me fall back and keep the rear guard, as he called it.

"We went on at a jog until we come back close to the house.

" 'That's all I need of you,' says Charlie.

"I takes off my hat to the lady, and then I cuts across country. I was best pleased to be away from that business —whatever it was.

"I get back to the bunk house, and there I rest on my oars, as you might say, and think things over, and it looks to me like a mean business, for sure, that was goin' on.

"After a time, Charlie sends for me. I go up to the house, and he's walkin' back and forth in the patio. He says to me, 'Chuck, I don't have to tell you to keep your mouth shut about this, do I?'

" 'No,' says I, 'I'll keep my face shut!'

" 'That's the talk,' says he, very hearty.

" 'But,' says I, 'I figger that I'm best out of any more of those dealin's.'

" 'Why?' says he, very sharp.

" 'By listenin' to the sound of her voice,' says I, 'and by seein' her cryin' in the starlight and makin' no sound!' "

A dreadful oath broke in a murmur from the lips of Rhiannon.

"You figger like me, do you?" said Chuck, gratified. "Well, Charlie looked me over, and finally he said: 'Well, I'm disappointed in you. That's all. So long, Chuck!' But I knew right then that I went down in his black books."

"And that's all?"

"That's all, up to the holler that I heard tonight, and I've told you about that. The rest of the boys laid still. I had to go and look around. So I went to the old wing of the house and there I tried to do a little explorin'—and you caught me comin' down like a rat in a trap—"

"One minute!" said Rhiannon, raising his hand.

Plainly across the night came a brief burst, like the rattling of a great drum. A pause. The noise again.

"Gunfire!" said Chuck Maple. "Hell's loose for real, now!"

Chapter Twenty-Five

THEY LISTENED again. The night was perfectly still.

"Rifles!" said Chuck Maple, "and from the ranch!"

"Rifles—*and* revolvers!" said Rhiannon.

"What's happened?" gasped Chuck Maple.

"Whatever it is, it's finished," said Rhiannon in a voice that rang like an iron bell. "Go back to the ranch. I'm going home. I think you'll find a dead man—or a dead woman back there, Chuck."

They separated with no other words.

Rhiannon went home across the dark field, his feet growing wet and chilled with dew as he walked. He found the house dark except for a lamp with the wick turned down low in the dining room. The Italian had left that burning for him as a sort of dim welcome, and Rhiannon leaned against the wall and blinked at the light. He should be across the valley, using his hands in behalf of the girl. So said his instinct. But how should he reach her? What was even his strength, his guns, against that trained battalion of desperadoes employed by the Dees?

The sheriff had not told him as much as the sheriff surely must have known. He wondered why!

Dim as the burning of this lamp, he saw into the strange affair at the house of Dee. A draft was making the flame rise and fall, and with it the shadows of the chairs rose and fell and writhed together along the wall. So it was with the adventure of the house of Dee.

It was all Charlie, he felt sure. Behind the garrulity of the father there was enough hardness, but not, he assured himself, the hardness which would deal with a young girl as Charlie seemed to be dealing with Nancy Morgan. But everything was wrapped in a mist. He could not understand. What had drawn the girl each night to the hill—what had drawn her so irresistibly into the hands of the enemies of her family—who was that other man, the Morgan to whom she expected that Charlie would take her? And why should she expect that Charlie would bring her to one of her kin? Those questions needed answering.

Other things, also, were odd, to say the least. There was the extraordinary cordiality of all the Dees toward him. The cordiality of Oliver Dee, of his wife (at least on his second visit), of Charlie, and finally and above all, of Isabella herself. Such cordiality that the door seemed continually open for him to come again and call at the house. Isabella would be glad to see him—the last touch of her hand and the last glance from her eyes had assured him of that!

Let him flatter himself that they had taken an instinctive liking to him—perhaps because he had shown himself a strong man of action? Yet still that hardly quite explained the whole affair. There remained something behind the scenes, a motive power for which he could not make an accounting. So he told himself. He yearned to have the wise sheriff with him, at this point, so that they could put their heads together and try to solve some points in the mystery.

He took the lamp to his bedroom, undressed, and turned in. When the light was out he lay rigid, staring into the darkness. A gentle wind blew through the window and brought the fragrance and the coolness of the night about him.

Was it not, in a way, strangest of all that the sheriff knew so little about the family of Dee? Or was it the weak point in the character of Caradac that he knew very well, and realized that the strength of this family was too great even for him to touch them? So he left them free to do as they would! On that unhappy thought, Rhiannon fell asleep and dreamed of Isabella Dee singing in the patio and horror and death lying about her.

It was a prophetic dream, in a way.

The morning was still young when a boy drove over in a cart from the Dee place to fetch the day's supply of milk and a roll of butter. He was running over with excited talk. The night before was an unforgettable moment in the history of the Dee ranch, it appeared.

Rhiannon was not long gone when there was a crash in the old wing of the house; the men ran out to investigate this noise and they encountered a stranger running away. He was told to halt and a bullet was sent over his

114

head. At that, he dropped to the ground and scattered the formidable Dees with a deadly fire.

Now Mortimer Dee lay with a bullet through his body. Would he live or would he die? That was the question. And Jimmy Dee had been shot through both thighs, the left leg bone probably shattered by the passage of the slug of lead. Most marvelous of all, the gunman who had inflicted this damage was still at large, although the Dees and all of their men were combing the countryside for him.

"And nobody's got an idea of who he is?" asked Rhiannon.

"Sure they got an idea," said the boy. "They seen him run right across the path of the light that spilled out of a window. It was the gent that used to work over here for you."

"Richards?" cried Rhiannon.

"That was his name. Richards. I heard them call him by that name!"

Rhiannon sat down suddenly on the edge of the rear porch of the house.

"Richards!" he said. "God a'mighty, I can't make nothing out!"

"No more can nobody," said the boy. "But the boss is pretty near crazy, he's so mad. And he says that if Mort dies, he's gunna burn the whole country to the ground to get at Richards and then feed him to a fire, inch by inch! I never heard of nothin' like it—droppin' two Dees in one shootin' match, and then gettin' off!"

"Without a scratch, eh?" asked Rhiannon.

"Him? Sure he got a scratch! They found blood where he was lyin'. They found more blood in the brush where he sneaked away, and the place where he must of stopped and bandaged up his wound. He ain't gunna get far away, and God help him when he's caught, is all that I got to say!"

He said it with great fervency, and Rhiannon was quite willing to agree that Richards would need more mercy than ever he would receive at the hands of the Dees.

But Richards! The dark of brow—the sullen, silent, maliceful Richards! What was he doing there at the Dee place? For what purpose had he, of all men, attempted to enter the old wing of the house?

Would Richards have tried to bring the girl away? Was

it she who had brought him there? Did he have any other possible purpose in going to the house? Or was it, indeed, that mere curiosity had taken him to the place—if the story of that cry in the night had by this time been noised about the countryside?

Anger rose in Rhiannon. He was closed about with a high wall of impossibilities. There was no gate by which he could escape into the open sunlight of understanding!

Then he said to himself that it was a matter of which he must wash his hands—until night came again upon the hills. And then, God willing, he would steal or smash his way into the old wing of the house, no matter how guarded, and either give up his blood like so much water, or else take Nancy Morgan away from the trap!

So he set his teeth and went to work like a bulldog, hardly knowing what his hands performed, but glad to have time slipping away.

In mid-morning he had almost a greater shock. A sweating rider came out to him with an envelope. He leaned from his foaming horse and gave it to Rhiannon.

"There ain't any answer!" said he.

Then he whirled his horse and galloped away.

Rhiannon was left with a letter which read:

Partner, things are starting and there's gunna be speed showed all round this part of the country, for a while. I gotta be on the job to help the Dees to find that man Richards. I always told you that Richards was a bad one! Now he's gone ahead and proved it.

Now, it's pretty sure that Richards is wounded and that he's wounded pretty bad.

That being the case, where will he go to hide? He may lie out a night. But with cold in his wound, he ain't gunna lie out long, I'd say.

He'll hit for shelter, and it may be that he'll come straight back for the farm and try to put up with you.

Now, if he does that, this is what you must do. Put him to bed and take the best care of him in the world, and don't let anybody come near him.

Don't tell a soul that he's there. Cover up his tracks, and keep it dark. If anybody asks you about him, you ain't seen him. And if I should be there when the questions are asked, still you don't know nothin'. I'll be there before dark, I hope.

*This may sound funny to you. Don't ask any questions.
Just stand between Richards and any danger that comes
his way, and stand between with guns, if you have to.*

*If you don't, you're gunna be the saddest man that
ever stepped on this here earth!*

So long.

Owen C.

This letter Rhiannon could not understand until he had
read it twice through, and then repeated all the words
aloud. Richards, the sneak, the spy, the crooked dealer!

And yet now his life was to be protected, if he came
there for shelter, as though it were the life of Caradac
himself. So it appeared from the sheriff's message.

It never occurred to Rhiannon to refuse to do what he
was commanded. But he sat on top of a fence and cursed
long, and steadily, and with wonderful eloquence, and the
sheriff's name was included among his blasphemies.

Chapter Twenty-Six

RHIANNON went to the blacksmith shop in the hope of
finding there something which might distract his mind. He
built up a forge fire and put into it a great broken iron
bar for welding, but his interest lagged almost at once.
He left the fire to die and went toward the barn. Out of
the distance floated the clear, sweet voice of Caracci
singing a song of his native land.

Rhiannon turned into the barn, and as he did so he
saw a tattered figure in the act of climbing over the
manger. At his call the other turned toward him a face
marked around the forehead by a broad bandage, blood-
stained; and more blood streaked the face of this fugitive.
His coat was in tatters, and at least half of his shirt had
been torn away—evidently to make the bandage.

Staggering with weakness, covered with caked mud,
blood-stained, horrible to behold—it was Richards! And
when he saw Rhiannon, he reeled, and grasped drunkenly
at the manger rail to support himself, and laughed.

Out of that great body, out of that huge throat came forth foolish, failing laughter—thin as the laughter of a woman, loose as the laughter of an idiot. "Rhiannon!" he said, and laughed still. "Rhiannon—the great Rhiannon!"

And still he laughed as Rhiannon went up to him. He was not drunk with alcohol. There was no trace of the pungent odor of drink about him. Obviously the poor fellow was simply on the point of collapse.

Rhiannon regarded him with an odd mingling of disfavor and wonder and curiosity. "Are you bad hurt?" he asked.

"Rhiannon!" said Richards, still feebly laughing. "Rhiannon!" He seemed to find infinite amusement in repeating that formidable name; then, losing hold on the edge of the manger, he staggered backward until his shoulders crashed against the side of the barn. The shock of that contact would surely have knocked him to the floor if it had not been that Rhiannon, following, caught him up and supported him.

Richards sagged, like a half-filled sack, in his arms. Rhiannon carried him from the barn. At the door he stared keenly about to make sure that no one was coming up the road, and then he started toward the house with his heavy burden.

Richards lay like a dead man. As in death, his mouth had fallen open, his eyes were half shut and glassy, his breast did not move with any sign of breathing.

As Rhiannon passed the shed, Caracci came out, and the song stopped on his lips as he saw his master passing with such a burden. But at once he turned his back and began to sing again.

There were all manner of good qualities in Caracci. And Rhiannon, seeing that the cat was out of the bag, called sharply to him:

"Joe! Hey!"

The other came on the run.

"Take his feet and help me in with him!"

Caracci took the feet willingly. They hurried on through the little gate and to the house. There they stretched out the unconscious body on the bed of Rhiannon.

Rhiannon went to find brandy. Caracci, unordered, hastily and skilfully began to remove the clothes from

118

Richards' body. The work was half finished before Rhiannon came back with the stimulant. After that, he had to examine the hurts of the fugitive. There were not many. A dozen bruises, more or less severe, and many small cuts and scratches, as though Richards had had to force his way at full speed through stinging thickets of thorn.

The main injury was a long gash along the side of the head, apparently put there by a glancing bullet. And the loss of blood from this wound, never properly cleaned or bandaged, was what had weakened the man so completely. Then Rhiannon cleaned the cut with iodine, and under the sting of it, Richards opened his eyes with a groan.

But his mind was far at sea. The strain he had been under must have been prolonged and terrible. Not only loss of blood but also physical fatigue had worn him down until he was a thin shadow of his old self, and now he lay on the bed with his big arms thrown out nervously to either side, and with his head rolling loosely back and forth. His eyes were wild one moment and half lost in feverish sleep the next; continually he muttered.

"Will he live?" asked Rhiannon, half of himself, as he stepped back and looked at the man.

"He live!" said Caracci with much conviction. "Plenty of life in him. He gotta sleep! He gotta eat!"

This brief summary of the case seemed convincing enough to Rhiannon.

He went into the kitchen to cook something for the hurt man, and, as he did so, he saw through the window a swarm of half a dozen riders raising the dust of his corral. At their head rode William Dee.

They were coming at a gallop from the barn. They dismounted outside the gate, threw their reins, and came hurrying in toward the house. Every man was armed. Undoubtedly they meant to have their own way, whatever that way might be. Among them he noted Chuck Maple, but, though Maple was a friend and a courageous fellow, it was most unlikely that he would show his friendship in the midst of this crew.

There was no fear in Rhiannon as he eyed that formidable gang. He stepped out on the rear porch and with his empty rifles he faced the men and their rifles, and their belts sagging at the hip with long Colts. "Hello, boys," said Rhiannon. "You look sort of hurried!"

Will Dee was leading the procession. He slowed in his pace a little. "We run down the rat to your barn, Gwynn. He came back here because he'd been here before, and I suppose that you thought that—"

"What rat?" asked Rhiannon.

"Him! Richards!" said Dee. "What have you done with him?"

"What should I be doing with him?" asked Rhiannon.

"Don't bluff," said Will Dee in anger.

He came to a stop, however, and frowned at Rhiannon. "Mort is lyin' just around the corner from death," said he. "We want the rat that shot him and dropped Jimmy, too!"

"Richards did that? Yeh, the kid told me about it this morning. But what brought you here?"

"Because he come here. We follered his trail right into your barn!"

"Then he's in the barn. Go take a look for him there, and good luck to you!"

"It ain't gunna do," said Dee with earnestness. "We've looked the barn over careful, and now we're gunna look over the house, and if you don't want any trouble with us you'd better—"

"Trouble?" said Rhiannon. "I hate trouble. I hate it like hell. But you don't bust into any house that belongs to me!" He said the last words with a naked revolver in his hand. It was an old gun. The trigger was filed away; so was the sight. It was simply a battered old Colt of the ancient single-action type, and the big thumb of Rhiannon's right hand was hooked over the hammer, which worked up and down a little, as though trying the strength of the spring.

He did not try to whip the gun up and cover Will Dee or any other man in the party, but the careless manner in which he allowed the weapon to hang at his side had an infinite meaning for those bold men and brave.

Will Dee took note of the situation with care. He was neither frightened nor very angry. Rather, he was much surprised. "Gwynn," said he, "I thought that you was a friend of ours?"

120

"And why not?" said Rhiannon.

"You're standin' between us and a fair proposition that I make to you. We ain't a pack of Red Indians. We ain't gunna bust up your place. We only wanta take a look around. Now, what's wrong with that? Especially, if you ain't got Richards inside the house," he added cunningly.

"From one way of looking at it," said Rhiannon, "there never was truer words spoke. But from another way of looking at it, there never was anything worse! In the first place, I won't let armed gents come into my house to prowl around unless they got warrants from the government. What warrants have you got?"

"There ain't a man here," said Dee with much coldness, "that don't carry one warrant on his hip and another in his hands. What you say to me, Gwynn? Be sensible, man. You're the last that we want any trouble with. The old man would raise hell if we had to do anything to you—but we're gunna sure see the insides of your house!"

"Don't talk like that, partner," said Rhiannon softly. "Because if you keep on that sort of a way of talking, you'll convince yourself. You'll talk yourself into being angry. Don't get angry with me. I'm a peaceable farmer, and I don't want any trouble!"

There was a slight murmur among the men who followed Will Dee. They began to stir a little and spread out to either side, their rifles at the ready.

As for Dee, his temper was getting the better of him. "It's plain that you got him!" said he.

"Is it?" answered Rhiannon, still perfect master of himself. "But I tell you this: Suppose that I *did* have him! Suppose that he was lying in my house—perhaps looking out at you now down the barrel of a Winchester—"

There was a swift shifting of eyes in the entire party. That point had told!

"Even then," said Rhiannon, "how could I let you come in to search for him? When a man walks into your house, he's got a right to be protected. It's the rule. It's the rule of the range, and you know it!"

That point also told. There was an instinctive nodding of heads in the search party which Will Dee cut short by announcing curtly: "We got six men here. Rhiannon, you see for yourself. If we're turned back by one man, we'd be laughed out of the county."

There was silence. They seemed to have come to a deadlock.

Chapter Twenty-Seven

IN THAT moment of pause, Rhiannon knew that he was as close to eternity as ever he had been in seven wild years. He was not disturbed, but he saw all things clearly and well. He could have closed his eyes and told the color of every one of the six shirts and the patterns of the bandanas, and the rig of the guns, and the looks in the faces.

"Dee," said Rhiannon, "suppose that you was beat and done, and that you got to a house, and the door closed behind you, and the wolves come howling at the door. And suppose that the gent of the house opened that door and throwed you out to the white teeth—I ask you to think of that, Dee!"

William Dee thought of it, and his face turned a fiery red. "It's a mighty mean picture," said he, "but it's got another side. That side is this: The hound has dropped two good men that belong to my family!"

"I'm doggone sorry to hear it," said Rhiannon. "He sneaked up and shot 'em in the back?"

He asked it pleasantly, seriously, as one requesting information, and Will Dee fell into the trap. "He didn't do that. When we rushed him, he dropped to the ground and blazed away at us from there!"

"How many was rushing him?"

"Seven or eight."

"Head on?"

"Surest thing!"

"Well," said Rhiannon slowly, "I dunno that that changes anything except in favor of Richards. Seven or eight gents rush him. He fights 'em off and drops a pair of 'em, and then he gets away—"

122

"By God, Gwynn, you're a friend of his!" exclaimed young Will Dee.

"Friend?" said Rhiannon. "I run him off of the place! Ask the sheriff if I didn't. I ain't even said that he's in the house, but I'm putting my side of the case."

"It may be a good side or it may be a bad side," said Will Dee with the slowest of thoughtful voices, "but this is the way that I gotta look at it. I was sent out to find Richards. I think that I've found him. I got five men behind me. There's one man in front of us. That's the way that I see the thing. That's the way that I gotta see it!"

"If Richards is in this here house, you got another man to pass," said Rhiannon, "before you go in. If you drop me—all of you won't be starting into that house. Two or three are just gunna lie down and go to sleep under the fig tree, here. I don't like to talk and I don't like to boast. But I'm telling you the facts!"

He looked them in the eye, one by one, and one by one they had to turn their heads away from him—not much, but the slightest shifting of the eyes.

And though it was apparent that they would not refuse their duty, or to follow their leader, yet it was equally apparent that they were flinching from the stern necessity. Will Dee seemed to feel the falling off behind him, and he flashed a look at his followers. "Look here," said he, "you remember that there ain't more than one man agin us!"

Then Chuck Maple put in: "If there's nobody in that house, then we've killed John Gwynn for nothin'; if Richards is in that house, the minute that we turn loose on Gwynn, Richards turns loose on us. I ask you if the job is worth it. That's all. Personal, I don't think that any one bullet is ever gunna kill Gwynn. He don't look that way!"

It appeared for the instant that the crisis would be passed over without any further difficulties, but all was not yet ended, for William Dee was worthy of his name, and he now threw himself headlong into the struggle. He did not shout or make any violent appeals. He simply remarked with the greatest simplicity in the world: "I'm gunna go into that house, boys, without you or with you. Gwynn—you better back up!"

And he actually took a step forward. There was a

slight wavering among the men behind him, and then they strode forward together!

Never did a balance sway in a more perilous fashion. The eyes of Rhiannon already were narrowed, and the cords of his wrists were beginning to stiffen. The fingers of his empty left hand worked a little. He was not accustomed to having that hand empty in such affairs!

Then their attention was snatched away by the rapid sound of gunshots, sweeping toward them—shots fired one by one—six in a row.

"What's that?" asked Chuck Maple, glad enough to divert attention from his benefactor, Rhiannon.

"No matter what," said Will Dee, who had halted for only an instant. "No matter what! The point is that we'll ask questions about other things later on—"

A high-pitched yell came over the fields. "It's a Dee!" said one of the men, and lowered the butt of his rifle and half turned.

The call came again. "It's Charlie," muttered the leader, and took a step back. "We'll let Charlie take command, then. He can make a decision a pile better than me!"

Charlie Dee came at a brisk gallop through the corral gate and up to the fence, and as he dismounted he shouted, "What's up, Will?"

He came hastily down the board walk, and Rhiannon watched his coming with a grim suspense. This would either make or break him, of course. "Hello, Gwynn," said Charlie Dee. "What's happened, Will?"

"We ran Richards down to the barn, out yonder. He wasn't in the barn. We came in to search the house, and Gwynn, here, won't let us do it!"

"Quite right, too," said Charlie. "Why should he let a crowd bust into his house? And even if Richards was there, it's Gwynn's right to show him hospitality. It's the law of the range, boys. You all know that!"

It was a most astonishing speech. No one was more surprised by it than Rhiannon. As for Will Dee, he was helpless with bewilderment. "He's got a right to keep anybody he wants?" he asked. "We got no right to finish off our search?"

"He's a friend of ours, ain't he?" asked Charlie Dee without hesitation. "Do we chuck away friends of the breed of John Gwynn? We don't. Not to finish off a hundred like Richards."

He nodded at Rhiannon. "I'm glad I got here," said he. "Will means the right thing, but he's sort of stubborn."

"I'm glad that you got here, too," said Rhiannon, and smiled a little—without mirth.

"I'd like to see you and Will shake hands," went on Charlie. "Just to show that you understand each other."

"Sure," said Rhiannon. "Glad to!"

He held out his great hand and Will Dee stepped forward to meet it. "Never was gladder to have anything taken out of my hands in my life," said Will Dee with a sigh. "I thought that we'd have to have guns talkin', before the finish, Big Boy!"

"We'll swarm out to the barn," said Charlie Dee, "and try to pick up the trail there, boys. Lead on, Will."

They started down the board walk, and Charlie turned back to Rhiannon. "Sorry that this happened, Gwynn," said he. "Mighty sorry. But I gotta say this: I respect you for keeping your house to yourself, but if you really got Richards inside of it, it's only fair that you turn him out again as soon as you can."

"Partner," said Rhiannon with real emotion, "there's nobody that I ever liked less than Richards. That's a fact!"

Charlie Dee waved farewell. "Come over and see us," he invited. "Then we can be sure that there's no hard feeling on your part about today. Will you do that?"

"Glad to, Charlie."

"So long, then."

He went off down the board walk with a springing step and leaped into his saddle; Rhiannon watched him jog toward the barn. The sheriff had been right at least in part about this youth. He was a man of quick decisions, a man of action, a man of strong will.

So Rhiannon went back into the house and found Caracci in the act of rising from the floor where he had been lying in the dining room with the muzzle of a Winchester pressed against a great crack in the outer wall! He gave Rhiannon a guilty smile and a shake of the head; then they went in together to the bedside of the wounded man.

They found Richards tossing his head from side to side,

125

his face flushed beneath the bandage, and his eyes wild with fever.

"Sit here and watch him," said Rhiannon. "I'll fix up a snack for him."

It did not take him long. He came in from the kitchen with soup and bread and found Caracci leaning insistently over the hurt man and demanding in a quiet, steady voice: "What's your name? What's your name?"

Rhiannon stood in the doorway, frowning with wonder. It was obvious torment to press questions upon a sick man delirious with fever. And why, after all, should the Italian wish to make sure of the name of a man who already was accepted throughout the district as "Richards"?

Every time the question was asked the wounded man answered in a jumble of words which suddenly became louder:

"Twenty-five paces from the entrance—turn left—turn left—"

Then his voice changed and rang with a sudden clearness as the remorseless question of Caracci beat against his dizzy brain: "My name is Morgan, if I die for it!"

Chapter Twenty-Eight

THEN CARACCI, seeing Rhiannon in the doorway, slipped from the side of the bed and stood against the wall, smiling, but with his eyes uncertain. It was plain that he had not expected his employer to return from the kitchen so soon.

Rhiannon went past him without more than a single glance. He sat down beside the wounded man.

Richards—Morgan! There were two Morgans left, Chuck Maple had said. Nancy, then—and this gloomy fellow!

Yet it seemed impossible. There could have been no greater contrast than that between bright Nancy, and this sullen, half-savage man, with his cunning, and his slinking ways. Yet there had been nothing slinking in that last announcement which had gone ringing through the room: "Morgan, if I die for it!"

"Morgan," and he nearly *had* died for it! But what had he been doing on the farm so long? Why had he spied upon Rhiannon? Questions to be answered!

As for the attempt on the old wing of the house of Dee, that was now explained. He had gone to get Nancy. It was the last and convincing proof that Nancy was indeed confined there! He had failed to find her, he had brought the full force of the Dees upon his head, but he had baffled them and had made good his retreat as far as this house.

Rhiannon could have laughed. The whole affair was growing absurd. Its confusion had reached a tangle which would need more than human intelligence if it was to be dissolved and made common sense.

He tried to feed the soup to the sick man, but Richards —or Morgan, perhaps—refused with a groan and set his teeth against the taste of it.

"Afterward," said Caracci. "He'll take it afterward."

Rhiannon left the room and motioned to Caracci to follow him.

They confronted each other in the dining room, Rhiannon with the tray of food still in his hands. "Now," said Rhiannon, "you out and tell me why you wanted to find out the name of—Richards, or whatever he is!"

"You know," said Caracci cheerfully, "when a man goes around he sees a lot of faces. You forget names. You remember faces, eh? I thought I'd seen him—not using that name of Richards. I thought I'd seen him somewhere, so I sit and ask. Finally, he says Morgan."

"Was that the man you knew?"

"I don't know," said Caracci. His eyes were wide open; they looked straight at Rhiannon.

"Twenty-five steps from the entrance—turn to the left," quoted Rhiannon. "What did that mean?"

He thought that the eyes of Caracci opened a little wider. "That was fever in the brain. Men talk nonsense like that when they're sick."

"Joe," said Rhiannon, "going around the world you meet with a lot of lies and you meet with a lot of liars, but

I never met with bigger lies than you been telling me just now."

Caracci expanded both his hands and shrugged both his shoulders. He rolled up his eyes at the same time. Never had there been a more complete and silent denial of all wrongdoing!

"What did I hire you for?" asked Rhiannon.

"To work—milk cows—patch fences—dig in the garden—plow—plant—take care of cows—skim milk—churn—"

"Wait a minute," said Rhiannon. "You don't have to recite off everything. But the fact is that I never hired you to lie on the floor with your rifle squeezed into a crack of the wall, all ready to start butchering good, law-abiding citizens! Did I ever hire you for that?"

His iron brow relaxed as Caracci made another helpless gesture.

"Between us, Joe," he could not help saying, "I figger that we would of given a hot time to them, eh?"

"There was two standing in a row. One bullet for two men—if you shoot low, through the belly. Those two would have dropped and squealed like pigs the first time I pulled the trigger." He said it with a sparkle in his eyes, and Rhiannon chuckled softly. He could understand this. He began to feel that, whatever was behind this man, he was a treasure!

"But look here, Joe," said he, "what brought you out here? Who sent you? Who put you in the path of the sheriff?"

"Sheriff Caradac, he wanted a strong man. I have pretty strong hands," said Joe Caracci with a grin.

"You're a liar," growled Rhiannon, "but I sort of like the way that you tell those lies! I think that you would of stuck by me. And what your real name may be, and who you are and who sent you and what you know, and what you want to know—well, I leave that for a smarter man than me to find out. Now you better get out there and look after the windmill. It's in need of oiling."

Caracci disappeared, and Rhiannon spent the rest of that day in close attendance upon Richards-Morgan.

Before noon, the fever of the wounded man seemed to diminish and he recovered his senses a little. He sat up in the bed suddenly and looked keenly at Rhiannon. Then bewilderment came into his eyes.

"How'd I get here?" he muttered.

"No matter how," said Rhiannon. "The point is that you're here and that you're safe."

"They'll be after me, and they're sure to come here for me!"

"They've been here and I turned 'em away. You're safe, I tell you!"

"Charlie Dee—" began the other, and then slipped back in the bed and lay still, with a groan.

"Leave off thinking," said Rhiannon. "Charlie Dee is the man that turned them back when they was about to jump me."

"He ain't a man. He's a red devil!" said Richards-Morgan through his teeth.

"I got some soup hot for you, Morgan," said Rhiannon. "Will you take some of that?"

"Morgan?" gasped the other. "Morgan? Good God, do *you* know that?"

"I heard you say it while you was raving."

"Then you know that the Dees would like to—"

"No matter what I know. I know that you're safe here. I know that you gotta try to get your strength back. I know that you'll never do that if you don't eat. Now shut up and lie still while I bring you in some chuck!"

Obediently Morgan lay back on the bed until Rhiannon brought in the bread and soup. He ate what was offered him, seeming to have to choke it down. But when he had finished he rested with his glance on the ceiling and a frown on his forehead. "I played the part of a sneak out here, Rhiannon," he said at last.

"Forget that, will you? Tell me one thing. Are you the brother of Nancy Morgan?"

"I am," said he.

"Then go to sleep. Nothing is gunna happen to you here," declared Rhiannon.

The other raised his head a little—then let it fall back with a sigh of weakness and relief. In another moment he was sound asleep.

So Rhiannon sat close to his bed and studied his face. There was no touch of resemblance to Nancy in his look, to be sure, but, now that it could be studied carefully,

Rhiannon noticed a good forehead, spacious and high, and a clean chiseling of the features. He began to feel that there might be some real justification of the strange actions of Morgan in the house. Even his unwillingness to fight might be explained with no detriment to his character. At least, so Rhiannon hoped with all his soul, and determined to leave judgment in abeyance.

Dusk came at last after that long day. The stars began, but still he waited, for he had determined that he would be patient until the full night had come before he started on the great expedition against the house of Dee.

Morgan had come on famously all through the day. In the midafternoon he had eaten well and then slept again. Now, for some hours, there had been no sound from the bedroom.

It seemed about the proper hour for beginning the expedition, but before he started, Rhiannon wanted a last look at the invalid. He went to the closed door of the room and tapped softly. There was no answer to that tap. So he turned the handle with care and looked in. The window of the room opened toward the west streaked with the last faint light of the day, not strong enough to bury the pale stars. But there was by no means enough light to enable Rhiannon to see more than the vague outline of the bed.

"Morgan!" he whispered. He had no answer. Undoubtedly Morgan was sleeping soundly, but he would make sure before he left the house on a trail from which he might never return. He stole forward. His hand touched the bed and he reached to find the sleeper.

Instantly his hand was on the naked sheet! He scratched a match. There was no Morgan. The heap of torn and tattered clothing which had been lying on a chair in the corner was gone, also, and the battered shoes which had been with them.

Morgan had got up, dressed, and left in silence! But why? And if he wished to flee, before the Dees returned on the following day, would he not have asked for help —even for a horse?

Rhiannon left the house on the run and hurried in to the barn. It was as he suspected. One saddle and the gray horse—his best one—were missing!

Chapter Twenty-Nine

HE DROPPED the match, by the light of which he had made this discovery, and cursed Morgan softly to himself. But as he stood there in the darkness, he thought that he heard the mumbling of voices behind the barn. He passed to the end of the stalls and could be sure—two men in close conversation.

After that, Rhiannon stalked them like a cat.

Through a rear window of the barn he crawled, working his bulky body with the utmost care, and so came to the open air. At the corner of the barn he crouched; for close to the brush he saw the outline of a horseman and another man on foot standing close by, and the first word that he heard, though muffled, came in the unmistakable voice of Caracci. "I saddled the gray horse for him. That's the best one we had."

"Where's Rhiannon?" It was the voice of Sheriff Caradac—the voice of the sheriff, using Rhiannon's real name to a hired Italian laborer! Caradac, here by stealth, talking by stealth of Rhiannon, the outlaw, with a price upon his head!

Of all the strange things that had happened to Rhiannon, nothing had been so strange as this. He knelt where he was. He could not have found the volition to move.

"Where's Rhiannon?"

"Resting on the front porch. He don't even know that Morgan's gone."

"No," said the sheriff, "he's a little slow in the head. There ain't any doubt of that!"

"He is," said Caracci. "He ain't too fast in the brain. I've noticed that!"

Rhiannon set his teeth.

But the sheriff—Caradac! How could it be that such talk should come from him?

So, stung with grief and bewilderment, Rhiannon sharpened his ears.

"What will Rhiannon do tonight?"

"I dunno. Sleep—if he don't find that Morgan's gone."

"He'll find that out."

"Then he'll probably sleep, anyway. He takes time to make up his mind about anything."

"You can't tell," said Caradac. "And mind you, Caracci, watch yourself plumb careful."

"That's what I do," said Caracci. "I'll be best pleased when I'm clear of this job, Caradac."

"Does he still think you're a Dago?"

"He never thought nothing else. I sing some tunes that might be Dago. He never doubts me."

"No," said the sheriff, "he's like a kid. No suspicion in him."

"And still, he's Rhiannon!"

"He is," said Caradac, "and if you doubt it—"

"I don't doubt nothing. I seen him outface the Dees, today. Oh, he's got poison in him, all right!"

"If he knew I was working behind his back," said the sheriff, "it would be a bad day in my life! But you'll keep your mouth shut, son?"

"I got a cause to!" said the false Caracci, softly.

"Could Morgan handle himself when he left, d'you think?"

"Sure he could. He needed a sleep, and that was all. He got that, some chuck, and his wound fixed up. He'll be all right! I asked him!"

"Did you give him a gun?"

"I did, and fifty rounds."

"That's right. I gotta go. You watch everything."

"As close as I can."

"So long. There'll be something to tell you in the morning, my boy!"

"They've got her, have they?"

"I dunno what they've got. Good night, kid." The sheriff pulled the head of his horse around and started across the field, while Rhiannon drew softly back along the side of the barn and reached the front of it. There he paused, almost blind with rage—and sick at heart, as well. For this double-dealing of Caradac's seemed to him a most unhappy thing indeed, and a thing he hardly could believe, even after hearing the words of the sheriff with his own ears.

He saw the form of Caracci darkly appearing, like a faint shadow among shadows, as he went back toward the house.

Then Rhiannon went into the barn and took the second horse. It was an old brown gelding, rather stiff in its joints, but once warmed to its work it could run fast enough.

After saddling it, he put a second saddle on his best mule, a gray veteran of many a day's labor, but able to raise a gallop, as well. The stirrups of the saddle on the gelding he shortened to what he considered a proper length. Then he went back to the house. As he came closer, he heard Caracci in his room, singing softly a song of Italy—or were they of Italy, these songs? Rhiannon gritted his teeth and went on.

He entered as softly as he was able, and took his best rifle. He rigged another holster under his right armpit. And now, with two revolvers and the Winchester, and a heavy belt of ammunition strapped around his hips, he told himself that he was ready for action.

He stole out from the place as softly as he had entered it. Back to the barn—where he took horse and mule and led them to the corral gate, opened it with the utmost caution, lest a single creak could be heard, and so mounted the old mule and leading the gelding, proceeded down the road. He was in no hurry. The complete darkness had hardly more than set in, and all the night was before him —a wild night it was to be, he made sure.

On his way from the corral, he had stopped at the blacksmith shop and added to his equipment a short bar of the finest steel. There was no more useful tool than this for the opening of doors, locked windows, etc. He slipped his hand into the saddlebag now and fumbled the cold metal with much satisfaction.

So he came winding down the road into the valley and through a cloud of trees to the vicinity of the house of Dee. That was his signal to dismount, for a horseman makes a lofty mark, almost sure to strike the eye of any observer even in the dim light. On foot he went on, wading the creek, because he did not wish to make a noise by crossing the bridge, which was sure to sound hollow under foot, no matter at how slow a pace he led the animals on.

133

He was under the steepest face of the creek bank on the opposite side when he heard a crackling of brush. He looked up and raised a Colt in readiness.

Two horsemen moved above him and then disappeared beyond the rim of the bank, but still he was able to make out their voices as they sat their saddles near by.

"I heard something in the creek," said one.

"So did I. It was a fish that jumped."

"A couple of 'em," said the first speaker.

"Sometimes they break water together, a lot of them!"

"Why they got us fanned out like this tonight?"

"I dunno. How should I know? I know we're here, keeping double hours!"

"For double pay!" suggested the other.

"Damn the double pay! I'd rather spend my time in my bunk. I'm fed up with this here wandering around in the night!"

"I'll take the money, boy, and you do the sleepin'."

"We might as well ride up the far end of the bank."

"Maybe. I wonder what the old man expects?"

"Trouble. That's all that I guess. He sent over for five extra men from the ranch of Sid Dee."

"I know. He's got the whole mouth of the cup pretty well blocked, by this time."

"Come on."

Their horses moved away, slowly, and Rhiannon waited until the sounds should die.

"The cup" to which they referred was that deep indentation in the side of Mount Laurel which enclosed the ranch house and the lands immediately around it. To the northeast arose the vast wall of the mountain itself, and northwest and southeast extended the double arms of ridges which opened toward the hills. It was a natural pocket, and it appeared that Dee was guarding all the outer lip of this reserve with his fighting men. Easy enough to slip through such a line of guards, of course, but only when one moved with care. Pursued, and traveling at speed, those armed men would be sure to be attracted. So Rhiannon pondered as he stood by the whisper of the water. He could not return this way, even if he were lucky enough to have reached the Dee house.

No, if Nancy Morgan once were with him, he would have to break straight back toward the face of Mount

134

Laurel itself, and if he were pursued closely, he would have to find refuge by passing through the hole-in-the-wall. But that would leave them floundering in his rear, as it had left them a hundred times in the past.

He should have made up his mind to that line of retreat before. But he had dreaded revealing his mortal secret even to Nancy Morgan. It had meant life to him too many times; he might have need of it how many times in the future!

Now that the sound of the horses had diminished, he turned to the side and quickly found an easier slope up which he led his animals to the level above; and almost at once they were in the shelter of the woods. He went through them slowly, pausing often. It was impossible that he should go forward without some noise, and he had proved that this night was filled with hostile eyes and ears. But so he came, at length, to the edge of the woods, close to the Dee house, and directly opposite the old wing.

Here he tethered the mule with a slipknot, the horse to the pommel of the mule's saddle, and finally took his rifle and turned toward the great adventure.

Chapter Thirty

IT WAS a black night. The stars were hooded over by high clouds; and yet it seemed to Rhiannon that he would have welcomed greater darkness if it could have been found— the dark of the pit, best of all! For from the inhabited wing of the Dee house shafts of lamplight worked through the blackness and stretched out long arms which would reveal him at a single touch.

Two things gave him a greater sense of security—the rising wind, which began to thrash the boughs of the trees and grind them against one another, and the first pattering of rain. Together, those noises should help him forward with his task. They should be a covering to any sounds which he himself happened to make.

Now, then, he went forward rapidly, keeping close to

the verge of the trees, and hastily leaving them when he had to, for the dash toward the old wing.

Under the shadow of its wall, he worked his way to the first window. It was very low. The sill was hardly higher than his knees, and, though he found it locked, as he had anticipated, he was not discouraged. With the strong steel bar he set to work as an expert should, loosening the frame slowly and in half a dozen places, before he applied more power. At length it sagged.

There had not been a sound, he was sure. He lifted out the lower section of the window, therefore, without much further trouble, placed it inside against the wall, and stepped into the house.

It was of course pitch dark, but the little bull's-eye without which he never traveled did away with darkness. He used it as an artist uses a pencil, making quick strokes and slashes here and there, so that in a moment he had sketched for himself the position and size of everything in the chamber.

Then he picked up the window and fitted it back in place with care. No one, passing, must notice that one of the panes, glistening like polished black basalt, was missing. He even put the back of a rickety chair against the frame. Then he went on in his venture.

The door to that room was unlocked, by a lucky chance, but even so it was not an easy task to open it, for the hinges were lodged with the rust of years and they moaned faintly at the slightest pressure.

Patience, then, and a certain trick which he had learned many years ago—never let the pressure relax, but send it forward as slowly as the minute hand of a watch. So he did, falling upon one knee and gently and firmly applying the pressure. With infinite slowness the door was drawn ajar, but when that happened, a strong draft entered, whistling.

Rhiannon gritted his teeth but composed himself to shut the door behind him as carefully as he had opened it. That business accomplished, he touched the darkness in which he stood with a few more rays of light, snapping them on and off with the well-oiled shutter of his lantern.

He was in a narrow hall—narrow but with a high ceiling from which the plaster sagged down in one place; at the farther end of the hall appeared a balustrade and the first of a flight of stairs. To this he made his way, and then started his climb. First of all, he tried the stairs with the weight of his hand and made sure, what he had dreaded, that the wooden structure was so extremely old and loose that it would screech at the first weight. The proper way to mount stairs in silence is to take the side closest to the wall, for there the boards or the stone slabs are most strongly secured and the weight of the man acts with the least leverage, but even this precaution was of little use. He had to fall back upon a bolder but more dangerous expedient.

Already there were noises in this house—the tapping of the rain and the moan and whistle of the wind, together wih those faint groans and murmurs which always live in an old house. For those noises he thanked his stars, and advanced.

He went rapidly up half a dozen steps, paused, took three more swift strides, paused, took another; and so, with irregular rhythm, climbed to the top.

No ear except the most clever would connect the squeaking of the stairs beneath him with the weight of a human foot, for we listen to stealthy sounds, regular, softly progressing. These were bold, loud noises, such, for instance, as a shutter of rusty hinges would make, when swayed to and fro by the wind.

He passed a landing, gained the head of the stairs. There he dropped on one knee to take his breath once more. For, strangely enough, there is no sound more piercing—for its small volume—than the loud breathing of a man. He waited several long minutes, until all was normal with him. Then he began to explore the darkness again with the lantern rays, making out that it was an upper hallway and the top of the house, unless there was an attic still higher.

A dozen doors opened to one side or the other, and he hesitated as to which of these he should choose. To shorten the search, he ventured to use more light, and so, examining the hall floor, he presently found a number of footprints in the dust and a door at which they turned aside. Here he paused and looked through the keyhole, but found solid, tarry blackness. He passed a knife blade through. The keyhole was not closed, but the room was simply in utter darkness.

However, on account of those footprints, he determined to enter this chamber at any cost. The lock was fast. He had to use the steel lever again, and with this he rapidly forced it, taking advantage of a loud squall of wind to cover the noise which he was making. The door gave with a sudden sagging. He found himself in a square chamber with a table in the center and two broken-down chairs. But most of all, there was a token that he had come to the thing for which he had searched so faithfully; a bright penciling of light was streaked across the bottom of the door which stood at the left!

No stalking cat could have moved more softly than Rhiannon now! Crossing to the door, he no sooner came opposite it than he saw that, in one respect at least, it was ideal for his purpose. For its face was widely cracked, and a strong ray of light broke through. At the same time, he heard a man's voice—and a woman's made answer. A man's voice—that of Charlie Dee; a woman's voice—

But he would not trust to his memory. He slipped closer to the door, and through the largest crack he looked into a tiny room, in the center of which was a table where sat Charlie Dee, in fact, and with him, Nancy Morgan!

A sort of great hunger arose in the soul of Rhiannon, and food never could feed it! He had waited, he had hunted, and the quarry was now under his hand.

He tried the knob of the door. To his delight and his surprise, it gave readily under his hand. Slowly, slowly he turned it.

They were playing cards—cribbage.

"Fifteen-four, and three two's are eight."

"You're not home to deal."

"I only lack three points."

"Three are as good as a thousand, Nancy. I'm going to beat you this time."

"You always do," said Nancy.

The cards flicked together. Then sudden silence. And, in his mind's eye, Rhiannon saw Charlie Dee turning with a swift and furtive movement in his chair to eye the door—saw that glance fastening on the turning knob—and then the ready hand make a revolver glide forth—

Sweating, grim of face, Rhiannon kept up the steady movement.

"Ten," said a voice within.

"Fifteen-two."

"Twenty for a couple."

"Twenty-five and I take six for that. Is it a go?"

"Not a bit. Thirty—and twelve—and I'm going out, Charlie Dee!"

Rhiannon, relieved, continued the movement, until at last there was the faintest of clicks—he had turned back the bolt of the lock! And now the door was free beneath his hand. A tenth of an inch he swayed it in. In an instant, he could sweep that door open and cover Charlie Dee!

Then, looking suddenly behind him, he was sure that a soft shadow was stirring at his back. No, that was imagination.

"I thought I heard something!" exclaimed Dee.

"So did I. The wind, of course."

"I'm not so sure."

"Charlie, you *want* to hear things."

It seemed odd to Rhiannon that she should be so friendly with Charlie Dee. But, after all, there was no reason to carry hostility past a certain point. Wrangling words bring only bitterness to the hearer and the speaker.

"Nancy," said Charlie Dee, "night and day I expect someone to try to break into this place and get you!"

"Are you going to keep on the stage till the last gasp?" asked Nancy wih a sigh.

Why did she say that?

But Rhiannon had no time to guess or to argue. He cast the door open with his left hand. With his right, he leveled a revolver at the back of the head of Charlie Dee.

Opposite him, Nancy slipped down in her chair and threw her hands before her face.

"Quiet!" commanded Rhiannon brusquely.

Charlie Dee had dropped a little forward—there was a gun in his hand as it lay on the table; but he made no real effort to turn about.

"It's John Gwynn, by heaven!" said he. "John Gwynn!" He seemed stunned by the sound of Rhiannon's voice. The latter thrust the door to, behind him.

It was the last time he would be known in the world as John Gwynn. By this night's work he threw that name behind him, and all his hope of a peaceful life thereafter. Henceforth, he was Rhiannon!

Chapter Thirty-One

"PUT YOUR guns before you, Charlie," he advised. "Slip them onto the table. The knife too, if you don't mind. I want to see 'em all."

One by one, Charlie Dee put forth two heavy Colts. And then a long, rather thin-bladed hunting knife. "That's all," said he.

"Not quite," hazarded Rhiannon.

There was a faint mutter in response, and then Charlie Dee took a small two-barreled derringer from inside his shirt and laid that beside the other weapons. "How did you know about that?" he asked calmly.

"I didn't; I guessed," said Rhiannon.

Nancy Morgan jerked down her hands from her face and stood up. "You've come for me!" she said faintly. "You've come for me, John Gwynn."

"He's come for you," said Charlie Dee bitterly. "And he's made a fool of me—an absolute fool! John Gwynn—the farmer!"

"My name is Rhiannon," he answered.

Dee turned slowly, at this, and confronted the big man. "Rhiannon!" he echoed.

"You've been square with me, Charlie," admitted Rhiannon, "and I'm sorry that I gotta do this. You helped me out of a tight hole the other day. I'm sorry that I gotta pay you back like this. Bad luck, I call it."

"Rhiannon!" murmured Charlie Dee. "But Rhiannon's a man of forty or so and—"

Rhiannon smiled. "It was the beard," he answered.

Nancy Morgan said not another word. She had pressed herself back into a corner of the wall and merely stared, as though this was an event to be seen but never to be comprehended.

"There's some rope in the corner," said Dee in the most matter-of-fact tone. "You'll need that, I suppose."

"Sorry," said Rhiannon. "I suppose that I gotta use it. Will you bring it here, Nancy Morgan?"

She picked it up and came to him like a sleepwalker, with a face of stone and staring eyes.

It was strong quarter-inch rope. With it he rapidly secured the wrists and the feet of Dee. Then he hesitated. "I hate to use a gag," said he.

"Matter of fact," answered Charlie Dee, "I wouldn't mind giving you my word that I won't call out—"

Then Nancy Morgan cried in a voice that trembled with passion: "Would you trust him? Would you trust Charlie Dee, of all the men in this world?"

Rhiannon shrugged his shoulders. "He's been hard on you. I know that. But I got an idea that he wouldn't lie to me about this."

"Thanks," said Charlie Dee. "That's a lot to say!"

"I'd like to ask you one more thing," said Rhiannon. "You look like a man to me, Dee. You never gave me the idea of a low rat that would badger a girl. You don't have to answer, but I'd like to know what made you handle Nancy Morgan this way!"

"Two reasons," said the other instantly. "She's a Morgan. That goes a long way with us. Second thing is, there's a lot of money up. About a quarter of a million, I take it."

"I don't see how that comes in."

There was a faint glimmer in the eyes of young Dee. "Someday you may!" he answered quietly.

Now all this time the wind had been rising in violence and in noise, and at this point a sudden draft worked through the cracks and made the lamp flame flutter.

"Someone's coming—there's a door open somewhere in the house—or a window!" said Nancy Morgan.

Rhiannon hung at the door only an instant. "I've got your word, Charlie?"

"You've got it," replied Charlie Dee, and he looked straight at Rhiannon with the blank eyes of a man deep in thought.

Then Rhiannon drew the door open. Nancy looked up into his face—a fleeting glance of fear and doubt and hope, he thought. Then she went past him quickly.

He closed the door as he stepped through and with a ray from his lantern he found the way across the room for himself and the girl. He carried the lantern in his left hand—the ready revolver in his right, and as they came toward the door, he almost used the gun.

For a flare of light appeared in the hall, instantly extinguished. And next he heard a man's voice speaking—the voice of Oliver Dee. Another answered, and another. Three men were coming down the hall.

Rhiannon flashed a beam across the room. The window was heavily shuttered. There never would be time to dash those shutters open and escape through—even if it were possible to climb down the sheer wall of the house from that point.

Nancy Morgan did his thinking for him. She caught his arm and dragged him into the corner just inside the doorway. She only whispered in his ear: "Wait—don't shoot! For God's sake, don't shoot!"

And then the flare of light turned into the doorway and filled the room! It seemed to Rhiannon, tense with his revolver, that behind that light eyes looked straight at him, but then the light went out and three shadows stalked across the room.

"We'll see how things are goin' with Charlie," said the voice of Oliver Dee. "Take a night like this, and anything is likely to happen!"

They gathered at the farther door through which the light glimmered down the jagged cracks. Nancy Morgan set the right example again, stealing softly away as soon as the three were well over the threshold of the room. Rhiannon followed her into the hallway—followed her to the stairs—followed her down to the first floor. And he had time to wonder at her greatly. This was the frightened and semi-hysterical girl he had met on the hill that other night! This was the shrinking creature! And now she was as stealthy and as strong-nerved as a hunting panther!

He bit his lip in wonder and in his first doubt of her. But there was nothing that escaped from doubt in these mad days. The sheriff above all—then Richards-Morgan—Caracci—all the Dees—and finally Nancy Morgan herself! He had no chance to develop these ideas, for as they reached the lower level at the foot of the stairs there was a heavy crash above them, and then a loud shouting, as of many men in a hot dispute.

"This way!" called Rhiannon, and, opening the hood of

142

the lantern, he led the way through the room by which he had entered the house. He jerked in the window, hurled it aside with a crash, and then lifted Nancy Morgan in his arms and passed her through into the wind and the rain.

He was instantly beside her. Inside the house, footfalls were thundering on the stairs; a gun was fired rapidly—no doubt to give a signal.

"Run!" said Rhiannon, and struck through the wet night for the trees. He ran with half his strength; instantly a lithe form was up with him.

"Faster!" she called. She was like a deer, so swift and light; and they dashed on together through the screen of brush to where the mule and the horse waited; and the old gelding whinnied a soft greeting to Rhiannon!

He pitched the girl into the saddle on the horse as if she had been a sack of barley. He himself sprang onto the mule—a mule against the fleet blood-horses of the Dees! They were hardly in the saddle when two riders went past, flashing dimly in the rain, the water cupping up from the hoofs of their horses and splashing far.

Then Rhiannon rode out and headed straight up into the hollow. The girl reined frantically at his side. She rode well, indeed, and, while her horse galloped, she tipped from the saddle and shouted, "You're riding straight into the trap!"

He answered, "The hole-in-the-wall!"

She answered something; he could not tell what, but the wave of her hand seemed to indicate that this solution was all she wanted. And on they went, the mule at its full gallop, the girl pulling the horse back to keep the slower pace.

They had to go past the face of the house at a comparatively short distance, and as they did so a shutter was opened—before a window, perhaps, and a shaft of light like a long arm reached at them. Nancy Morgan, a length ahead, rode full into it, and Rhiannon saw the wet gleam of her yellow hair, and that her clothes were already black with the downpour. He himself had no time to swing the mule aside from the same telltale illumination.

A voice shouted; a gun cracked and a bullet hissed above their heads. They had been spotted and now it was a chase indeed!

143

Rhiannon sent the spurs home. Every second unpursued meant priceless rods gained; but looking back across his shoulder he saw shadows plunge out from the gate of the patio at high speed and then swerve to the right, and come streaming after him—horsemen riding for their lives!

He remembered then what the sheriff had said—that Oliver Dee needed merely to whistle, and he could fill the hills with armed men!

Certainly on this night he had planted a legion around his house. How, then, had Oliver Dee known that the attempt was certain to be made at this moment? Had he really feared simply that Morgan, the wounded man, might come back and make another attempt?

There was a shrill cry from Nancy. She pointed with a stiff arm to the right, and he saw a horseman break from the trees and bear wildly down upon them.

"God help him!" said Rhiannon. He fired. The horse leaped high and fell, and the rider rolled headlong. And now the clifflike side of Mount Laurel rose close before them.

Chapter Thirty-Two

JUST AT THE base of Mount Laurel was a small apron of fallen rocks of all sizes. Some of them were boulders as huge as a house, and sometimes time had weathered away the stone, so that soil had formed, and there was a cloud of brush and small trees standing out a bit into the level of the valley. Straight at that fringe of trees Rhiannon bent his course. Then, on the verge of the greenery, he checked the mule and leaped to the ground. Fast as he was, Nancy was instantly at his side. The girl seemed all springs and fiery resolution.

Glancing to the rear, he saw the dim shapes of the riders from the House of Dee swiftly coming up, but still well beyond accurate eyeshot. He turned the mule and the horse north; cut them with his quirt, and saw them dash off, snorting.

Instantly the shadow shapes to the rear swerved to the left to follow the apparent course of the fugitives, and Rhiannon strode into the brush. The girl was behind him, one hand clutching at the tail of his coat to make sure of him in this utter blackness of whipping branches.

They came out on a swift, smooth slide of water that ran past the edge of gigantic rubble, for here the boulders were at their hugest.

It was hard for Nancy to stand. The wind, deflecting from the polished face of the cliff, shouted with a human fury, and tore at her with hands.

Rhiannon picked her up in his arms and stepped into the current. It was so strong that he had to lean well back against it. Every step had to be made slowly, fumbling forward, a foothold at a time. He went down the stream a matter of forty or fifty yards and walked straight at the face of a vast black boulder. He dipped under its edge. Half the clothes of Nancy Morgan were soaked as he stooped, though he raised her so high in his arms that she had to turn her face from the upper surface of the stone. Straight on went Rhiannon for half a dozen steps, then climbed from the water into still, warm air. He dropped Nancy to her feet, and sand gritted beneath them.

They had entered the hole-in-the-wall! "That finishes off that little job," said Rhiannon with a sigh. "It was a mite closer rub than I expected—but it's over!"

He flashed on his lantern and stood before her, dripping from his shoulders down, but with a stern smile of triumph.

And he found Nancy Morgan not a trembling, frightened, collapsing child, but a triumphant woman with joy in her eyes and her cheeks flushed. She actually laughed at Rhiannon. "And they thought that they could match you!" she said.

"Did they speak of me?" asked Rhiannon sharply.

She seemed to wince a little. "If you *should* have come," said Nancy Morgan: "They feared nothing. Charlie Dee said nothing in the world could break through to me tonight. He said that every inch of the valley was watched. Not even Rhiannon could manage, said Charlie! But you have! And here we are—and this, this is the hole-in-the-wall!" There was a ring of the wildest exultation in her voice. She took his hand which held the lantern and made him turn it from side to side and reveal the long, sloping shoulders of the cave and the ragged roof above them. And finally she pointed the light down the narrow passage which opened just before them, not more than three feet wide, and cleaving, apparently, through the dark heart of the mountain.

He looked down at her with wonder—with doubt, as well. That first mention of his name, and the way she had flinched ever so little when he asked the hasty question— he did not like it! But he thrust the doubt from his mind. He felt as though he were losing his mind; was not the first sign of madness a feeling that all the world is wrong?

"And that's the way out?" she asked.

"That way," he answered. "Shall I make a fire first to dry your clothes by?"

He pointed the light at a heap of dry wood, long ago laid in here by his foresight for just such emergencies.

But she answered: "No, no! Let's go on—let's go on! We're just at the edge of the mystery! Let's go into the heart of it!"

"What mystery?" he asked her sharply.

She lifted up her face to him and laughed, for she seemed ever bubbling with laughter, now—mirth which she could not repress! And her blue eyes were as gleaming and as cold as steel in the midst of this rejoicing!

He had not known her—that was plain. She was no more what he had thought than a house cat is like a mountain lion!

Beautiful, yes. Too beautiful, almost, with those changing, brilliant, thoughtful eyes. He never had seen eyes before like those, unless he called to mind the eyes of Charlie Dee, when that young gentleman was excited.

"Walk ahead," said he, "and I'll shine the light over your shoulder."

"Walk ahead?" She hesitated.

"Why not?" asked Rhiannon, surprised.

"You go first," she answered anxiously. "You go first —I—don't want to walk first into that—that darkness, you know!"

Rhiannon knew in his heart of hearts that she was lying

most grossly, and disgust and a sort of despair rose up in him for nothing that he touched—nothing human that he touched—remained sound and honest. All crumbled and became false under his hand.

She, Richards-Morgan, Caracci, even Owen Caradac whose life he had held in his palm, whose life he had given freely back. Even Owen Caradac had proved a traitor in the end!

So, half blind with a sort of weary sorrow, Rhiannon turned from the girl and took the lantern ahead of her. "Keep close behind me," was all he said to her.

"Yes, yes," she answered. There was a touch of impatience in her voice. And he remembered then she had not spoken a word of gratitude to him; she was vastly excited and pleased, of course, but her attention seemed bent forward to what was to come.

For that matter, perhaps she had reason!

He had not spoken to her about the man who claimed to be her brother. He would wait until later for that. Wait until some of the soreness had left his mind.

So he walked on until the passage narrowed a bit more and became lower. "Here's a funny thing," said Rhiannon to the girl, without turning his head. "You look along the walls, here, and you'll find that there's been pick strokes and blasting. Once a long time ago this was a drift in a mine, maybe—or a shaft that was sunk through the rock. Think of the work that they done on it! And all to give me a hole-in-the-wall!"

She did not answer. He paused. There was no sound behind him and, turning in surprise, Rhiannon saw a bright spot of light shining against the side of the wall twenty or thirty yards behind him, and above it leaned the girl.

Odd indeed that she should have an electric torch, and one of such power! Most amazing of all that she had found something in that tunnel which interested her so much. How had she found it in the thick darkness behind his broad shoulders?

"Nancy!" he called, and the narrow tunnel took up his voice and magnified it like a megaphone. "Nancy, what's the matter?"

She straightened, and her laughter came down to him clear as a bell, and hard, indeed, as metal chiming.

"There's nothing the matter!" said Nancy, "but you gave me the ticket out, and now I'm going to see the show!"

He started back toward her, and then she threw up her hand. "Go back, go back, Rhiannon!" she called.

He halted. "What's up, Nancy?"

"I tell you," she cried in greater excitement, "go back at once, or you're dead, Rhiannon. Go back—you great fool!" she added in a burst of impatient anger.

He winced back a little. "Nancy, have you lost your head?"

"You idiot!" cried the girl, "you'll be losing yours! Back down that tunnel—or else—God help you!"

The brain of Rhiannon spun. "I'll come to you and find out what's up!"

"You'll never see me again!" rang the hard voice of Nancy Morgan. Then, as he persisted in going forward: "Take it, and God help you—you fool! You fool!"

She jerked violently at something which he could not make out. It seemed like a ring fixed against the wall. And as she did so a mass of solid rock dropped with thunder straight down past the face of Rhiannon. He barely had time to wince back from its fall; it would have torn him in two as a meat knife cleaves a block of meat!

A violent shudder came in the top of the tunnel above him. A shower of small stones and dust rained down, and Rhiannon turned and fled for his life as another whole ragged mass of stone was loosed and beat down into the tunnel at his heels. Half sick, bewildered, he leaned against the side of the rock and played his light over the ruin which filled his tunnel. The hole-in-the-wall was gone. And the secret salvation which had been his for so long was ended. He hardly cared.

But what weighed like lead upon his very soul was the knowledge that blue-eyed Nancy Morgan, beautiful Nancy, delicate Nancy had deliberately tried to take his life and leave him buried under countless tons of rock. And she? What had she to gain by that?

Chapter Thirty-Three

OWEN CARADAC had an office in the Laurel jail, but he rarely used that room. He preferred to work from his own little shack at the corner of H and Fourth Streets. There was a vacant lot on each side of him and at his rear. Across the street stood a carpenter shop, equally framed in vacancies. For Laurel was a boom town of the old days. It had been laid out in the most magnificent manner, with public parks sketched out, and sites for post office, city hall, and other buildings of importance that never came into being. Those who had bought lots had run up frame buildings on their holdings, and sometimes found themselves a quarter of a mile from the nearest neighbor. In fact, Laurel looked like a burned town which has been partially rebuilt, and which will never be restored fully. It seemed to stand upon ruins, which were the ruins, one might say, of its own hopes.

But the sheriff liked the situation of his place. It commanded a clear sweep of the adjoining ground, and during the day that was a great advantage, for people were apt to have a keen respect for his eyesight and his guns. During the night, he had a brood of savage bull terriers more dreaded by dangerous men than guns ever could be! There were only two rooms in this little shack—where he had been born and bred. One of them was the kitchen-living room-dining room-bedroom, which stood at the rear. The other chamber served the sheriff as an office. For this office, having collected his mail for the day, the sheriff started from the post office.

He walked with a loosely swinging stride, his head high in the air, whistling as he went. And he pretended not to notice that people who saluted him did so with stiff, jerky nods as they went past him. He pretended not to notice—as he did repeatedly from the corner of his eye—that they turned after they had passed him, and then

149

scrutinized him with care, as though they never before had seen him.

The sheriff made his whistle louder and tilted his sombrero a little more to the rear of his head. But darkness gathered in his eyes.

He was opposite the front door of the bank when a fat little man ran out at him. He had a bald head that bobbed upon a lean, weak neck. His fat, soft stomach bobbed up and down, also, with every stride. He shook a pulpy forefinger at the sheriff as he approached. "What have you been doing, Owen Caradac?" he called. "What have you been doing to yourself?"

"I dunno," said Caradac, and paused, towering.

"I'll tell you, then!" said the banker. "You've kicked yourself right out of your job, if that's what you want to know."

"I didn't ask to know it," answered Owen Caradac. "How come you by the information, might I ask? And who's gunna do the kicking?"

"The whole population of the county!" declared the president of the bank. "They're gunna ask you to step down and out, and if you refuse—"

"There ain't any danger of that," said Caradac. "I can find other jobs in other places. This ain't the biggest town in the world, and it ain't the best town!"

"Is that the way you talk?" cried the other. "Owen, Owen, isn't there any shame in you—the town that raised you? And what am I going to do when you leave? How can I be sure that the bank will be safe! I'll have to buy new vaults and hire two night watchmen—and all because you've been and made such a roaring fool of yourself!"

"Have I?" asked Caradac.

"Have you?" shouted the banker. "You been associating with Annan Rhiannon, ain't you?"

"I have," said the sheriff.

"You've put him on a farm. You've treated him like a brother."

"Did he do the farm harm or good?" asked the sheriff.

"That ain't the question! The question is, for what did the people of this county pay you a salary and—"

"All right," said Caradac. "Let it drop, will you?"

He walked on past; the little man followed and pulled at his arm. "But I want to help you, Owen! I don't want to

150

lose you. It'll cost me thousands of dollars, if we get another sheriff in this county. It's you that have kept the crooks out!"

"Except Rhiannon," said the sheriff.

"Oh, damn Rhiannon!" exclaimed the man of money. "What harm did he ever do? Scratched the surface once in a while! Just scratched the surface. Good for our systems. He stirred us up when we got too settled! But on account of him—what made you do it? Will you tell me that?"

"You know all about it, do you?" asked the dry sheriff.

"It's spread all over from the Dee place," said the little banker, "that John Gwynn was nobody but Annan Rhiannon!"

"All right," said the sheriff. "Did it strike you, then, that Annan Rhiannon was nobody but John Gwynn?"

He walked on up the street, and still he pretended to notice nothing odd in the greetings with which he was met as he advanced. So he came to his shack and he stood a moment in front of the garden gate to admire the place.

The garden had no part other than the gate. Within was smooth-beaten ground out of which the bedraggled remnants of a few rose bushes thrust themselves. They never bore anything other than thorns, in these days, but the sheriff kept them on out of sentimental attachment to the memory of his mother. For, in her day, this front yard had been made to blossom wonderfully and give up armfuls of flowers of all sorts. And never had the housework been so heavy as to keep her from moiling and toiling in the garden soil—while he and his brothers played in the dust of the street. The sheriff thought of this as he looked at the smooth, hard face of the ground today.

He was a hard man, was the sheriff, but something stirred vaguely in him and rose in his throat like words, unspoken forever though they must be.

To the left had stood the remainder of the house—the three rooms which burned down when he was a youth. The shock of that burning had killed his mother. He always felt it was not the loss of the rooms and the furniture in them so much as the destruction of her beloved climbing roses which, twice a year, covered the

151

whole house with a network of white and crimson fragrance. Some stubs of those vines remained, and that was all.

So, to the passer-by, this house, sun-and-wind-worn, unpainted always, surrounded by bare ground, was typical of the sheriff himself. But to the sheriff it wore a different aspect and always appeared to him partly as itself—just large enough for a bachelor to take care of with ease, and therefore perfect—and in part as a mere section of a whole. Ghosts stood before it—ghosts of people and of flowers and of voices.

Once—it was only last winter—he had come out and sniffed the bitter January morning. "This here frost will do the roses no good!" the sheriff had said. Then he had looked about him and smiled a little. Of course the roses were gone and in their place were half a dozen bull terriers who now frolicked in the sun, sleek and shining as so many white seals.

When he stamped inside the gate, they came bounding toward him, barking in sharp, high-pitched yelps; but when they were close they flattened their ears and wriggled forward as if through water to lick those heavy, terrible hands.

The sheriff cuffed them aside and went forward to the porch. There he turned and surveyed his six white guardians. No dogs even ventured into his yard. Or if they did, a white bolt struck them down. No men ventured, either, until he, Caradac, had whistled to the pack and called them off.

Let come what might, the sheriff was content with life —and yet not content.

He turned hastily away from his own rising thoughts and went into his office. There he cut open his letters and read. There were at least a dozen, all of them from ranchers of the community, all of them asking one question: Was it true that the sheriff had actually sheltered on his farm for months the desperado and man-slayer, Annan Rhiannon?

The sheriff crumpled these letters one by one and dropped them into his waste basket. Then he picked them up, smoothed them, and reread them with apparently loving care.

He looked about him with rather a vague eye. This

office was his idea of a perfect place. He had a swivel chair at his desk. The desk itself was of bird's-eye maple, varnished to a wonderful brightness. It was like a thing of gold, to the sheriff. Then he had a bright rug on the floor. He had paid fifty dollars for it, and he rarely entered the room without leaning to feel its texture and to admire the straightness with which the long seams ran down its face. In one corner was a tall, narrow cabinet, also of varnished wood, in which he kept the overflow of papers from his desk. In the two other corners were stiff-backed chairs for visitors. Never make a man too comfortable. Keep him wriggling if you want to get the truth out of him.

Now, having surveyed all of these possessions, the sheriff tilted back in his chair and placed his feet on the top of the desk. His trailing spurs raked long furrows, turning the varnish to a white powder. He lay back in his chair and smoked one cigarette after another and dropped the butts on the floor. One of them found the rug, burned a fuming hole in it, and at last went out.

Still the sheriff smoked until a voice called: "Hey, Caradac! Sheriff Caradac!"

Then he sat up straight, and through the window he saw that a cheerful young man was waiting outside his gate. It was the governor's secretary and right-hand man, and Caradac knew why he was here.

"Hey, Caradac, call off your white lions, will you?"

Caradac whistled. The sleek white brigade gave way and then followed at the heels of the stranger, sniffing the calves of his legs, their lips curling hungrily.

Chapter Thirty-Four

"HELLO," said Sam Nearing from the door. "You still got that old bitch, I see."

"Yeh. I still got her. C'm in and sit down."

"Shade more foreface and she would take some beating!" said the governor's secretary.

He knew bull terriers; therefore he knew the sheriff

well. "And you've got the young dog, too. I thought you'd sell him. He's not up to the rest."

"He suits me," said the sheriff.

"Of course he does," replied Sam Nearing. "You want dogs, not pictures."

The sheriff waited. He knew that all of this was merely the premise to serious conversation. He knew what that conversation would be.

Finally he said, "You made a special trip down here to see me?"

"I did," said Nearing. "The governor wanted me to look things over in this section of the state and tell him about—"

"Rhiannon?" asked the sheriff.

He held forth the makings. "Roll one?"

"Don't mind if I do," said Nearing.

He made his smoke with deft, active fingers.

Then he lighted it and said suddenly through the smoke, "Yes, I came about Rhiannon."

"What about it?"

"If it's true, he wants you to get out."

The sheriff smiled a little. He knew that this frankness was a tribute to him from a busy man. "It's true," said Caradac.

Then Nearing went on: "Of course it's true. The strange things always are true. But the governor wants the full truth. Not just the scraps that the chickens pick up."

The sheriff considered and then shook his head.

At this Nearing went on, "You're one of the best guns in the governor's holsters."

"What in hell am I to him?" asked Caradac bluntly.

"You keep about half the state straight," said Nearing. "Killings make discontent. They don't have killings when Sheriff Caradac is around."

"Thanks," said the sheriff.

"That's why he wants you to talk. You don't have to make a speech, either!"

Caradac tapped the scarred surface of his desk. He looked out of the window, but the secretary looked at the desk. He saw the freshness of those scars. The white powder still lay beside the furrows. "I don't have to make a speech," said the sheriff. "No, of course I don't. I won't, either."

154

"You can't explain, Caradac?"

"No. Everybody knows the truth. I took in a crook. And I'm the sheriff. Those are the facts."

"Part of the facts."

"I'd have to undress to show you scars, if you wanted the rest of the facts," said Caradac.

Mr. Nearing looked keenly at him; then he looked at the ceiling. "The time you disappeared?"

Caradac nodded.

"That was Rhiannon?"

The sheriff nodded again, and Nearing waited politely.

"I don't publish this," said the sheriff.

"Of course you don't, man! I'm a mummy. So is the governor. All he wants is a fair excuse for himself. He'll back you up, and he's strong enough not to have to give reasons."

"He'd have to pardon Rhiannon to back me up," remarked the sheriff.

At this, Nearing made a wry face. "How many men has Rhiannon killed?" he asked.

"From behind—from the side—sneaking by night, or ever taking an advantage—not one!"

"He's killed a good many, though," murmured Nearing.

"George Washington killed a lot more."

"That's that," grinned Nearing. "I see how you feel about it. Can you tell me anything more?"

"I dunno that I can." He reflected. "This ain't for a newspaper."

"Not a word."

"Well, I met Rhiannon and he licked me. He beat me. I had the drop on him, too. Nacherally," added the sheriff, "I kissed the hand that beat me. That's all there is to it!"

Mr. Nearing, with truly wonderful tact, said not a word. He remained respectfully attentive; he did not even watch the drawn face of the sheriff too closely.

Suddenly the sheriff said softly: "I could of saved him. I let him chuck himself away again. I was too smart. I held back what I knew. That's what I done! I run him back to the wild again!"

Mr. Nearing was as still as a mouse, for he saw that this man was talking to himself.

155

Then the sheriff added: "I'm an old-fashioned man, Nearing. Him—he was my partner!"

Nearing leaned forward a little in spite of himself. "Did you break with him, Caradac?" he asked gently.

The sheriff did not hear.

"You're not seeing him any more?" asked Nearing.

At this, the man of the law turned slowly toward him and laughed a little. His throat worked. The great veins stood upon his forehead. "I'll see him when he comes for my scalp," said Caradac. "It won't be long," he added.

They smoked through a long silence, during which Nearing discreetly studied the floor, but at length he managed to say, "The governor realizes that this affair may mean to you your social position in your community, and your office, as well as the—"

It was the beginning of a prepared speech for the occasion, and the voice of the sheriff was like a projectile tearing the speech asunder. "What in hell do I care for community, and office, and position? To hell with them all! It's him that I had—and it's him that I lost!"

Said Mr. Nearing, "It's plain that he's a man, and a real man, Caradac."

"You never seen his like before," declared the sheriff. "Nor no man will ever see his like again!"

"He made a regular flower garden of your farm, I hear," suggested Nearing in the same gentle voice.

"Him?" said the sheriff.

There seemed little connection when he went on, "My mother made gardens."

But politicians are lovers of human nature, and they love humanity because they understand. So young Mr. Nearing caught a dim hint of the meaning of the sheriff. It was as though a beautiful ghost had swept past his face. Tears came for an instant into the eyes of the governor's secretary, for he was a Westerner, and west of the Rockies hearts are as soft as hands are hard.

Nearing stood up. "We'll have to think out some way," he said, and turned toward the window.

"Good God!" said he. "Caradac, call them off!"

A girl had just passed inside the front gate and a volley of six white projectiles leaped at her. They sprang as high as her shoulders. They cascaded like water from a fountain around her.

156

But there was no more danger in those six professional devil-dogs than in six white angels. They licked the hands of the girl. They tried to lick her face. She went forward through them half laughing, defending herself—as if she were leaning into a white hurricane.

So she gained the steps.

Even Caradac was moved to rise from his chair. "The sneaking, worthless brutes has turned into lap dogs," said Caradac, but his grin belied him. "Kind of a cool one, ain't she, Nearing?"

"A lovely girl, by God," said Mr. Nearing, his color quite changed. "Who is she?"

"Her? That's the young Dee girl."

"Come to you for what?"

"About Rhiannon, I guess. Everybody comes about Rhiannon."

Nearing smiled. He took out his handkerchief and brushed some dust from a sleeve; he pulled down his coat in front and kicked his feet lightly to knock the wrinkles out of his trousers.

The sheriff observed with a smile that appeared in his eyes alone. "You better go into the back room," he said. "She didn't come to a dance. She come to the sheriff of the county."

"I just want to meet her, Caradac," whispered Nearing.

"You jus' get out of here before you're throwed out. You may find some coffee stewing on the back of the stove. Help yourself."

"Lovely girl!" sighed Nearing, and went slowly into the kitchen.

A light quick tap came at the door.

"Come in!" roared the sheriff.

The door opened. He was revealed in his newly discovered position, feet on the desk, hat on the back of his head. "Hello, Miss Dee. C'm in and sit down. Whatcha want of me this kind of hot weather?"

She took the chair Nearing had been in and drew it up close to Owen Caradac. When she sat down, she could lay one hand on the edge of the desk. And there she laid it—a slender olive-brown hand like the hand of a Mexican girl, except that the nails were pink and white. And her eyes were as dark as the eyes of a Mexican, but there was no hint of smoke in them.

"You've come about Rhiannon," said the sheriff harshly.

"I have," said she.

"Well," said he, "what do you want?"

"Him," said Isabella Dee.

Chapter Thirty-Five

To THIS frank statement the sheriff replied by interlacing his big fingers and wedging them under his chin, so that his head was supported as on a tripod, and his grin, half savage and half amused, was turned full upon her. He looked like a primitive creature, this Caradac; a creature of an earlier type before the long millenniums had refined humanity with more delicate features, more supple limbs. He was simply rough-cut flesh and bone. His hands looked like clay studies, blunt and enormous. His brows were heavy and irregular masses of bone, deeply hollowed beneath for the eyes. They gave him a look half thoughtful and half wild—those deep-set eyes.

And Isabella Dee was another type, the product of a later age, made with precise delicacy.

"You—Rhiannon!" said the sheriff.

She nodded with perfect cheerfulness.

"Him—that lump!" said the sheriff.

"Exactly," said Isabella.

"Him—he's the same kind of a dish as me," said Caradac.

"But the devil salted him," said Isabella.

"Of course," answered the sheriff, "you may see it that way. But what about the way that he settled down and become a regular farmer?"

"He didn't settle down. He burned up," replied the girl.

"He worked as regular as a ticking clock."

"And he worked day and night—like a clock, not like a man."

"Now how d'you know that?"

"Everybody talked about it. And from an attic window I could see the farm. There'd be a light there at two in the morning, often! I've come back from a dance at three, and heard his anvil clanging."

"Ever see him swinging a hammer?"

"Charlie did. I didn't have to."

"You didn't?"

"No, he looked that way."

"You sound kind of partial about him."

"I am partial about him. Terribly!"

"He's new, that's why," said the sheriff. "He's rough and you're smooth."

"D'you think that I've been raised among lambs?" she asked him.

"I dunno, Isabella. This sort of beats me. You forget him. You chuck him over your shoulder and leave him lay!"

"He's too big for me," chuckled Isabella.

"He'll get small in time," declared Caradac. "You'll take on with some of these boys that you've been raised with."

"Maybe I will," answered she, as frankly as ever. "But I don't feel that way about it now."

"He's gone wild and he'll never be tame again," said Caradac with gloomy conviction.

"Look here, Owen Caradac," said she. "I come to you crying with a hurt finger. You ought to tie up the finger and make a fuss over me, and say how sorry you are. Instead, you say the finger will get well—some day. Then you give it another whack. Is that kind?"

"How bad are you hurt?" asked Caradac.

"Very bad," said she.

"You don't look it."

She opened her purse and took out a little mirror in which she viewed herself critically—at close hand and then at arm's length. "Well," she sighed, putting the mirror "I've missed a lot of sleep, anyway."

"Lemme ask you. How do your folks take the idea?"

"I haven't spoken to them about it. Mother would take it pretty hard."

"I don't see your father asking for congratulations, either."

159

"He wants me to marry some land," said she. "That's the only trouble."

"Not worried about the way that Rhiannon smashed up his place—and then got away from all the Dees?"

"Oh, he says that he'll tie Rhiannon over a slow fire and cook him and feed him to the birds. That's the way that Dad talks. He's never half-way."

"And he don't mean what he says?"

"Of course not. Annan Rhiannon's a man. Dad knows that, you see!"

"Humph," said the sheriff. "You talk like a baby."

"I could talk a lot more like one," declared Isabella. "I'm just around the corner from tears this very minute!"

"Look here," said the sheriff, and placed a square-tipped forefinger on the desk, "look here, Isabella. You got sense. You listen to me."

"I'll listen, Owen. But say it in words of one syllable. I'm not a student this day."

"He's wanted. Rhiannon is wanted a lot. For a lot of things. He's held up a train. He's killed men!"

"Self-defense," said Isabella.

"Self— Oh, damn it, Isabella, if you're gunna talk that way!"

"I dunno," droned Isabella sadly. "You don't seem to help me much. Of course I know that he's not a Sunday-school boy! But he can settle down. He's proved that on your farm."

"His farm," corrected the sheriff.

She opened her eyes a little.

"If he'll take it. But I could only make him take a half interest. He's that way. But you see, Isabella, you never would have a chance to marry him."

"Marriage," said she, without emphasis, "wouldn't stop me a bit."

"What?" cried the sheriff.

"Not if he'd have me along," said Isabella.

Caradac struck his hand on the desk and raised a sound like thunder from it. "You mean that!" he said. "But he wouldn't have you!"

"Maybe not," sighed Isabella. "He's lost his head about that Nancy Morgan, of course. I suppose he'll marry her?"

"What do you make of her?" asked Caradac.

160

"She's a gold-digger," said Isabella. "Of course I hate her for taking him."

"That's nacheral. But if she's a gold-digger, will she waste time on Rhiannon?"

"I don't think so. I hope not! She just wants to get something out of him."

"What?"

"I don't know."

"Who does?"

"Charlie does. Charlie knows nearly everything about everybody, it seems."

"But, getting back to Rhiannon. The more he cared for you, the less he'd come close to marrying you. His life ain't worth a nickel, he knows that. You ought to know that."

"I'm going to go to the governor," said she.

"And what'll you do there?"

"Fall on my knees and cry."

"What good will that do?"

"He's one of these strong men with a strong chin," said Isabella. "You take a man like that—he never can stand to have a girl cry. I'll keep at it till he pardons Rhiannon for me."

The sheriff grinned.

"D'you really think that would work?" he asked.

"No," she replied, "but that's something to do, at least. It's better than sitting still with my hands folded in my lap."

"And what do you want me to do about it?" asked Caradac.

"You'll see him before long, of course."

"Perhaps," said Caradac, and made a wry face.

"Why do you do that?" she asked.

"No reason," said Caradac. "Go on. When I see him, what am I to do?"

"Tell him that the latchstring is hanging outside."

"Your door or your father's door?"

"Both," said she. "I'm going home to tame Dad, now."

"Can you do it?"

"It's easy," said Isabella. "He's really just a baby, if one knows how to handle him."

"All right," said Caradac. "Now, suppose you get Rhi-

161

annon pardoned, which you can't. Suppose that you marry him, which I doubt. Then how you gunna live?"

"With Annan Rhiannon, of course."

"Look here. You're all polished up. You been East. You been finished."

"Not so finished," said Isabella. "Not so polished, either. Not so polished you could see me in the dark!"

"You'd like a lot to settle down and milk cows and fry bacon and make butter, you would!" said the sheriff with irony.

"Wouldn't I, though!" said Isabella. "And take care of the baby, too!"

"Well," grinned Caradac, "you're willing to look on the dark side of things, I see."

"I am," said Isabella. "Now look here, Owen. Tell me what it's all about—Nancy being kept at our house, and all of that? And what do you know?"

"Honey," replied the sheriff, "I'm all tangled up like a calf in a rope. I got a few ideas, but they ain't worth trotting out now. I'm working. That's all I gotta say. How's Mortimer?"

"He's going to get well."

"That's good news."

"I'm going back home," said Isabella.

She hesitated at the door. "When you see Annan Rhiannon—" she said.

"I'll tell him everything."

"But gently, Owen. Gently, please!" She paused, laughing back at him, but when he watched her down the steps, he saw that her face was very sad indeed. The bull terriers swarmed about her again, leaping, barking. She gained the gate with a struggle, and was gone down the street.

Chapter Thirty-Six

WHEN YOUNG Nearing came into the room again, his eye was on fire. He walked nervously up and down.

"Never heard of such a thing in my life!" said he. "But she's a jewel—she's a fairy princess—"

"She is," said the sheriff.

"She's worthy of a king!"

"Or a millionaire," said the sheriff, and yawned.

"Damn it," said Nearing, "something has to be done!"

"About what?"

"About her."

"Well?"

"She's got to be brought to her senses."

"How?"

"Must be shown that she's throwing herself away!"

"She'll never throw herself away on him. He wouldn't take her."

"Caradac, be reasonable."

"I am, son! He wouldn't have her. He ain't that kind. Would he break her life in two? No, he'll simply bust her heart instead. Because he's a good man!"

Nearing answered with violence: "You're out of your head about that fellow. He's a killer—a thief, Caradac."

The sheriff raised one finger. "You say it because you don't know," he replied gently. "But don't say it again."

"Man, man," groaned Nearing, "would you really trust him?"

"Look!" said the sheriff. "I hounded him for years. I trailed him everywhere. I went around and solicited folks so's to get a higher price put on his head. I've killed hosses to catch him. He's killed hosses to get away. It's been a war between us. Outside of me, life was a joke with him. But finally he got me good. Fair fight. I was down and out. Look what he done! Here I sit. He brought me through. He worked on me day and night. He never made no bargain, neither. Now, Nearing, that ain't all. I couldn't tell you all. All I say is, Rhiannon is white!"

"A white train robber, eh?"

"He begun young. He had a wrong steer when he was a kid. Seventeen or eighteen. What does a kid know about anything at that age? You go back and, if Isabella wants to see the governor—give her a chance to cry on his shoulder, will you?"

Young Nearing drew himself together with a sigh. "Look at the way she talked," said Nearing. "Right from the shoulder. Starts right off—she wants him—Rhiannon. She loves him. No beating about the bush. God, God, what a woman she is! And broken already. Smashed, done for. Damn it, Caradac, what a shame we can't do something!"

"Like marry her—one of us?" said the sheriff. "I tell you what, we ain't big enough!"

This the governor's secretary paused to consider. "I see what you mean," he said at last. "Of course she's a cut above. Rhiannon's a cut above the other pirates, too. Well, I'll go back and do what talking I can for him!"

"If you succeed," said the sheriff, "I'll tell you what. I'll give you one of those dogs—cheap!"

"Thanks," grinned Nearing. "Not enough foreface to have in my yard. So long, Caradac!"

The storms in the souls of the young never last long; Nearing was whistling as he went down the street, and the sheriff turned slowly to his work.

He began to sort out papers from his desk drawers, from his cabinet. He took out files, and fat manila envelopes lined with linen for greater endurance and wearing ability. From the envelopes he took photographs here, photographs there. He picked out papers from the files and arranged them. He began to pin this odd assortment together, with infinite care, worrying and sweating over his labor.

The day wore on. The evening came. He was still at his toil when the dusk grew so thick that the ache of his eyes made him look up and see that the night was almost there.

Then he went to the kitchen and cooked his supper. He was so absent-minded that he allowed the bacon to burn in the pan. He allowed the coffee to boil over.

He sat down to cold potatoes, pale coffee, burned meat, and ate mechanically. Then he went out to his front porch and watched the stars. The sickle of Leo was high in the sky; the Pleiades like a puff of diamond dust. It eased the heart of Caradac to watch those distant faces, for everything human about him was a burden to his very soul.

A buckboard jogged up the street with creaking wheels and rattling bed. It halted opposite his house. He heard two men speaking together; then they drove on. It was as if they had stopped to look at a house in which a murder had been committed. Somehow that small thing carried home to the mind of Caradac more clearly than all else the knowledge that his life work was ruined. He had spent his years and his blood to win the total confidence of the community. He had made his name a symbol of courage and of honesty up and down the far-flung range, and now in a moment the work was undone.

He, looking backward, could see clearly that he never could have succeeded, because, sooner or later, Rhiannon would have been recognized. True that his face was utterly disguised by the shaving of the beard, but nevertheless, some men are like burning glasses. Focus them long enough on anything, and the smoke will eventually rise, and Rhiannon was that sort—he could see it now—his personality would have shown itself in some fierce, rugged gesture.

In the meantime, his own life was ruined. Rhiannon's, also. And into the vortex Isabella Dee was being drawn. He tried to remember her careless laughter, but he could not close from his mind the thought of her sad, still face as she left.

He brushed his hand through the air before his face, as one does to drive away mosquitoes. Then he forced himself to concentrate on the street. Boys were playing in the deep dust, rolling, yelling. One of them began to cry. He was taken into the nearest house. But there, through an open window, he continued to sob until the pulsing sound entered the mind of the sheriff.

Life, he decided, was like that; there were always tears near by, and happiness was more name than reality. Men followed it, hunted it, but never could have it; just as

165

men hunted the wild deer but never could have that, either. For when it was taken, it was dead!

A man passed, flicking his fingers on the picket fence with a subdued rattle. The terriers rushed at the fence with a fury of snarling, and the stranger jumped to the farther side of the walk with an exclamation. "Damn brutes!" said he, and hurried on.

Another man came, a large silhouette in the night. He leaned on the gate and the dogs rushed at him with their savage clamor. He thrust the gate open.

"Look out!" cried Caradac, standing up.

But the dogs had fallen to either side and grown silent. They swirled in a dim white pool about the feet of the big man as he came slowly up the path to the porch. He climbed the steps. He stood over Caradac. "Rhiannon!" said the sheriff.

"It's me," said Rhiannon.

"Take a chair," said Caradac. "You walked in."

Rhiannon did not take the chair. "I walked in," he said.

The sheriff was silent. He had planned exactly the words which he would use, but now they failed in his throat, which labored but brought forth no sound. After all, words were of little purpose, here. Action alone counted with Rhiannon.

"They're stirred up a good deal, Annan," said the sheriff at last. "They got three posses out."

"And where's your posse?" asked Rhiannon.

The sheriff did not reply.

"Why don't you take the trail?" asked Rhiannon.

Again Caradac was silent.

"There ain't much light," said Rhiannon, "but there's light enough, I guess."

"I guess there is," said the sheriff.

"What'll you have," asked Rhiannon. "What'll you choose? Knife, or gun—or just bare hands?"

Caradac sighed and looked up at the sky. It seemed to him that all the stars were beginning to whirl. "I dunno," said he. "You pick what you want."

"Hands," said Rhiannon, "will take longer."

"Guns, then, if you want."

"All right," said Rhiannon. "Where'll we stand. Here?"

"If you want," said the sheriff.

He rose from his chair. Once more words stormed up against his teeth but he could not speak. Then he added: "Maybe down in the yard would be better. There used to be a garden—" He checked himself. He saw that the words had no meaning.

Then they stood opposite each other, dimly visible, ten paces apart.

"When that dog howls again," said Rhiannon.

"All right," said the sheriff.

But he subjoined: "If you need a hoss afterward, you'll find 'em in the shed behind the house. The black one is the best."

Rhiannon said nothing.

And then the dog howled in the distance, shrill and long.

The sheriff drew his Colt with practiced speed and fired from the hip—fired from the hip at the far-off Pleiades.

There was no answering shot. He saw the gleam of a gun in the hand of Rhiannon, and that was all.

"Damn you!" said Rhiannon slowly. "Damn you black! You won't even finish what you begun?"

Only then did the sheriff understand.

Chapter Thirty-Seven

HE COULD speak the words, but it was not easy to understand the fact that Rhiannon had come there not to fight but to die—as if some famous gladiator had taken sword and shield against a no less famous foe and then held his shield aside and allowed the first deadly thrust to speed home. But Caradac's bullet had split the air in the general direction of the Pleiades, and life still remained to Rhiannon.

He came striding closer through the night, but whatever his intention, it was put aside by the slamming of a door down the street and the sudden emergence of several men, who came toward the sheriff's house on the run.

Caradac caught the arm of his friend and dragged him back into the shadow of the wall.

"They're coming in a swarm!" said Caradac.

"Why not?" muttered Rhiannon. "Let 'em come. It's the best way—I should of thought of that—"

"Be quiet for one minute. I'm gunna talk to you in a minute, Rhiannon. And if you don't believe what I say to you then, I'll take my own gun and blow my own head off!"

From the fence a loud voice shouted: "Caradac! Caradac! Heard a shot over here! Anything wrong? Where are you, Caradac?"

"I'm here," said the sheriff, "and there's nothing wrong. I seen a coyote—or a dog—or something sneaking down the fence line."

The others turned slowly away, not convinced, murmuring with one another. And when they were out of earshot, the sheriff said: "You've come here figgering me as a double-crossing hound. Ain't that it, Annan?

"Don't answer me, then," went on Caradac. "I know that I played some in the dark. I thought it was better. But you figger that I turned you down—that I hired Caracci to spy on you—that maybe I did the same with Richards—that I played hand in glove with the Dees, maybe? Is that what you think?"

"I don't think," said Rhiannon. "I can't think."

"Come in with me," said the sheriff with sudden force, taking command of the situation. "Come in with me. We're gunna have a cup of coffee." He expected scornful refusal. Instead, Rhiannon submitted to the hand which fell on his great arm and was dragged into the kitchen of the little house. There he sat with his head hanging forward, his eyes staring. One hand lay upon his knee. The other arm dangled toward the floor. He seemed unnerved by fatigue and without will power to rally himself.

Caradac roused the fire in the staggering little stove, and filled the coffeepot and stood over it through interminable minutes waiting for it to boil. He dared not turn to look at that haggard face and sagging body; but he perspired freely and not with the heat, as he leaned above the coffeepot. It fumed up at last. He settled the grounds with a bit of water through the spout and then poured out two large cups of black liquid. "Will you have some chuck, too, Annan?" he asked.

"I dunno," said Rhiannon. "No, I ain't hungry."

Caradac sat down at the table. "Try that coffee," he urged.

Rhiannon fumbled at the cup but did not raise it.

'Go on," commanded Caradac, and automatically Rhiannon obeyed. He drained the cup and another brimming like it.

"Now," said Caradac, "will you hear me talk? First, in the beginning I give you my oath that I never had no thought agin you, and when you listened to me talking with Caracci behind the barn—"

Slowly the fallen head of Rhiannon raised, and the sheriff explained: "Caracci worked out the tracks the next day and seen where you stood. I'll tell you about him. I've known him for years. There was a time when he wasn't very straight. Caracci ain't his right name and nobody but me knows what that right name is. But I helped him out of a bad hole, and since then he's done jobs for me, now and then. I wanted him out at the farm. I felt that things was happening out there that might need him."

Rhiannon made a vague gesture. "Owen," he said at last in a harsh voice, "if you're lying to me, God rot you to the soul!"

"If an oath would make you believe in me, I'd swear any oath that you'd name. Annan, I'll tell you what I know, beginning at the beginning. I'll tell you what I guess, too!"

Some of the dullness left the eyes of Rhiannon. He looked straight into the face of the sheriff and the latter said: "There was the Nancy Morgan story that you first told me. That was the first thing that sounded queer to me."

"D'you mind telling me why?"

"She rode down there across the fields every evening?"

"Yes."

"After dark?"

"No, in the dusk of the day."

"All right. She rode down in the dusk of the day. Why was it always the dusk of the day?"

"I dunno," murmured Rhiannon.

"Why was it always at the same time of the dusk?"

"Because she had to be on the hill a certain time."

"Annan, she didn't want to be seen, she said? That was why she cut across country and didn't follow the road?"

"Yes. She said that."

"Old son, the way she chose—for hiding herself—lay right straight in front of your house. And she must of known that you used to sit out there. Why would she ride like that, jumping the fence? Because she wanted to catch your eye. Wanted to seem sort of mysterious. Can you find any better reason?"

Rhiannon waited, silent.

"And she did that every day, until you followed her, and laid for her; and, as soon as you found her, she let you know where she was bound for, didn't she?"

Rhiannon lifted his head a little higher. An angry flame was in his eyes.

"And as soon as she'd planted that idea in your head, she quit riding across country in the evening. She showed up at the Dee house, instead. She knew that you'd follow her."

"She seemed clean broken up. She wasn't flirting that night," said Rhiannon.

"She wouldn't be that much fool. She's smart! And she learned acting on the New York stage."

Rhiannon gathered himself, like one ready for a spring.

"I'm talking gospel," said the sheriff.

He explained, "I got it from her brother."

"Richards?"

"Morgan his name is, like hers. He's resting quiet in the jail. Not because of crooked work, but because he's safer there in case that a Dee should have sight of him and get careless with his gun! I got the thing out of him. He told me everything that he knew, and it was plenty. That's the story that I want to tell you, if you'll listen to me."

"Hold on," said Rhiannon. He rose from the table and flung up the window. Then he leaned into the night and breathed deeply.

At last he turned and faced Caradac.

"Owen," he said, "I been walking through a mist. Now I sort of begin to see through it. It sort of breaks up and lets me see that you been straight all the time; it was only me that was wrong in the head. I ain't gunna apologize for what I tried to make you do tonight, but I'd like to shake hands with you, old son."

The sheriff wrung that great proffered paw. Then he dragged Rhiannon into his office room.

"I'm gunna show you what I've found out about the Morgans, unless, Annan, you simply got your mind set not to hear the truth about that girl."

"I could afford to hear the truth," answered Rhiannon.

"You can see a part of it. Then I'll tell you some more." He jerked open a drawer of the desk and took out of it the two long documents which he had pinned together. They consisted of photographs, newspaper articles and letters, pinned in long scrolls. The sheriff unfurled them and explained, pointing out the items:

"There's Jack Morgan, as the police know him, alias a lot of other things—Dago Jack, Bill Alexander, and a lot more. Here's the way he looked when he was mugged for burglary. Here he is when he was arrested for his second job. Take a look, will you? Look this list over. He's been busy! He's twenty-eight, and he's spent ten years of his life in the pen or reform school. Never anything important could be hung onto him, but he was suspected of a lot of stuff. He was straight with a gun. He was damn straight. The Dees learned that, finally!"

He went on: "This here ain't the real Morgans of this here Hill Country, Rhiannon. They're just cousins. But they got the last scraps of the Morgan property from out this way. That was just a couple of trunks full of old clothes and letters and a few books, and such like things, y'understand?"

"I understand," said Rhiannon. "Even that was a lie —her being a Morgan?"

"Are you gunna take it hard, what I'll show you about her?"

"I'll stand it," said Rhiannon grimly. He added: "I got her away from the Dee house, old-timer, and there was no other place for me to take her—the other ways was all blocked—except straight back toward Mount Laurel. And there was only one way out of that. They was coming fast behind us."

"You went through the hole-in-the-wall?" asked the sheriff with excitement.

"I did."

"I gathered that from what I heard. Then, by God, she's done what she come here for—in spite of hell, she's done it!"

"I dunno what she come for," said Rhiannon, "but, once inside, she acted like she'd been there before."

"She did?"

"She pretty near murdered me," said Rhiannon. "And I seen her face with murder in it, as clear as ever I seen it on the face of even a man, I tell you! She pulled something—I dunno what. It dropped a ton of stone past my face. I just got back from another half ton slug of rock out of the top of the tunnel! That's the last I've seen of the lady," ended Rhiannon.

The sheriff looked earnestly at him. It was enough to explain a great deal of the condition in which Rhiannon had arrived at the house that evening. "Now," said Caradac, "I'll tell you some of her story!"

Chapter Thirty-Eight

HE TURNED out the other scroll and said: "Here you have her start—detention school for girls, a little shoplifting and picking of pockets. She began early. She was eleven. You see here?"

"Interesting," said Rhiannon.

He settled himself in the sheriff's comfortable chair.

"This here is her mug. Pretty, ain't she?"

"Like a picture!" said Rhiannon.

And it was true. It looked like an ideal face, not an actual photograph of flesh.

"Kind of face that makes a man turn soft and sappy and wish for children of his own, eh?"

"It looks that way. Now, this here ladybird was kept till she was fifteen, and when she got out, she'd sort of graduated, y'understand? She went into bigger things, She got deeper right away. Slippery, too. They tried her for smuggling diamonds in. They tried her for smuggling dope. They tried her for stealing the pearls of a Lady Whatnot from England. There's the article about that.

"Things begun to look a little too hot even for pretty Nancy. She tried her hand at something else. She tried the stage. She done the chorus. She had a face and she could use her feet. So she climbed up out of that and got a better job. Y'understand? Not leading, but song and dance in musical comedy. She was that good!

"The stage is too lively for some, but pretty soon Nan begun to get bored. She turned back to the old ways. Smuggling again. They got her this time. Pen for three years. Then out on good behavior. But she chucked her parole. After that, she was plain underworld. She had to use disguises, keep switching names, and keep on the move; and she made money, and she lost it. She took up cards. And she got trimmed. A big job in Pittsburgh. She'd lose her wad in some gambling dive when she got to Chicago. A good sport was Nancy. Cards wasn't enough. She'd take a flyer at the ponies when she was real flush. Got to a jockey in Brooklyn, finally, and got him to pull his hoss, and Nan cashed in on the second best contender. A little sweetheart, was Nancy, and a quick worker, always. One meeting and she had her man hypnotized."

"She done that with me, dead easy," said Rhiannon.

"But, after a while, she dropped out of view, not many months ago, and that was when she got herself started on this business out here. It was her brother that give her the flying start, old son. Her brother, Jack Morgan. He told me a little about it in the jail. He'd done part of a stretch in the pen. He come out and, having nothing to do, he went up and started to rummaging through the old trunks that had come from the Western Morgans. And while he was working through those trunks, he come across something that looked interesting. Something scratched onto the flyleaf of a book—a little diagram and a few words. That was all. He couldn't make nothing out of it. He thought that he'd see his smart sister.

"He done that. She never had much use for Brother Jack, nor him for her. They didn't have exactly the same kind of talents. She was a cut above him, as a crook.

"So she turned loose on the trunks with Jack, and she

173

went through them with a fine-toothed comb and got some more scraps of information.

"Then she bought a couple of tickets West—Jack was broke, as usual—and they come and begun to work up this country to see what it might be worth.

"It wasn't a clean bust for them. Jack didn't tell me everything, but what he did say was that the thing that they wanted to find was the hole-in-the-wall. They come all the way from the East about it!"

"Ah!" murmured Rhiannon.

"You see where you begin to come in, son? No sooner they come out here and ask a few questions than they learn that there's always been talk about a way through the face of Mount Laurel. And finally Rhiannon come along and he found that way through, and, on account of it, the police, particularly meaning Owen Caradac, had been made fools of a dozen times, and Rhiannon still at large, so to speak.

"Now, just how it worked, I dunno, because Jack the Gunman, and Jack the Thief, he didn't tell me all the details. But anyway, he spotted you as being Rhiannon one day when you come to the town. He come out to work for you. That was the reason that he waited until he could get the job on your place. He wanted that job because, one day, he hoped that he'd have a chance to find out about the hole-in-the-wall! He waited and he watched, and he sneaked around and listened when he could. But he never found nothing about the hole-in-the-wall, although he finally did overhear you and me talking, and by that he knew that you really was Rhiannon, as he'd suspected before."

"The greasy snake," said Rhiannon calmly.

The sheriff looked at him with a smile of delight. "You feel kind of more nacheral?" he asked.

"More nacheral than ever," said Rhiannon. He explained: "I was beat, Owen. Now I think that maybe we got a chance to do something, still!"

"We have," said the sheriff, "maybe. But let's get on with the yarn that Jack the Thief told me. He said that he used to come in from the farm to the town and have a talk with pretty Nancy on the side, and finally, one day she was gone. He waited, hoping to hear some message. She'd got herself a couple of smashing fine

174

horses, and she used to ride out after the heat of the day; and sometimes she'd come out past the farm after dark, and he'd slip away and talk to her, and compare notes. You see?"

"Yes. That would of been easy."

"But after she disappeared from town, she never come back no more. He never seen her at the farm, nor in the town. She was clean gone.

"When that happened, Richards—Morgan, I mean— got more and more worried. He figgered that his dear sister had up and arranged to do the work and cop the money all by herself, though how she was gunna get the information about the hole-in-the-wall from you, he couldn't imagine. But she was a crafty worker and he put nothing past her.

"And there," said the sheriff, "is the end of the story as far as I know it. Maybe you can add something?"

"Nothing at all. But she came to find the hole-in-the-wall, and she's got what she wanted to get."

"She shut you off in the middle of the tunnel that you talk about?"

"She did."

"She thinks you're dead?"

"She's plumb sure of it," said Rhiannon. "The first fall of rock shut off her sight of me. The second fall she heard rumble. She must of been sure that it nailed me."

"You're a dead man, then," chuckled the sheriff. "Is that right?"

"To her—yes," said Rhiannon grimly.

"Did you think of coming around right away and trying the front end of the hole-in-the-wall?"

"Sure I thought of that. But what was the good? A man entering the hole-in-the-wall would be killed dead easy by anybody inside. Still, I come around the shoulder of the mountain, and then I seen that the Dees had the hollow filled with men!"

"And they still have," remarked the sheriff.

"Which makes me think, pretty sure, that Nancy has been working with the Dees all the time."

"I dunno," said the sheriff. "Suppose we put down what we don't know. We don't know just what the pair of Morgans—brother and sister—have been after. Some-

175

thing worth while. There ain't any doubt of that, of course!"

"No, of course not. Something—worth murder," remarked Rhiannon with a singular smile.

"What would you do if you had her?" asked the sheriff curiously.

"I dunno. Nothing," said Rhiannon. "But I'd like to see her again. To pass the time of day!"

Caradac nodded. "We don't know what they're after. That's the first thing. I couldn't get it out of Jack. He shut his mouth tight as a clam. He only talked at all because he was worrying to death for fear that she's double-crossing him—which of course she's doing just that! Then, besides, we don't know where the Dees figger."

"They figger strong," said Rhiannon darkly.

"Not all of them, maybe."

"All," said the outlaw. "The old man and his wife. Charlie is the center of it, I guess. And they even used the girl to work on me! They even sunk as low as that!"

The sheriff looked sharply at him. Then he went on: "We know that the likely thing is that she wanted to get into the Dee house, and she wanted you to come after her. That's pretty plain, I'd say."

"It looks that way."

"And then what did they do? They covered the place with men. And they arranged what?"

"They arranged," said Rhiannon with a sudden oath, "that I'd be headed straight back toward Mount Laurel. Damn it, why didn't I see through that? Why else would they choke the mouth of the hollow with their gunmen? Why else?"

"Ah," said the sheriff. "You got the right of it."

"I got something more," said Rhiannon loudly. "Twenty-five paces from the entrance and turn to the right, and there you'll find a—"

A bullet hissed past his face, the window glass crashed, and the short, deep cough of a revolver boomed through the room.

Caradac dived for the door. He did not wait to turn the handle but gave it his shoulder and lunged out, Rhiannon behind him; and then they saw a fleeing form in the darkness that was swerving round the corner of the horse shed. They bolted in pursuit, but when they came to the corner of the shed they heard the departing beat of hoofs. The would-be murderer was gone.

"Search the ground," said the sheriff. "You got your lantern?"

They moved straight back toward the house, swinging the ray of lantern light across the ground, and it was Caradac who saw a glitter and picked up a ring—a large man's ring, too big to have fitted the finger of any woman. "Look, Rhiannon," he murmured. "It's got the same sort of a blue stone in it as your ring, and it's got the same things cut into it!"

Chapter Thirty-Nine

THEY WENT back to the house and sat on the veranda.

"Where did you get that ring, Rhiannon?" asked Caradac.

"On the floor of the hole-in-the-wall."

"And now a man with the same sort of a ring takes a crack at you through the window! Who was it?"

"I don't know," said Rhiannon. "I'm going back to the hole-in-the-wall, if I can get there. I think it'd be easier to answer questions there."

"I'll get the hosses."

"Hosses?"

"We go together, Annan."

The outlaw did not argue the point. They went to the shed and there they found that of three horses one already was gone.

"He helps himself to a hoss," said the sheriff without heat, "leaves him cached over here near to the shed, then comes and takes his shot at you."

"How could anybody miss at a short distance like that?" asked Rhiannon.

They began to saddle their mounts.

"Look out through a window of my house and you'll see

why," chuckled the sheriff. "That's the worst glass that ever was put in a sash. All full of waves. It makes Mount Laurel look like it was breaking in two. He took his shot, but the glass showed him the wrong way. He may be a handy man with a gun, in spite of that!"

A voice called near the house: "Hey, sheriff! Oh, Caradac!"

Caradac went from the horse shed. He came back again, shortly, with the terriers around him. "Morgan has left the jail," he said dryly. "I gave word that he was to be let go whenever he wanted to start. I wasn't holding him for anything. And there, Annan, is the gent that took the shot at you!"

"Ay," said Rhiannon. "But why should he of wanted to sink lead into me?"

"Were we talking over his references?" answered the sheriff. "Besides, did you treat him like a dog, the last night that you had him at your house? He'd rather forgive you for murder than for making him take water, Annan."

They led out the saddled horses, mounted, and went out through the back gate of the sheriff's yard. Then they rode through the trees toward the black, towering mass of Laurel Mountain. Under its side they swung away to the westward again, and carried on at a brisk pace. The sky clouded. A whipping shower fell. Then the vapors began to break up and roll down the high vault of the sky, and the stars came out in bright patches, whirling among the dissolving clouds. Their trail was spotted, here and there, with patches of tarnished silver—the little pools which had collected on the roadbed. But the long-striding horses dashed through these and carried them steadily on toward their goal.

So they rounded the shoulder of the mountain and came out on the hills toward the house of Dee—hills high and broken, like the hollow-faced waves of the Agulhas Current. They found a thick copse between two hills. There they hid and tethered their horses. Then they went on cautiously, turning to the right and making for the top of the southern arm that extended from the breast of Mount Laurel, one of those two ridges which half embraced the house of Dee.

178

They gained the ridge. Looking down from it, they could see the lights of the house twinkling.

"Like a nest of hawks," said Rhiannon grimly. "That's what I think of when I see that house!"

"Lemme tell you about one of those hawks," said the sheriff. "She's gone to see the governor and beg for your pardon."

"My pardon!"

"Ay."

"Might as well ask for a slice of the moon!"

"I tell you what she's doing."

"That's Isabella?"

"Who else would try such a thing?"

"D'you mean that there's a chance that she's straight, while all the rest are crooked?"

"Everybody's innocent till you can prove 'em guilty," said the sheriff with decision.

"And I'm a dead man unless I get the pardon," said Rhiannon. "But—let it go. We gotta get down into that hollow. We gotta get under the face of Laurel Mountain! How many men will they have down there guarding us, Owen?"

"God knows. We'll go and chance it."

"You're the sheriff," answered Rhiannon. "If they found you with me, you'd be as bad as me. They'd salt you away as quick as they would me."

"Don't argue," commanded the sheriff almost wearily. "I'm old enough to know my business. Come on, Rhiannon, and shut up, will you?"

They went on, side by side, moving stealthily from one cover to another, until they had worked their way down the slope of the hill. There was no one sighted, no stir among the brush before them, no shadows slipping toward them among the rocks. But when they came down into the center of the hollow they heard a quiet voice, answered by another. The sheriff and his companion flattened themselves against the ground. They had before them a low outcropping of rock which gave them perfect shelter. But straight up to those rocks walked two men—a third came with them, a little to the rear. Not five yards away lay the sheriff and Rhiannon. They dared not raise their faces, lest the flesh color should appear pale in the dark of the night.

179

"There was nothing," said one of the watchers.

"I thought I seen it agin the sky line."

"There's been a lofer wolf, up there."

"Lofers wouldn't be hunting, this dark night."

"It's blacker'n hell."

"I'll go up and scout around."

"Keep here. We ain't to move out. We're to keep tight."

"And what's gunna be goin' on, anyway?"

"I dunno. It's something they're working at on Mount Laurel. I heard Chuck say that he thought they'd found the hole-in-the-wall."

"The hell!"

"Rhiannon would thank them for that!"

"Plug that hole and they'd soon run that fox down."

"You never can tell."

"Has big Jerry come in?"

"I dunno. The old man was foamin' about him a while back."

"It ain't the old man's game. It's Charlie's. He marches the old boy up and down and won't tell him nothin'."

"And what are they after?"

"Rhiannon, most like."

"That'll be a fire to warm all our hands at!"

"Oh, I dunno. The bigger they are, the easier to hit."

They shifted to the side. They disappeared, but still their faint voices were perfectly audible. The sheriff worked closer and whispered in the ear of Rhiannon: "You gotta get through. Work down the valley, then come on back, walking as big as you please. You try this side. I'll try the other, beyond the trees on that hummock. We're both big Jerry. Understand? We're arriving late, and we're walking through the lines. Suppose that we both get through, where do we meet?"

"Walk straight in toward the toes of Laurel Mountain. Follow up the run of water that you find there. Where it flattens out smooth and wide, there you'll find me!"

"So long, Annan."

"Old-timer," said Rhiannon, "it's my party. You back up and be a rear guard, will you? Why should you try to break through?"

The sheriff returned no answer. He simply wriggled himself away like a snake through the surface mud and grass, then disappeared into some brush.

Rhiannon obeyed instructions. He went back a little distance on his hands and knees.

Then he stood up and walked boldly out from the trees, swinging his rifle in his hand. Yonder, to his right, was the very place where horse and rider had fallen before his revolver shot. It gave him an odd tingle of confidence, as he remembered that. He strode on more lightly. God give luck to the brave sheriff! If Rhiannon were caught, it would be mercifully swift death. If the sheriff were caught, it would be worse—lifelong disgrace!

"Hey, you!"

A hard quick voice out of the dark.

"All right, all right!" snarled Rhiannon. "Whatcha want? My money?"

"Some damn smart gent, out there," growled an answering voice. Then, "Who are you?"

"Who in hell should I be?" asked Rhiannon. "Somebody that'd rather be in bed than here, if you want to know!"

"I'm gunna pop him under the chin," cried an angry man. "I'm gunna soak him, damn him!"

A silhouette appeared before Rhiannon, nearing him rapidly.

"Where are you?" asked a voice that rose high, to a squeaking point of rage. "Where are you? I'm gunna bust you one, you flat-faced hound!"

Chuck Maple, swelling with instant anger, and striding toward him in the dark.

"I'm here," said Rhiannon loudly.

Maple came at him on the half run.

"Chuck!" said Rhiannon in a loud whisper.

The rush of the latter was checked. He stood swaying, gasping.

"It's me," said Rhiannon.

"God—God!" breathed Chuck Maple.

"I'm Jerry, and what do you want of me?" asked Rhiannon loudly. "What d'you want with me, runt?"

Chapter Forty

"It's JERRY," said someone in the bushes.

"Sure it's Jerry," said Chuck Maple. "I can tell him by his fool way of trailin' straight into danger."

"Lemme be!" said Rhiannon. "I can't be bothered with you gents and your ideas!"

He walked straight on, Maple at his heels.

"I never seen Jerry look so big," said someone.

"Talk would make anybody look puffed up, wouldn't it?"

"Maybe it would. Hey, Jerry, come here!"

Rhiannon stepped on. There was a shudder of apprehension down his backbone. They were on either side. Half a dozen men, half a dozen fighting men, all guns in hand.

"Jerry!" This was an angry shout.

"Well—well!" said Rhiannon, pausing. "Whatcha want?"

"Come back here."

"Who are you? Who you mean to be ordering around?"

"If your own uncle ain't got a right to call you, boy, who has? Come here this minute!"

"My own uncle didn't send for me. My own uncle, he don't know my business, here!" said Rhiannon. "My own uncle has got nothing to do with me tonight."

There was a stifled burst of laughter. The uncle burst out in a rage: "I'll make you sweat for this, you pup. I'm gunna make you sweat for this."

"Aw, leave the poor fool be," said another. "He never made nothin' but trouble. I dunno why Charlie wanted him here, tonight."

"Budge," said the uncle in still greater anger, "who you callin' a fool?"

Rhiannon walked on. In an instant, a screen of trees was behind him. He lengthened his stride and went swiftly on toward the mountain, whose face, wet with the recent rain, glimmered before him, tall and vast.

He was through the line, thanks to the invention of Caradac! But Caradac himself? What would have happened to him?

Nearing the foot of the mountain, he saw a tall shadow come from the brush to the left. The shadow halted, then came on more slowly. "Who's there?" asked Rhiannon loudly and confidently. "Stand tight there and gimme your name!"

The other halted. Then very soft, deep laughter reached the ear of Rhiannon.

"It's all right, Annan!" And there was the sheriff beside him, crushing his arm in a reassuring grip.

"Meet anything?" asked Rhiannon.

"Not a thing. I walked right through a hole in the line. But I heard voices over to my right."

"Must of been the boys stopping me. But I got through. I'm Jerry. Kind of big for Jerry, though, it seems!"

They chuckled, guardedly. Then they went on, side by side, and cleared the last shadowy screen of brush, and stood on the verge of the water. Smoothly it ran, with a whisper of speed, and Rhiannon, stopping, buried his hand in the current to test the weight of the running water.

Then he said to his friend: "Owen, straight in from us there's the opening of the hole-in-the-wall. You stoop under the rim of that rock which looks like it touches the water. But it don't! You can pass right on under it. Keep straight on through the dark. Pretty soon you'll come to a shelving of the side of the bottom. It'll bring you up into the cave itself. Now, Caradac, I'm gunna try that passage. And if you don't see me again in ten minutes, you come on under after me. Is that right?"

"Right," said the sheriff.

"Move careful. Don't make a splash. There's been people in there before us. The woman, anyway. And probably she's in there now. Otherwise, why would they be watching the hollow so careful?"

"True," said the sheriff. "I ain't a water-rat, but I'll try to go plumb careful."

They shook hands, and Rhiannon stepped into the water. He advanced straight across the stream, bowed his head beneath the rock—and almost instantly was lost above his head in the icy water. The force of the current jerked him sidewise. Only by luck he caught the upper rock, and so, after steadying himself, he was able to turn.

He went back to Caradac. "More than the girl know about the hole-in-the-wall now," he informed the sheriff. "They got things now so that there's a pit at the entrance. You'll have to let go with your feet and just float yourself in. You'll get soused. Can your gun stand it?"

"A few minutes under will do me no harm, or the guns, either."

Rhiannon returned. He found that it was perfectly easy, once forewarned of the trap, to take the lower face of the rock, and so draw himself inward. At last he put down his feet, found the bottom, and waded on through the utter darkness.

The shore shelved. He went in softly, for as the upper portion of his body came above water there was danger of the dripping garments betraying him. At the same instant, he tried a flashlight and ventured a rapid ray which, cast around the cave, showed him that work had indeed been forward there since his last visit. For in the center of the space, a yard or two from the lip of the water, there was a heap of what looked like old chests or boxes.

He went on through the new darkness in the direction of them, sat down in the sand, and began to pass his hands firmly over his clothes, hoping to press out most of the water with which they were loaded. So he waited. The cold increased every moment. He shuddered in the darkness. But he remained quietly sitting there until a slight stir in the water broke him to his feet, ready to assist the sheriff.

However, he now heard a sharp gasp, and then, "Is it all right, Nancy?"

"Oh, no! The infernal oilskins didn't keep the water out. I'm soaked to the bone again!"

"You didn't pull the strings around the wrists and ankles tight enough," replied the voice of Charlie Dee.

Rhiannon retreated cautiously to the side of the cavern. When they showed a light, he could only hope that they would not throw the beam straight at him. He stretched out flat on the sand, one arm exended before him, and a gun in that hand. If they shone the light at

Rhiannon, it would be the last moment for one of them!

They were coming on through the darkness, careless of the noise they made, sputtering and gasping. Then they were stamping on the sand.

"Show me a light!" commanded the voice of Nancy. "My boots are full of water. I'm frozen!"

A strong light instantly flashed, and Rhiannon shrank with discomfort when he saw the extent to which the sand around him was illuminated. He could only pray that that beam would not be directed toward him—or if it were, that they would not be suspicious of the dark, irregular shadow on the sand.

In the meantime, what of the sheriff? Had he seen these two pass him and enter the water? Would he follow on immediately behind them? And would not the noise of his coming cause the light of Charlie Dee to be focused on him? Bullets from the gun of Dee would then end the matter.

He could hear every word that was spoken, even when the voices were much lowered, for the curved ceiling of the cave reflected the sounds—almost magnified them!

Nancy was sitting on the sand, stripping off her boots and emptying the water from them. She was covered with yellow oilskins, so that she glistened like a heap of gold.

Charlie Dee stood beside her, sympathetic. "You brought a little flask of brandy, Nan. Why don't you take a shot of that?"

"After we finish the job. I'll have a drink then. They're keeping a close watch, Charlie."

"They are. I thought that Budge was going to stop us and have a look at you."

"It was a narrow squeak. But what if they *had* seen me? We could have bluffed it through."

"Maybe. But—"

"But your father. When is he going to suspect what we're after?"

"If he knew we were here—if he guessed what we're after—" Charlie Dee laughed, and there was an unpleasant ring in his voice.

"He'd put the rates up?"

"Sure. He's a regular miser," said Charlie Dee.

"He don't like to see his boy get on in the world, eh?" chuckled Nancy Morgan.

"Never mind. He don't know a thing. We're going to get the rest of this stuff away tonight."

They stood up and began to examine the boxes which were piled on the sand. These they handled carelessly, throwing some of them to a little distance. Over one that remained they leaned with care. Nancy was dipping her hands into the contents.

Suddenly Charlie Dee exclaimed: "Careful, Nan. Just let me have a look at everything that you put your hands on!"

She straightened, stamping with anger. "D'you think that I'd try to hold out anything on you?" she demanded.

"I don't think," he answered her, perfectly cool. "I know."

"You know, do you?" A little animal whine of rage came into her voice.

"It's no good throwing a bluff at me, Nancy," he told her dryly. "I like you fine. You're a pretty picture of a girl. But we'll go on at this as if it was business, not just pleasure. There's no use having to trust each other too far."

She said, after a little pause: "You're right. Of course there isn't. Show me a light here, again."

He obeyed, throwing the strong glare into the inside of the box. Only the reflection of it passed out over the cavern, over the water. And now, from the pale surface of the latter, Rhiannon saw the dark head and shoulders of a man lifting.

Chapter Forty-One

THE MONSTROUS width of those shoulders enabled him to recognize the other even in the dim half-light. It was Caradac, coming cautiously in toward the edge of the water. Rhiannon lifted himself a little and began to work in on hands and knees. He took his time. It was plain the sheriff was taking no chances. So slowly did he advance

186

through the water that his forward movement was almost imperceptible, and Rhiannon imitated that caution.

The girl had lifted out several small, heavy bags. Then she began to fumble at something else. Cloth ripped under her strong hands.

At last she straightened for a rest. So perfectly audible was every sound and movement that Rhiannon could hear her excited breathing. "I think it's there," she said. "I think that's the main part of the boodle, Charlie my dear!"

"It's been worth while, anyway," said Charlie. He added, "In five minutes we ought to be shut of the hole-in-the-wall."

"Then let Rhiannon come back when he pleases," said the girl. "He'll find that the nut's been picked out of his shell! The fool! The fool! Living on top of this stuff all those years! But you can't make a half-wit see the light."

"Look here, Nan," said the other, "why d'you hate him so?"

"Why shouldn't I?"

"That's a woman's answer," said young Dee. "I asked you for a reason. Didn't we use him? Without him, would we ever have been able to find this place?"

"I hate a fool!" said Nancy with violence.

"You're pretty enough to make any man foolish," said Charlie Dee.

"Except you, Charlie," she suggested.

"I'm not romantic," he answered.

"Not romantic! You're a cold-blooded fish!"

"You have a tongue of your own, Nan."

"God gave me that," she replied with a shrug of her shoulders. "But what about you? You pretend that you like Rhiannon—the big heavy-handed brute?"

"What did he do to you, Nancy? What did he say to you? Will you tell me that? Didn't he come and *rescue* you from us?" He chuckled as he said this, and she laughed sharply in return.

The looming shadow of Caradac was drawing closer and closer to them. Rhiannon, also, was working nearer every moment. He almost wondered why, with a turn of the head, they were unable to see either of the two dangers which focused upon them so certainly. But then he understood that it was the absorption of their thoughts

187

in the work that lay under their hands, and more than that because their eyes were dazzled by the brightness of the light which flared before them.

"He rescued me—after you'd planned the rescue," she said. "You want me to give him credit for that?"

"Sure," said Charlie Dee. "But it was a job that only a brave man and a clever man could have done!"

"Why d'you tell me that?" she snapped. "Didn't you sit there *ready* to be surprised—even after you heard the floor creaking under him in the next room?"

"He had to get through the ring of Dad's watchers," said Charlie Dee. "And *they* weren't in on the secret. They were ready to shoot. Shoot at shadows, even! Even as it was, he'd barely got you out when the 'rescuers' were with me! But tell me, Nan, what makes you think he wasn't buried under the fall of rock?"

"I wish he had been," said the girl, "but he wasn't. I don't know how I know, but I do. I can feel him. I can feel that he's sort of still living. I can feel him near us, Charlie."

Charlie Dee actually turned and cast a glance over his shoulder at the figure of Caradac—and that instant the gun of Rhiannon steadied upon him. One move for a weapon, and Charlie Dee would have died. But he saw nothing. It had been merely an instinctive glance at the mention of the danger from Rhiannon.

So Dee turned back to his companion. "All right," said he. "You got voices to guide you, maybe—like Joan of Arc, eh?" He chuckled sneeringly at the comparison, and, as he laughed, the girl lifted her head and fixed her glance steadily upon Charlie. Even Rhiannon shuddered as he saw that glance. But Charlie Dee seemed oblivious of it.

"Leave Joan of Arc be," said the girl. "No matter what I am, I've led you to some money, Charlie. Is that right?"

"Oh, that's right enough. I don't deny your talents, honey."

"Leave that word out, too!" she snapped at him.

"Look here, Nancy, did you ever care for a human soul in the whole of your life?"

"I've never known anybody except fourflushers and cheap smart guys," said Nancy Morgan. "I could appreciate a *real* man as good as anybody."

"You would have liked Caradac, then," said Charlie

Dee surprisingly. "There's a real man. He's done for now, though."

"We've picked him off his high place," said Nancy, chuckling with a malicious pleasure. "We rolled him in the dirt, too!"

"Does that please you?"

"Why not?" she snarled in answer. "Have the damned elbows and cheap dicks ever done me any good? Haven't they made life hell for me?"

Charlie Dee stared at her. "Tell me, Nan," he said, "how you worked Rhiannon. Weren't you scared a little when you faced that big man?"

"The first second," she admitted. "After that, he was easy. I was a little hysterical. That always gets the big men. It makes them feel bigger and stronger. But never try it with a small man. It makes him feel smaller and meaner. Rhiannon—he was dead easy. He's one of those square heads. He never would lay a hand on a girl. Even a poor working girl like me!"

She laughed again, and Charlie Dee cut curtly into the laughter. "Let's get on with the work, Nan. Let's finish it off. There's only that last parcel."

She leaned over the box without a word. Again there was the sound of cloth ripping.

"Shall I help you?" asked Charlie Dee.

"Leave me alone, will you?" she snapped at him. "We agreed that I was to do all of the opening up of things! I know how fast those skinny, long fingers of yours can work!"

To this insult, Charlie Dee returned a perfectly good-natured insult. The sheriff was now not five steps from the pair of them, and Rhiannon was no greater distance. One bound would bring him upon them; therefore he rose to his feet. He prepared the flashlight in his left hand. The revolver was ready in his right.

Now there was a stifled exclamation from the girl. She lifted a small box in both her hands. "Look, Charlie!" she said savagely. "You don't know what's in this box. Neither do I. I'll tell you what. I'll stake all my share of everything else. You take the whole caboodle. I'll just take this little old box—without even opening it! Maybe there's nothing in it at all—I'll—I'll take my chance of that!" She had bowed a little over the box, holding it to

189

her body with both arms, and such an insensate greed was in her voice as Rhiannon never had heard in his life before.

"I'll have a look at the box, dearie," said Charlie Dee. "I'll take a look at it."

She stiffened, and stood straight. "You fool!" she said to him. "You smart—fool!"

Then she snapped the lid of the box open—and the next moment her low cry rang through the cave. Rhiannon himself could hardly keep from exclaiming. For the whole interior of the box gave back the light of Dee's torch with a blaze and a flare of many colors—green and red and blue and crystal white all shuddering in the trembling hands of Nancy Morgan.

"Ay," said Charlie Dee. "You would have taken this little box for your share, all right!"

"My God—my God!" whispered Nancy with a voice like a sob. She raised the box and pressed her face against the cold, gleaming jewels. It was like the caress of a mother for a child. Never had Rhiannon seen such passion, and horror went through him, chilled him, hardened him.

"All right, Nan," said Charlie Dee. "Just close up the box again—before a couple of those beauties happen to fall out—and roll up your sleeve!"

Nancy Morgan threw back her head and laughed and laughed again, and the mirth rang in the sweetest music through the cave. "I've got it!" she cried. "I've waited. But I've always known. Some day I'd have my hands full. I'd have them heaped and loaded with the beauties— and I got 'em now—I got 'em now!"

She snapped the lid of the casket shut.

"I'll carry that," said Charlie Dee sternly.

"Of course you will," said Nancy Morgan. "D'you think that I don't trust you, honey? Of course I trust you! You've been square as a die with me. You take it!"

She put the casket into the hands of Charlie Dee. There was such cordial warmth in her voice that, even from the brain of Rhiannon, so long forewarned and forearmed against her, the memory of her crimes melted away like smoke before the pure wind.

"We'll have a touch of brandy, Charlie," she said. "We've worked hard enough—brain and body. We deserve something!"

190

"A grand idea, Nan."

She took out a little silver flask. It glistened like crystal. This she uncorked and offered to him.

"After you, Nan."

"No, Charlie. You've done the biggest share of the work."

She kissed the flask and offered it with a laugh to him. "I give you my good luck with it!" said Nancy Morgan.

"And good luck to you, Nan," said the other. "I drink to you!"

He raised the flask high and bowed, laughing a little in turn at this odd moment of courtesy which had stolen upon them unawares, as it were.

"If you take that drink," said the calm voice of Caradac, hardly two steps behind the pair, "you'll never take another!"

Chapter Forty-Two

AT THE FIRST sound of his friend's voice, Rhiannon had flashed his own torch full upon the pair, blindingly bright; and, though Charlie Dee had put out his own light the instant that he heard a sound, the two were caught and helplessly snared in the radiance that fell around them. From big Caradac's hand a second shaft of light flamed at them. Two walls of brightness crushed them helplessly together. They could see the leveled, gleaming guns which were held beside the torches, and they understood their meaning.

"Offer it to her, first," said Caradac. "Let her have a taste of the stuff, Charlie, and see if she ain't glad to have it!"

"I will," said the girl, and snatched the flask. "I'll finish—"

She lowered the little silver bottle when it was already at her lips. "No," she said. "What's the good? I may pull through even this!"

"Just shove your hands up, Dee!" commanded Rhiannon.

A faint scream from the lips of the girl. "Annan Rhiannon!"

"It's him," said the sheriff. "Got a nice voice, ain't he? Dee, you hear the talk about sticking your hands up?"

Charlie Dee obeyed. He was wonderfully cool and collected. Nancy Morgan shrank against him, shuddering, her hands clenched. "I told you we should have finished the job last night!" she said fiercely.

"Then I would have had the poison a night earlier, honey. Is that it?" asked the quiet voice of Dee.

"Oh, damn you—and you—and you!" gasped Nancy Morgan. Her voice broke in a dry sob of passionate regret. "I've missed my chance! I've missed it! I wish I were dead!"

"You've got a short cut in your hand," said the sheriff. "Nobody would hold you back!"

She flung the bottle at Caradac's head. It missed narrowly and plumped in the standing pool of water.

"Take her hands," said Caradac. "I'll watch the pair of them. Mind you, Dee, I have a thumb on the hammer!"

"I'm a lamb, Caradac," replied Charlie Dee, still perfectly self-possessed. "I won't make a move. You can understand that I'm even glad to see you boys!"

Rhiannon took the slender round wrists of Nancy Morgan and saw her lips wrinkle back from her teeth as though she would sink them in his hands. She hissed at him like a cat, and like a cornered cat's were her eyes.

He was glad to turn her around and bring her hands behind her back.

A few turns of twine secured her. The sheriff, in the meantime, made Charlie Dee helpless in the same manner.

"Will you talk to me?" asked Rhiannon quietly.

"I will, man, of course," said Charlie.

"What part has your father in this—your mother—"

"And Isabella?"

"Yes."

"Not one damned scrap had any of them to do with it. I promised the old man that I could give him fifty thousand if he'd let me have command of every whit of his power for ten days. That's all. It was just a business deal between us."

192

"I believe you," said Rhiannon. "And about Nancy, here—you knew what she planned to do with me when she got me in here?"

A pereceptible shudder ran through the body and the voice of Charlie Dee. "So help me God," he said, disgust in his face, "I didn't dream it. You see through the trap now, of course?"

"Nacherally, Charlie."

"I tried to persuade her to put the case straight to you, or let me do it, and trust to you to split the stuff with us, after you'd found it. She wouldn't trust you."

"Nor any man!" sneered Nancy Morgan.

"Sweet little bird!" said Caradac. "Sweet little singing bird, she is!"

He threw his light full in her face. "Reg'lar lamb, she is," murmured the sheriff.

"What'll you do with me?" asked the girl defiantly. "What *can* you do to me?"

"Attempted murder. That's a little something, honey."

"On Rhiannon—the outlaw? There's a price on his head!" She laughed in her triumph.

"Maybe you're right," said the sheriff. "Maybe there's nothing that we could do to you—"

"Not a mortal thing!" she assured him, teeth bared.

"Except give you a trip back to good old Manhattan and let the police there look you over, honey."

She turned a little and looked up in his face. "Bluff, dearie," said she. "Thin bluff, too!"

"Or," said the sheriff, "maybe the Pittsburgh boys would be glad of a sight of you, or in Chicago they might even meet you with a band!"

She looked earnestly at him and was silent.

He said in conclusion: "I know all about you, Nan. A good many of your names, a good many of your jobs." She was white. She looked suddenly older, but never for a moment did her self-possession diminish. She simply said: "All right. Everything is queered. The devil is up to his old tricks, taking away the cake just when I have my hand on it."

She added: "Charlie goes with me, though. Criminal conspiracy. I guess that we can work out something like that on you, Charlie, for your share in this case! If I rest in the coop, you'll be chirping in the next cage, dearie!"

Charlie Dee shrugged his shoulders and turned his back on her. "I sort of hope so," said he. "Damn if a prison term wouldn't be about the only thing that would give me a clean feeling again! I've been rolling in soot, Rhiannon. Worse soot than *you* were ever dipped in! But I give you my word—I never meant harm to you, man. Not directly. It was just the unlucky chance that you knew about the hole-in-the-wall—the only person in the world who could take us to it!"

"Caradac figgered that all out," said Rhiannon. "He did the real work to puzzle the case out."

Caradac said: "We'll go to where the rest of the stuff lies. You'll show us the way, you two."

"Not a word to 'em, Charlie!" breathed the girl. "They gotta pay for what we know!"

"Not a cent," said Charlie Dee. "I'm fed up, honey!"

"Are you gunna hang me because you're fed up?" she screamed at him.

"I'm through," said Charlie Dee. "I'm through with all short cuts to quick money! Caradac, I'll take you to the spot!"

The girl began to scream at him.

"Gag her," suggested Charlie Dee calmly. "She's going to raise hell when we get into the open—unless you want my father and his crowd down on you!"

The sheriff undertook that task. He pried open her set teeth by a pressure of his iron-hard thumb and forefinger against the base of her jaw. A rolled handkerchief made the gag. Then Caradac shouldered her like a log and marched down into the water. Charlie Dee followed, his hands free, but Rhiannon and his mighty hands close behind. As for Rhiannon himself, he had been loaded down with the last of the plunder—the heavy little bags, the box of jewels. So they passed through the water and came up wet and dripping on the outer shore. They found all black again. A close rain fell with a steady drumming and the sky was sheeted over with darkness.

"If anyone speaks to us, I'll do the talking," said Charlie Dee. He led off up the hollow. But not a challenge did they receive and not a shadow of a human did they see, except for one dimly revealed silhouette of a horseman, lost in the rain and the darkness.

"The boys are earning their money," said Charlie Dee.

He led the way to the left, close to his father's house, where now all lights were out. Then he turned again into the woods. Close to the bank of the creek he stopped beneath a tree.

The sheriff set the girl on her feet but did not untie her hands or remove the gag.

"Lift the flat stone, Rhiannon," said Charlie.

Rhiannon obeyed. The large slab came up under his fingers, and beneath he was looking down into a close pile of such small bags as he already had in his pockets.

"There is three hundred pounds of coin—gold," said Charlie Dee. "That's around forty or fifty thousand dollars, I guess? But the jewels are the real stuff."

"Will you tell us what it is, Charlie?" asked the sheriff, in a voice whose kindness promised many things.

"Nobody knows," said Charlie. "Nobody knows for sure, except that the Morgans never laid in old Spanish gold coins, and they never bought jewels in heaps like these. That's plain and clear. Then how did they get the stuff? Well—the Morgans were kind of a wild lot. Is that right, Nancy?"

Caradac turned the light on her face. She could not answer because of the gag, but there was such coldly concentrated fury in her eyes that they spoke more eloquently than words.

"The roads used to be kind of unsafe in the days of old Jim Morgan," said Caradac. "I heard tell about that— long before my days of work out here in the hills."

"And it was Jim Morgan's handwriting that was on the flyleaf of the book," said Charlie Dee. "We found that out. What did he do? Why, took the loot that he found. The gold—I dunno. Something he got south of the Rio— God knows how. That's probably the way of that. The jewels—well, he picked and chose on the high road. The boys used to sink a lot of money in diamonds and what nots, during the mining days. Anyway, I suppose that Jim Morgan cached the stuff in the hole-in-the-wall. This is pretty much guessing, but I think it's close to the truth! Now, Caradac, I'm ready to go with you!"

"If you're ready," said Caradac, "you go home. I'll— call for you when I want you!"

He had been removing the gag from the girl's mouth as

he spoke. "I'll yap!" snarled Nancy Morgan. "You can't grab me and let that bird fly loose, you crooked—"

"You fly free too," said the sheriff. "I dunno, maybe I'm wrong, but I can't see the life of a man like Charlie Dee—with what he's got in him—dragged through hell for the sake of jailing a—lady like you, Nancy."

Chapter Forty-Three

NOTHING human has so swift a pair of wings as Rumor. Rumor had flown through the hill country and through the town. The sheriff went back to a new atmosphere.

It was true that people no longer hailed him in the same hearty and cheerful manner to which he had grown accustomed in the old days. They watched him, however, with a bright interest and nodded to him as though they were prepared to smile. Public Opinion was not informed, and nowhere are people more slaves to Public Opinion than in the West, though every man has a vote in the making up of its voice. But Public Opinion in the little town was ready to be determined, now, in favor of the sheriff, whereas before this, it had been prepared to damn him almost without a hearing as the conspirator through whom Annan Rhiannon had escaped from the hands of justice.

There had been talk of bringing him before a court, under arrest, and charging him with the crime. And all that kept the most discontented from doing this was a dark doubt as to who would be willing to go and arrest Owen Caradac. Now all this air of foreboding was gone.

Just what had happened, no one knew, but there was a rumor of strange doings among the Laurel Hills. There was a whisper of the hole-in-the-wall, that much doubted place which was so intimately connected with Annan Rhiannon and his long career. No one had much that was definite to offer, but it was said that there would be a great surprise.

It was pointed out that the sheriff had made two trips

to the capital of the state, and it was well known that he had conferred with the governor on each of those occasions. It was known, also, that Caradac had been accompanied to the state capital each time by Charlie Dee.

What had the Dees to do with this business?

Isabella Dee, for instance, had been away for weeks. She was not yet back. She, too, had been seen with the governor.

So the whole range waited for what would happen to the sheriff. Their favorable impression was increased by another thing—there had been no further depredations by Annan Rhiannon. That giant no longer descended from Mount Laurel.

Again, small, heavy boxes of unknown content had been shipped from the town under the name of Sheriff Caradac and sent to an Eastern bank. And upon the finger of Caradac appeared a ring, set with a bit of lapis lazuli, curiously carved. So all people held their breath. What had happened? What would come to the sheriff? What was Rhiannon doing? What had the Dees in this case? What had meant that heavy mustering of men between the arms of Mount Laurel?

It would have been small wonder if Sheriff Caradac had relaxed and grown gay during this interval; but, as a matter of fact, he seemed to age every day. His face became more grim. His step was heavier. Wrinkles appeared around his eyes. It was said that he was turning gray. Certainly the good sheriff never had been so sober. So he appeared, seated this evening, not in front of his shack in town, but on the veranda before the little farmhouse in the country. It had a cheerful look, even in the autumn of the year, for the alfalfa was growing thick again, and, though the fig trees were bare, they made a pleasant design against the sky. And those who passed by listened to the clanking of the gears of the windmill— the soft, well-oiled sound—and looked at one another.

"That Rhiannon—he done a job," they said.

And they went on, with their heads turned, admiring the green fields as if they had been great emeralds. Others had been attempting to follow the good example set for them, but their locations were not so lucky. Wells were expensive things to dig. Others invested thought and money, but not the fierce energy of Rhiannon.

So the admiration for Rhiannon had grown. "A gent like him—he could do anything. He was a fool to take up crooked work!" said someone.

The whole hill country echoed that thought.

The sheriff, as though irritated by a thought, now rose from his chair and paced slowly back and forth on the veranda. The shadows increased. The short autumn dusk began.

He left the veranda and walked up and down the path, to the gate, and back to the porch.

Caracci came out of the house, looked at him, and disappeared softly again.

At length, Caradac heard the sound of a horse galloping far off, and he leaned on the gate and watched the rider come closer—a small rider, on a tall horse. A vigorous rider on a good horse. One could tell that by the slant of the body, the way the horse shot across the bridge—one loud beat as the hoofs struck the center of the wooden arch, and then again the sounds muffled in the dust.

Caradac grew so interested that he went outside the gate. There he stood, and presently he made out the flutter beside the saddle flaps. Too quick a flutter for chaps to make. Divided skirts, then?

The rider swept straight up to him, swung from the center of the road, brought her horse to a sliding halt, like a cowpuncher, and, throwing the reins, sprang straight down into the arms of the sheriff.

Twice upon either cheek she kissed the sheriff—the brown, stubbly cheeks of Caradac. "Honey, honey, honey—" said the sheriff. "You won out, finally?"

She merely laughed!

"Say it in words, Isabella!"

"I won!" said Isabella.

At this, the sheriff turned his back upon her and went through the gateway, not even pausing to hold it open for the girl. He went down the path with great long strides. He disappeared into the house, and the little place echoed under the beating of his heels.

So he came to the kitchen where a pair of huge shoulders and a great head were bowed over a pan in which brown-skinned potatoes were turning to white crystal as the worker plied a deft knife. "Annan," said the sheriff.

"Leave me be," said the outlaw. "I gotta finish this pan of potatoes. Leave me be, will you?"

"I got something to tell you!"

"Tell it to me after dinner. I'm busy. I'm tired of your fool ideas, too," said Rhiannon.

"Annan Rhiannon," said the sheriff, "stand up!" There was something in his voice that made the other put the pan aside and slowly rise, until he stood beside the other, equally enormous.

He kept flicking the edge of his tough thumb over the blade of the knife. There was a thoughtful look in his face.

"Go on," said Rhiannon. "What's up now?"

"Annan, I'm sorry to say, I gotta arrest you in the name of the law!"

He laid his hand on the shoulder of Rhiannon. "Anything you say might be used agin you," said the sheriff. "I gotta warn you of that!"

"Is this straight?" asked Rhiannon gravely.

"Are you gunna resist?"

"God—no!" said Rhiannon. "I'll never doubt you again, Owen. If you was to lead me to a rope, I'd hang myself if you said so."

"You fool!" cried the sheriff, "don't you understand? She's been lucky at last! God knows what she said. I couldn't do it, nor Charlie Dee. But she finally done it. If you'll stand your trial, the governor has promised his pardon to you if you're convicted! D'you hear? It ain't legal. God bless our governor, he's too damn big to be legal! There she is out in front. Waiting for you. Go out and tell her something!"

Rhiannon gasped. "I dunno that I—" he began.

The sheriff seized and dragged him to the hall.

"Look here, Owen—for God's sake go easy. I don't hardly know how to talk to her! I—she—"

"Hey, Isabella!" called the sheriff. "He says he don't know how to talk to you!"

And a voice from the veranda answered quietly, "I suppose that I'd better come in and teach him, then!"

ABOUT THE AUTHOR

Max Brand, pseudonym for Frederick Faust, was one of the most prolific writers in America until his death in 1944. He averaged a wordage equal to a full-length book every three weeks, dictating to one stenographer after another while he sustained his energies on incredible amounts of black coffee. A splendid talker, he could hold his listeners spellbound by the hour while he discussed anything from Western round-ups to China Clippers. He was killed on the battlefront in Italy in May, 1944, while serving as correspondent for *Harper's Magazine*.

2P 35/1

MAX BRAND

MB

EXCITING WESTERNS